Family
Jewels

Kate Christie

SECOND GROWTH

DEDICATION

To our newest players to be named later:
We're all waiting to meet you!
No pressure. Really.

Love, Mama, Mimi, Alex,
Maggie, & Corona

CHAPTER ONE

The year everything changed seemed to start out happily enough. I rang in the new year with Dez, my best friend since Women's Studies 101 freshman year at University of Michigan, and Maddie, my girlfriend of two and a half years who I was thinking of asking to move in with me on Valentine's Day. We stood together on the deck at another friend's party in downtown Ann Arbor, my arms looped around each of their necks, humming along to "Auld Lang Syne" and shivering as we watched fireworks light up the clear, unusually snow-free sky. None of us knew the words to the penultimate New Year's Eve tune, but that didn't matter. Sure, I was another year closer to thirty without having accomplished much that other people—my family, specifically—would consider significant. But I had a pair of jobs that I liked, my best buddy at my side, and a future planned with the woman I loved. What more did I need to be happy?

Later, after Dez showed up on my doorstep with melted snowflakes clinging to her short hair, her eyes damp with weather and what she could no longer bear to keep from me, I would remember that night on the deck, the three of us lit up by rainbow-hued skyrockets and exploding chrysanthemums, the pyrotechnic cracks and whistles a sibilant accompaniment to our traditional invocation of the end of one year and the beginning of another, and I would wonder if their hands had been clasped together behind my back. There I was, clueless, the two people I thought I loved most flanking me for what would be the last time, and I didn't even know, would never know, what had been in their heads or hearts as the sky exploded around us.

I don't remember Valentine's Day, which arrived shortly after Dez's confession. I do remember weeks of waking up at the same time each morning, my digital clock broadcasting 4:03 as if I had set the alarm. Anxiety, it seemed, was just as capable of jarring me from sleep as the morning news report on NPR.

Every morning, as I lay in the dark picturing Dez and Maddie in bed across town, naked and entwined about each other, I would kick at my sheets and gnaw my chapped lips until the radio turned itself on at seven. My stomach hurt constantly, a tight, visceral pain that made me worry I would die of a bleeding ulcer. Any thought of food made my stomach contract unhappily, while the sight and scent of it actually made me retch a few times during those first early, post-apocalyptic weeks. Not exactly convenient given that one of my jobs was serving food in a café.

"What's wrong with you?" Dr. Margaret "Fitzy" Fitzgerald, my boss and mentor at U of M's Matthaei Botanical Gardens, my other job, finally demanded one drizzly morning when I arrived fifteen minutes late for my shift.

"Nothing," I muttered, ducking my head beneath her legendary gaze. Fitzy, it was said, could pick out differing species of Goldenrod from twenty paces or more.

"Bull honkey. Lately if you turn sideways I can't even see you."

It took me a minute to realize she was saying I was too skinny. I didn't bother arguing. After a couple of weeks of wallowing in the mire of my sorrow, I was thinner than I could probably afford to be.

Fitzy put her hands flat on her desk and pushed herself up to face me. "Tell me you're not doing any of that heroin, Junior. Tell me you're smarter than that."

I looked up, startled. "No, ma'am."

A committed beer drinker and weed smoker, I had never dabbled in anything harder. I preferred my highs to come from barley-based beverages or good old-fashioned ganja.

She nodded, the gesture brief and compact. "Are you sick?"

"No."

"Well, something must be wrong. Are you going to tell me about it, or are you going to make me keep guessing?"

I sighed. "It's Maddie," I admitted. "And Dez. They… The two of them…"

When I trailed off, swallowing hard, Fitzy made a sound of impatient sympathy in her throat as she came around the desk. Then she was at my side, her arm engulfing my shoulders, her touch surprisingly gentle.

"I'm sorry, my girl," she said, patting me the way she used to pat her dog, Curly, a cheerful, rust-colored mutt who had succumbed to cancer the previous fall.

This uncharacteristic display of empathy from Fitzy, along with the thought of Curly, whom I had loved nearly as much as Fitzy had, made my throat tighten. I closed my eyes and rested my head on her shoulder, crying silently as she held onto me and made comforting noises I had never heard from her before.

I wasn't surprised, exactly, to be consoled by Fitzy. Known for her mannish boots and the cigars she sneaked when she wasn't taking oxygen for her increasingly debilitating emphysema, Fitzy usually seemed happier interacting with plants than with human beings. But for some reason, she had taken a shine to me, as she had stated gruffly more than once, usually with a shrug that implied doubt as to her own powers of judgment. When I was still in college, she would drill me on the Latin names of plants during my shifts in the conservatory or out on the grounds. Long before I'd left the ranks of the U of M student intelligentsia, she'd let me know there would be a position on her staff waiting for me, if I wanted it. Five years later, I still did.

"There, there, my girl," she murmured. "They didn't deserve you, that's all. You'll be better off without them. Just wait. You'll see, my dear child."

A knock sounded at the open office door, and Chris Jenkins, a student intern, stopped short as he caught sight of Fitzy embracing me.

"Well?" she demanded. "You have eyes, don't you? Come back later, boy."

Stuttering an apology, Chris backed out into the hallway.

I pulled away and rubbed my face. "You didn't have to scare him."

"Of course I did. It's part of my job, particularly for the ego-challenged—as you will no doubt recall."

I laughed a little, the first time in what felt like decades, remembering how I had come into Fitzy's entry-level Botany course convinced I knew more than anyone else, including, perhaps, her. Quickly and deftly she'd whittled my ego down to a more manageable size, causing me at first to despise her and then, gradually, to respect her. Eventually my love of all things green had led to an internship at the Botanical Gardens under Fitzy's tutelage, which had in turn led to spots of generously paid manual labor at her house not far from campus. By the end of my sophomore year, I had evolved from respect to affection for Fitzy, whose crotchetiness, I'd learned, masked a brilliant, genuinely caring and truly contradictory persona.

Eight years in, our relationship was still based on the mentor/mentee model. Fitzy regularly gifted me with greens and vegetables from her home garden, the only payment I would accept for helping around the house these days, and gave me books that were "no longer needed." Sometimes after fundraising or other events, she and I would linger at the Arboretum and talk for hours about the state of the world, American politics, the movement to return native plants to local landscapes—a passion I had picked up from her over the years. Fitzy, a widow who I had caught on more than one occasion talking to the framed photos of her deceased husband and daughter she kept around her home and office, had known I was gay since day one—I was a bit, shall we say, *vehement* about my sexuality when I was younger. But she, my one-time professor and eventual boss, had never seemed to give a whit.

The one time we'd talked about it, my junior year after a couple of gay boys had been attacked outside a GLBT event at the union, Fitzy had scowled and said, "I've never been able to see what the fuss is about, frankly. Homosexual behavior has been documented in most species. Surely even the Christian crazies wouldn't dare to find fault with their creator given that fact, would they?"

"I'm not sure they've thought of that angle," I'd replied.

Over the years, Fitzy and I had freely shared our less than charitable views toward Michigan's increasingly vocal cadre of right-wing Christians. Academia and religious fundamentalism rarely mixed well, which was one of the reasons I was only too glad to be employed by my alma mater.

My other employer also leaned to the left. Toby Anderson owned

Boadicea, a crunchy café near the University of Michigan's main campus. I'd started out at Boa as a lowly dishwasher my first year of college, but had since worked my way up to assistant manager. Like Fitzy, Toby took it easy on me in the weeks after Dez and Maddie's collective defection, letting me show up late and not giving me too hard a time at first when, in early March, I demonstrated potentially bad judgment by entering into not one but two rebound hook-ups. In my defense, my self-confidence was at an all-time low. When two equally hot Boa regulars asked me out within days of each other, I couldn't find a compelling reason to refuse either.

Boadicea was a well-known boon for the social life of any lesbian lucky enough to work there. Like the barely spring night that set the change in my life to rolling in earnest—from the main counter, looking out across the booths and tables that filled the café almost to overflowing, I counted a handful of potentials, at least one of whom had been giving me noticeably un-subtle looks over the top of her paperback. As I watched, she closed her book, unfolded deliciously long legs clad in skinny jeans, and approached the counter.

A couple of weeks of rebound sex with two enthusiastic partners had improved my overall outlook on life in the month since my busted Valentine's Day. My stomach no longer hurt as much, and I had begun to remember what life had been like Before Maddie. *BM*—that seemed to sum up the ending of my relationship with Miss Madeline Stanton perfectly.

Thinking about bodily functions had distracted me from the cute college student standing before me, so I offered her the rakish smile that lifted the right side of my mouth in symmetrical opposition to my silver nose stud and asked, "Was that hummus with avocado or roasted red pepper?"

"Avocado," she said, her smile almost as suggestive as mine.

I rang up the order and watched my customer saunter away. Maybe a little later I would go out to bus tables and strike up a conversation. Life was too short to overlook a smile—not to mention an ass—like hers.

"Eyes back in your head, Junior," Toby said, elbowing me as she passed.

"Like you need any more girls," Elissa, one of the sandwich makers, added.

They were always ganging up on me, which I had learned to expect from my three older sisters but not from my supposed friends.

"There can technically never be 'too many' girls," I said. "Besides, I'm single."

"Not what I hear." Elissa wiped her knife on a rag.

Steph and Caitlyn, the attractive co-eds I was "hanging out" with, knew about each other, and each had professed to accept that I wasn't ready for a committed relationship. So far, both women seemed fine with the casual nature of our situation(s).

"Whatever. I'm taking a break." I untied my apron and threw it at Toby, who laughed as I withdrew to the alley behind the building for a smoke.

Outside, the patch of gray sky visible from the back steps was crisscrossed by jet tracks. I leaned back on the wooden steps that led into the café's kitchen, shivering in my shirtsleeves, and wafted a couple of smoke rings up between the buildings.

"Is this a solitary sulk, or can I join you?" Toby asked from the doorway.

"Only if you promise not to lecture me on the evils of tobacco."

"Deal," she said, and sat down beside me on the steps. "Dinner with

7

the family tonight?"

I nodded. Every other Sunday, my parents held court at the old Victorian house on the hill, which meant that twice a month, my three sisters, their respective partners and children, and I dropped whatever we were doing and high-tailed it out to the edge of town. We didn't dare miss an official dinner at our childhood home. But then, I was likely the only member of the Starreveld clan who wanted to.

"You could always come home with me instead," Toby offered. "Sheila's whipping up a Tofurky with mashed potatoes and stuffing."

Early spring Thanksgiving dinner at Toby and her wife Sheila's house, a cozy bungalow not far from Boa, sounded wonderful. "I wish."

We sat quietly, me staring at the glowing tip of my Marlboro Light and thinking about how I needed to reduce my dependence on cigarettes now that I was no longer in the throes of romantic despair, Toby smoothing splinters from the bottom step with her boot and probably thinking about her motorcycle. She'd just brought her Harley out of winter storage and insisted on riding it everywhere now that much of the snow had melted. More of the white stuff was probably on the horizon, seeing as it was only mid-March, but no one seemed to want to mention this fact to Toby.

"How's the ride?" I asked.

"Excellent," she said, and waxed lovingly about her bike as I smoked my cigarette and nodded occasionally. Sometimes I thought she adored her bike almost as much as she did Sheila, her partner of nineteen years. But that was Toby. She never did anything halfway, which was how she'd built Boadicea into a mainstay of Ann Arbor's alternative scene.

After a few minutes, she seemed to realize she was gushing and cleared her throat. With a square jaw and a fondness for leather, Toby liked to believe that other people saw her as a tough, manly dyke.

"Anyway, enough about me," she said. "Did you have a good time last night?"

"I think so."

"You don't sound convinced."

"I'm not exactly. Alex and I had a couple of beers and sang some Karaoke, and then we saw Maddie and Dez and I had a few more beers."

"Tell me you didn't sing Katy Perry again."

"Sorry, they didn't have any Neil Diamond."

"Too bad—he's a musical genius." She paused. I knew what she was going to say even before it came out of her mouth: "Did you talk to Dez?"

"No," I said, not looking at her.

Toby had never been a fan of Maddie's—*ice queen control freak*, she'd pronounced after the fact—and hated to see me chuck a decade of friendship over such a *useless excuse for a lesbian*. I didn't tell her I wasn't the one who had chucked the friendship, exactly. Dez hadn't tried to get in touch with me even once since the night she'd appeared on my doorstep looking to unload the mother of all secrets. I wasn't sure how I would have responded if she had.

I crushed my cigarette under the heel of my Doc Marten boots. "I better get inside. My boss can be a real tyrant."

"Nice."

I felt her eyes on me as I headed back in. She meant well, I knew, but I hadn't yet managed to quell my nausea from the previous night's outing to Lucky's, Ann Arbor's women's club. Like a scene from one of my nightmares, Maddie and Dez had been wrapped around each other on the dance floor, radiating mutual adoration for all the world to see.

At one thoroughly tipsy point, I had accidentally drifted near them, but they hadn't appeared to notice. Probably it would have taken some kind of calamity to make them take note of the outside world. Or, at least, of me.

Which didn't matter, I told myself now, swallowing against the telltale burn of acid in my esophagus. I was fine. Better than fine, even—after dinner tonight, Caitlyn, a former gymnast and current U of M cheerleader, was planning to come over to my place for a pre-arranged booty call. I pictured her spread-eagled on my bed, her eyes closed in anticipation as I lowered myself between her legs. That was more like it.

A line from an Ani DiFranco song drifted into my mind, about how her ex was never that good of a lay or even much of a friend. It always reminded me of Maddie. Unfortunately, the next line confirmed that in spite of those failings, Ani still adored the unnamed "you" of the song.

As I passed through the kitchen, I paused beside my backpack to pop a couple of Tums, just for good measure. Back at the main counter, I checked the booths. Sure enough—the cute girl from earlier had finished her sandwich and appeared to be engrossed in a Jane Austen novel. Upon my word, there was nothing I loved so much as nineteenth century British women's fiction. I tied my apron strings, rolled up my shirtsleeves, and set out to clear some tables.

CHAPTER TWO

"Elizabeth, dear, please set the table," my mother directed.

Elizabeth was my given name. Only my friends called me Junior. The nickname had been bestowed upon me by certain older members of the Ann Arbor GLBT community when, at sixteen, I started hanging around Boa and the local queer bookstore.

In the formal dining room, the long oak table was already covered in a lace tablecloth. I set out cloth napkins, silver, and china from the antique armoire, trying to tune out the high-pitched buzz of my mother and sisters' voices from the kitchen. My niece and nephews were in the den off the kitchen, no doubt enthralled by one of the many children's DVDs my mom kept on hand. Meanwhile, my father and brothers-in-law were out on the deck guzzling light beer and grilling red meat. The fact that it was only the second week of March made no difference to my relatives. True Michiganders, they barbecued year-round.

I counted the place settings again: parents at either end, me and my three sisters scattered along the sides, two husbands, three small children, one infant. Wait, where was the high chair? I found the ancient wooden infant seat in the pantry and set it up at my father's end. Jane, the eldest, traditionally sat beside him facing Mike, her husband. But since Mary had to be able to reach the high chair, she'd taken over the Seat of Honor, as Cat and I referred to it. Cat was three years older than me, Mary a year and a half older than her, and Jane another two years older again. My parents had been busy there for a while, especially if you counted the baby boy my mother had lost between Cat and me. After I came along, the doctors had warned my parents against further pregnancies, so they'd given up on producing a male heir.

Having me was almost like having a son, I frequently said to Toby. But I'd never cracked this particular joke anywhere near my family.

Setting the table had long been my responsibility. I could barely make breakfast for myself, let alone dinner for a dozen people. Early on, when my mother was teaching my sisters the ins and outs of the kitchen and they were taking swimmingly to it, as they appeared to do with all traditionally feminine tasks, I had refused to sit still and listen. I would run from the kitchen, hands over my ears, chanting, "I can't hear you," and escape the block and a half to my friend Jody's house. His mother didn't try to make me learn to cook; I couldn't understand why mine did.

A boy with a girl's name, Jody was being raised in a "gender-neutral environment," I had once overheard my mother confide to my father. What that meant exactly, I wasn't sure at the time. I did know, though, that Jody was the only boy in the neighborhood who thought it was cool I could outrace him on foot or by bike, or that I could throw a football as far as he could. His parents, too, were the only adults I'd encountered who didn't seem to have a problem with my aversion toward dresses and dolls.

I loved hanging out at their house, even though they tended to leave the bathroom door open no matter what they might be doing in there, a habit that had resulted in more than one horrified moment for me. But when we were in ninth grade, Jody's father got a job out-of-state, a twist of fate I'd always bemoaned. Not only had Jody's family appeared to accept me unconditionally, but their house had provided a safe haven from my sisters' frequent attempts to inflict make-up or girly clothing on me.

My sisters, models of traditional femininity, had loved playing dress-up with me, their life-sized doll. When I was little, I would try to sit still while they brushed powder over my nose, wove my shoulder-length hair into wispy French braids, slipped shoes they had outgrown onto my feet. I admired my older sisters. They were fascinating creatures who participated in strange personal hygiene rituals and always smelled good. I would watch them in the mirror while they styled my hair after their own, listening to their conversations about boys they liked and trying to figure out what it was that made them like them and me, me.

Because no matter how skilled their designs, I always looked like a boy in drag. I alone had inherited our father's broad shoulders and narrow hips. A one-time star U of M running back, Dad had always looked more like a longshoreman called Sven than a jeweler named Eugene, except for his metrosexual wardrobe. By the time I hit high school, I was already taller than any of my sisters, even Jane, the oldest. Secretly, I was relieved that their hand-me-downs no longer fit. I preferred shorts and beat-up sneakers, faded jeans and T-shirts adorned with athletic logos. On those long-past dress-up afternoons, I would rather have been roaming the woods with Jack and Will, nearly feral twins who lived one street over, or rehearsing original musical scores with Jody in the unfinished room above his garage. Or later, after Jody moved away, mucking about the garden.

As a teenager, I'd spent what felt like entire summers shadowing Felix, our gardener, and his crew as they tended the plants, bushes, and ornamental trees scattered throughout my family's estate, which contained a pond with a working fountain and an English garden complete with a maze. I loved to transplant annuals into the rich earth near the house, shovel damp mulch from the back of Felix's truck, wield sharp shears against a truculent hedge. Working outside, I didn't have to worry about fitting in. Felix and the guys on his crew didn't appear to think I should be at the mall hoping to catch a glimpse of a cute boy. They seemed to accept my interest in plants as a given, and patiently shared what they had learned about tending gardens. My sisters, on the other hand, couldn't understand why I spent so much time outdoors. But even as they tried to wrap their pretty blonde heads around my floral sentiments, I knew it wasn't only my fascination with photosynthesis that set me apart from them.

Even now that we were all grown up and out of college, my sisters remained this trio of Stepfordesque girls, feminine and sociable like our mother. At least now that we were adults I finally had something major in common with them: I, too, had refused to take up our father's career gauntlet—management of Starreveld & Sons, the jewelry shop that had been in our family for more than a hundred years. By now, my elder sisters had opted for careers in orthodontics, housewifery, and law. And while I had yet to formally choose a career—Toby claimed I'd been auditioning for the role of professional lesbian for some time now—I knew that I didn't want to take over the shop. Nor did I think my father wanted me to. Since I'd dropped the lesbian bombshell on my family the summer after I graduated from high school, my father hadn't seemed to want to have much to do with me, store or no store.

"Is the table ready, Lizzie?" my sister Jane called from the kitchen for easily the nine hundred and forty-seventh time in our lives together.

"Yes, ma'am," I hollered back. Scary—the older she got, the more she sounded like our mother.

Jane poked her head out of the kitchen. "I heard that, brat." She crossed her eyes at me and ducked back into the kitchen.

Okay, so she wasn't exactly like Mom yet. But there was still time.

Dinner that night was the usual melee, with competing conversations, children's high-pitched tones, low adult exclamations and seemingly contagious laughter rattling the panes of the dining room windows that overlooked the wide lawn where I used to accompany Felix on his rounds. Now, hovering between winter and spring, Michigan was in thaw mode, trees and grass gray and brown, shrubs and raised beds almost expectantly empty.

I've always loved the smell of fresh dirt and melting snow on the first warm day when the sun returns. In the dead of a Michigan winter, when nearly every living thing is buried under several feet of monochrome snow beneath a leaden sky, it's hard to believe that green grass has ever waved languidly in a late summer's breeze, or that in a few short months multi-colored roses will once again creep over the backyard trellis, brandishing blooms and spikes aplenty. But on the first real day of spring when sunlight penetrates the hard ground, you can almost smell the color green on the breeze.

That night, the sun was still too weak to assert itself, and I was trapped in the familiar dining room yet again wishing I could be outside the fray, peering in through steam-blurred windows. Unlike the weather, my family was reliably predictable. My parents admired Jane and fawned over Mary and nine-month-old Brittany, who to me was still hairless and formless enough to be genderless. With a name like Brittany and the frilly, pink outfits Mary favored, however, I imagined she would end up just as feminine and tractable as her mother.

Everyone adored Mary—children, adults, babies, animals. She'd never seemed to realize, though. As lovable as Mary was, we all knew she wasn't the sharpest knife in the drawer. Her husband, Joe, who was neither as sweet nor as lovable as Mary, nonetheless worshiped her just as much as everyone else did, and seemed to take genuine pleasure in working long hours as a contractor so that she could stay home full-time with the baby and their older son, Joey.

Jane, on the other hand, the oldest of the Starreveld sisters, was sharper than the rest of us combined. Although how someone who'd scored in the top one percent on both the SATs and, later, the MCATs, ended up in a profession that required her to spend the majority of her days peering into the mouths of children and pre-teens was not obvious to those who loved her. But being an orthodontist suited Jane just fine, and that was all that really mattered, she'd reminded us often enough. Her kids took after both her and Mike, her software programmer husband—barely able to tie their own shoes and already obsessed with books and computers. Meredith, the oldest grandchild at six, would probably be designing cutting edge apps before I even owned a smartphone or tablet.

Meanwhile Cat, my other sister, was the proverbial middle child, even though she and Mary technically shared middle honors. Unlike Mary the domestic goddess, Cat was prone to vocal outbursts any time she thought she was being ignored. Fitting, we all concurred behind her back, that she'd decided to become an attorney—the law offered its practitioners nearly unceasing monologue opportunities, as well as plentiful money to pay for the designer lifestyle Cat had always coveted.

What my sisters said behind my back was not something I liked to ponder. At family dinners, I mostly hid out in the corner furthest from my father and brothers-in-law, who, while decent enough guys, occasionally still appeared uncertain what to make of me, an unabashed lesbian sporting body art and a faux hawk. My mother and I would engage in small talk, or Cat and I would spar, or Meredith or one of my nephews would fill me in on life in their world. Talking to the kids was my favorite dinner pastime even if they did occasionally mistake my gender. Unlike the rest of the people seated around the table, they weren't old enough yet to understand that they didn't have anything in common with me.

As the dinner conversation at the other end of the table skipped from mortgage rates (the lowest in years) to building demand (also, unfortunately, markedly low) to orthodontia and diamonds as common markers of discretionary wealth, I talked to Meredith about her first soccer game of the year, which we'd all attended in the pouring rain the previous morning; helped the two four year-olds (hyperactive Joey and dreamy Owen, Jane's youngest) cut their food into bite-sized pieces; and chatted with my mother about gardening. Every once in a while I noticed my father glance furtively in my direction, but mostly he seemed to pay attention to nearly everyone except me.

When I was younger, my dad and I had never seemed to run out of things to talk about. He taught me how to throw a baseball, catch a pop fly, and shoot a free throw. In summer, we would spend hours together in the driveway after he came home from work, shooting baskets as the sun set and the mosquitoes buzzed about our heads. Sometimes he didn't even change out of his suit, just rolled up his sleeves and kicked off his wingtips. But by the time I reached high school, a slightly puzzled look had replaced his easy smile when he looked at me. He still attended my sports matches and appeared proud of my academic achievements. But while he teased and fussed over my sisters, he treated me politely and a little distantly, as if he weren't sure anymore quite how to talk to me.

My father's uncertainty had caused me to doubt myself long before I fell in love with my best friend on the softball team. Even now, looking back on my early teen years is difficult; that's something I have in common with most people, probably. But just recognizing the commonality of a particular experience doesn't necessarily lessen the accompanying ache. In my case, middle school signaled a transition from being comfortable in my own skin, confident of my worth and of my parents' unconditional love, to a period of painful insecurity. As a child, I never doubted my father's love, never suspected either of my parents would look upon me with anything other than pride, affection, love. This security was their gift to me, the emotional platform they had built, consciously or not, for each of their children. Did my faith in their devotion make it harder later when their affection for me seemed to waver, to flicker in the face of the public condemnation of the type of person I was becoming? Their friends, other business owners and housewife moms, looked askance at my blossoming from a tomboy in pigtails and overalls to a baby dyke with boy-band hair and clip-on ties. Our church, Dutch Reformed, was neither open nor affirming when it came to gays, lesbians, or genderqueer teenagers. Which meant that neither, particularly, were my parents.

But that early boost of self-esteem they had given me was exactly what made me able to soldier on beneath the critical stares of neighbors and family friends, fellow congregants and school officials. The faith and encouragement my parents provided early on made me not only accept my own differences later but proclaim them, loud and proud, to anyone who would listen. Sometimes I thought my father wished I had stayed silent, that I had allowed him and my mother and everyone else to continue along as they were, ignoring my deviations from their version of normalcy. But I'd been raised to be honest, to honor those I cared about with the truth. And anyway, coming out the summer after high school graduation had merely been a confirmation of the message I'd been broadcasting underground for years.

The sense of self I'd learned from my parents and older sisters was also what allowed me now to continue to come home every other Sunday, to sit through dinner pretending that it didn't hurt when my father's gaze skittered away from me, his disappointment palpable after all these years. Sometimes I sat at the table daydreaming about leaving Ann Arbor, setting off for distant locales where I wouldn't have to bear constant witness to what I'd lost. Friends from college had invited me to move with them to London, New York, Chicago, and, the most attractive option of all, Seattle. But if and when I left my hometown, it would be to head toward something compelling in its own right, a new experience I couldn't wait to begin—not simply because I couldn't stand another day among people I knew had once loved me but wasn't so sure still did.

Not that the idea of fleeing wasn't tempting.

Dinner that evening seemed to be following the usual script—me passing the time with the younger generation, my father ignoring me—until dessert, when a new plot line abruptly developed. Taking advantage of a lull in conversation as everyone chowed down on blueberry pie, my dad clinked his glass with a fork and announced, "I have a proposition. For you, Elizabeth, actually."

Movement around the table ceased as all eyes shifted from the head of the table to me tucked into the corner seat at my mom's right elbow.

When I'd first graduated from college—like my sisters before me, I, too, had said yes to the University of Michigan—my dad had used family dinners as a chance to enquire regularly after my career aspirations. I would try not to squirm in the high-backed wooden chairs hand-crafted long before I was born and explain once again that I, a graduate of the U of M Honors program, was still working part-time at Boa and the Arboretum. Eventually he'd stopped asking.

Now I cleared my throat. "What kind of proposition?"

"More of a favor, really. I'm going to the annual IAJ convention next month. Keith was supposed to come along, but since Becky is on bed-rest until the twins are born, he isn't available. Everything is already paid for. I was hoping you might take his spot."

Keith was the store manager, and the International Association of Jewelers was one of numerous professional organizations to which they both belonged. I pictured the convention—the Hilton in Cincinnati or the Marriott in St. Louis packed with mostly male jewelry designers, manufacturers, and sales people, clean-cut and conservative like my father, and then pictured myself with my David Beckham hair, tattoos, and preference for ripped jeans trying to blend into such a crowd.

"I don't know, Dad," I hedged.

All eyes in the room swiveled to me again. Except the baby's, of course. She was too busy jamming uncooked blueberries into her mouth with both adorably plump little hands.

"IAJ is in Antwerp this year," my father clarified. "I also have business in Amsterdam. We'd be in the Netherlands for the tulips."

Tulips? In the real Holland, as opposed to the small West Michigan town?

"You know, I could probably make it," I said. "I just have to check with work."

"Good. We can talk more as I get the details ironed out. Now, Jane, did I hear you say that John DeSalle's daughter came into the office last week?"

The conversation moved on. Across the table, Cat's perfectly plucked eyebrows settled into an ominous *v*. She'd asked for a trip to Europe for her law school graduation the previous year, but my parents had reminded her that travel was a luxury, and luxuries did not constitute suitable gifts. Except jewelry, of course. But jewelry was a necessity, my father claimed, not an extravagance.

Like his father before him, he often said that he loved three things in life: family, diamonds, and tulips. In our world, family and diamonds were indelibly intertwined. Before my Y chromosome-free generation appeared on the scene, Starreveld & Sons Fine Jewelry had passed from four generations of fathers to their sons. My father was nearing retirement age, but his attempts to buy each of my sisters and their husbands into the store with tuition aid, partnership offers, and guilt had all failed. Though hardly the prodigal son, I was generally believed to be my father's last hope at keeping the jewelry shop in the immediate family. The invitation he'd extended had to mean he was more desperate than I'd thought—this trip must be a last-ditch attempt to woo me into coming back into the family fold.

I squared my shoulders. I had no intention of breaking under the pressure. More than likely, my father would be busy at the convention and with his other business, leaving me free to tour Belgium and the Netherlands at the height of the spring flower season. The Netherlands. As in, Europe. Awesome.

The best thing about a trip to Europe, besides springtime and the free plane ticket? I would be thousands of miles from Maddie and Dez in a place I had never visited with either of them, with zero possibility of an unexpected run-in. Surely such a vacation was worth a little family strife. It might even be worth a lot.

I smiled sweetly across the table at a still-scowling Cat and shoveled pie, homemade by Mary, happy housewife and mother to two children under the age of four, into my mouth. Wait until Toby heard.

CHAPTER THREE

"He's trying to buy you off," Toby announced, tossing her apron on the counter.

"Duh." I lifted the Specials chalkboard from its hook above the register. "Doesn't change the fact that I'll be in Amsterdam next month."

"Now, that's a city with real coffee shops. Smuggle me along in your suitcase, will ya?"

Toby was five foot five and stocky. Stowing her in my rucksack might prove difficult.

"Can't," I said. "Someone's gotta cover my shifts." Which was why she was here this late tonight—one of the baristas had called in sick last minute. The joys of business ownership.

"Ingrate," she said. "I'm off to count the till. I expect you to have this place ship-shape by the time I'm done."

"Sir, yes, sir."

I cranked up Lady Gaga on the CD player and set about cleaning up. I didn't mind the end-of-shift routine. Other workers bitched and moaned about closing, but I liked running the dishwater hot and soapy and tackling exposed surfaces. At the end of the night, when everyone else had gone home or headed off to Lucky's to kick off their weekend (or weeknight) partying, I would blast the stereo and whirl about the café, a furious cleaning dervish singing loudly off-key. As I scrubbed and rinsed, I liked to imagine attractive women walking past and peering in through the steam-frosted windows to see me guzzling decaf coffee among the murals of Celtic women warriors. Every lesbian in Ann Arbor knew Boa; working here automatically made you part of the scene, and I loved it. Even if Toby could get bossy sometimes.

I thought of what she'd said, that my father was trying to lure me into working for him. My sisters and I, one-time junior gemologists-in-training, had all worked at Starreveld & Sons throughout high school, just as our father had done and his father before him. We'd each started out as janitorial assistants and worked our way up to the floor. Well, my sisters had made it onto the floor, anyway. Somehow my father hadn't ever seen fit to approve me as a customer service representative, even before my interest in piercings had emerged.

As I moved around the café, I mentally compared the two establishments: Boadicea, with its bright murals, colorful booths, and wide windows at the edge of the student ghetto, where our dread-locked and tattooed customers lived en masse in run-down Victorians and brick apartment buildings, versus Starreveld & Sons in historic Kerrytown, where high-end shops stocked imported wine, gourmet cooking supplies, and upscale home furnishings. In its earlier incarnation, the store had been located on State Street not far from main campus. But when the lease had come up for renewal in the late '60s, my grandfather had decided to move the premises to Kerrytown, where business owners were just beginning to attract a more genteel crowd. In moving the shop into a building that had formerly housed a bank, he hadn't changed the interior much—teller windows edged in marble still lined the central display area now dominated by a bevy of glass showcases, while the back wall of the main room contained a heavy circular door that opened into a classic bank vault where the store's most valuable pieces were secured each night.

By this time of night, Starreveld & Sons would have been dark and silent for hours already, the only lights coming from the security beams along the floor and the red neon exit sign over the front door. I could picture the interior easily, as if it hadn't been years since I'd set foot inside. I could almost smell the faint scent of sandalwood that lingered about the store, thanks to my father's habit of burning a stick of incense each morning and evening. The incense cleared his mind and helped him stay alert, he said, the way coffee did for other people.

"You done out there, or what?" Toby called from the back.

I blinked, and Starreveld & Sons faded. Counters and espresso machine clean, I shut off the music and carried the last of the day's trash outside, where the air was cool but no longer freezing. Spring was close, I could feel it. By the time it hit southern Michigan, I would be in Europe, wandering the spring flower festivals. True, my travel companion would be my father, a man who openly disapproved of my "lifestyle choice" and seemed to have little to say to me these days, but the fact that he'd invited me surely indicated that he hadn't completely written me off as his daughter.

Didn't it?

Toby had responded well to my travel news, but I still had to inform Fitzy of my impending absence. Or, rather, request the time off—I was scheduled to work at the Arboretum on four of the eight days of my planned European adventure. Spring was the busiest season at the Botanical Gardens, so it was hardly a desirable time for anyone on staff to up and leave on vacation. Fitzy, I knew, would not be happy at the prospect of me gallivanting about the world while everyone else toiled to make the spring opening of the Arboretum its usual success.

Normally everyone worked extra hours throughout April, with unpaid volunteers helping out every day of the week. It was worth it—we all enjoyed what we did, and Fitzy, the center's long-time director, was an accomplished leader, despite her preference for the company of green, leafy matter. Hers was a big job. The Arboretum complex included the largest conservatory owned and operated by an American university (as those of us who worked there liked to brag), along with more than a dozen cultivated display gardens, several managed trails, a library and visitor's resource center, and a handful of other buildings at two separate Ann Arbor locations.

Throughout winter and early spring, I worked in the greenhouses and conservatory, helping with pruning, planting, and anything else that needed doing. In late spring, as the Michigan soil slowly warmed up, I transferred outdoors, where I remained through the fall. By the time I returned from Europe in mid-April, some of our early perennials should be well on their way. Assuming Fitzy let me go.

A couple of days after my father emailed me the final itinerary for the trip, I knocked on Fitzy's open door at the back of the visitor's center. Seated at her desk, she was peering at her computer screen and pecking at the keyboard. At my knock, she glanced at me over the top of her bifocals, her frown an expression that I recognized as one of her more inviting looks.

"Hello, my girl. To what do I owe the pleasure?"

"I was about to check on the rhody cuttings," I said, "but I wanted to talk to you first."

"Excellent. I could use a distraction—working on the weekly

accounts, don't you know."

She waved me toward a chair, the lone paper-free surface in the small room with its old-fashioned radiator and a window that looked out over the recently raked but still bare perennial gardens bordering the visitor's center. Fitzy's desk was piled precariously with folders, receipts, plastic pots, and several plants, from a jar of bamboo to a Christmas cactus that, since I'd been on the scene, had bloomed in just about every month except December. The bookshelves and counter space were similarly adorned, while the walls bore native art from Africa, South America, and Asia, all places Fitzy had traveled during her long academic career.

I took a breath and dove in. "I have good news and bad news." When she folded her arms across her chest, an eyebrow raised, I continued. "My father wants to take me to Europe in a few weeks, which is good news for me—"

"And bad for us." She leaned back in her seat and eyed me curiously. "Where would you be going?"

"To Antwerp for a jeweler's convention, and then to Amsterdam. We'd be in the Netherlands in time—"

"—for the tulips. But this is surprising. I thought you and your father weren't on the best terms?"

It was my turn to eye her. As far as I knew, I hadn't ever spoken to her in detail about my relationship with my father.

She waved a hand. "It was what you didn't say. If you go with him on this trip, does that mean you're thinking of going to work for him, too?"

"No," I said quickly. "Though honestly, he's probably only bringing me so he can try one last time to talk me into it."

"Somehow I doubt that," she said. "You know, Junior, I believe a trip would do you some good, put some color back in your cheeks. You could use a break from our fair city, couldn't you?"

I shouldn't have been surprised that she was putting my emotional health before the always frenzied spring season here at work. And yet, I *was* surprised. Fitzy's whole life seemed to revolve around work, and here she was encouraging me to abandon my duties at a critical time. It didn't add up. I peered at her, noting the dark circles under her eyes, the pallor of her skin strange even for someone suffering from seasonal sun-deprivation. Had she lost weight, too? I had been so caught up in my own drama recently that I hadn't taken much notice of what might be going on around me.

Nodding slowly, I said, "I could probably use the break."

"Then it's settled. But in the meantime, we'd better try to get your hours filled." She pulled her laminated schedule for April out from under an intermediate botany text. "Couldn't be a worse time, could it. Then again, you'll be in the Netherlands in spring, so your timing couldn't be any better, either. Now, which week will you be gone?"

I pulled my chair closer, and we went over the calendar together, her alternately lamenting the scheduling changes and offering suggestions on tourist activities in the Netherlands—her favorite travel destination, she had often told me, in the entire world.

"Tell you what," she said finally, leaning back in her rickety wooden office chair. "I'll let you go, but only on one condition."

"What's that?" I asked, even though I was pretty sure I could guess.

"That you go to Keukenhof with your father and take a mountain of photos. It's only an hour outside of Amsterdam."

How had I known this would be Fitzy's demand? Because on the wall beside the window hung a calendar featuring the Keukenhof Gardens, the fabled Spring Gardens of Europe. For all the years I'd known her, she'd had this same calendar on her wall here and in her kitchen at home, swapping out the old edition for the new promptly on the first of January each year.

"Deal. Or at least I'll try," I amended.

"You'll do more than just try if you know what's good for you," she said, staring at me over the top of her bifocals. Then, all at once, she gripped the edge of the desk, her eyes sliding out of focus behind the lenses. Her breath started to come in short gasps, and I thought I could see her lips turning blue as she reached for the oxygen tank tucked behind her desk. She turned away and held the mask over her face, turning the handle with a shaky hand.

I reached out, my hand hovering uselessly over her shoulder. She'd been having more and more of these episodes lately. It couldn't be good.

After a few long minutes, she removed the mask and cranked down the handle on the tank.

"Are you okay?" I asked, even though I knew she wasn't.

"Fine. Damned cigars. Anyway," she added, her voice unsteady as she reached for her keyboard, "why don't you go check on those rhodies?"

And with that, I was dismissed. I hesitated only a moment before heading out into the conservatory, for once glad to escape the confines of her office. Fitzy was sick, and she wouldn't be getting any better. She knew it, and everyone who knew her knew it. But as she liked to say, we were all dying, every single living being among us. It was just a matter of spending the time you had left in a meaningful way.

As I joined Chuck, a retired auto executive and longtime volunteer, at the plant table at the back of one of the greenhouses, I tried not to think too hard about the meaningful nature of casual sex, manual labor, and coffee.

In a typical week, I worked six out of seven days, even though I averaged thirty hours or less of actual on-the-job time. Tuesday through Friday, I spent my mornings at the Arboretum, adding regular shifts at Boadicea on Friday, Sunday, and Monday, along with any other time Toby asked me to cover a shift. That had made Saturday practically the only time Maddie and I had had to be together for more than a handful of hours.

A PhD student at the U in French Language and Literature, Maddie had dealt with our mutual limited availability by tightly scheduling when and where we would see each other, and for what activities. Despite the fact I had my own apartment while she lived in a shared house with three other grad students, all just as continually amped up on caffeine and stress as she was, Maddie insisted we stay at least as often at her place as mine. Most Fridays, our designated date night, we grabbed dinner and a movie, spent the night together, and went to brunch the next morning with Dez and a cadre of other friends. After spending Saturday together, our weekends were usually capped off by separate Sundays. She settled in at the library while I worked out or hung out with friends before my afternoon shift at Boa. I rarely saw Maddie on weeknights, either. "I have to study," had been her constant refrain, but now I wondered if she'd really meant, "I have to fuck your best friend."

Maddie's careful regimentation of our encounters was fine with me, I'd told myself for the two-plus years we were together. After all, my work schedule wasn't exactly ideal, and she was a grad student from New Hampshire. She couldn't help being uptight, could she? I had met her mother, a frosty former Bostonian, and could attest that the stick up Maddie's ass had been genetically implanted. In hindsight, though, I was beginning to view her aloofness for the red flag it clearly had been. God, I'd been unforgivably blind. And not just about my best friend shagging my girlfriend. While most of the lesbians we knew were shacking up after only knowing each other a few months, Maddie had taken most of our relationship just to work up to giving me a key to her apartment. Never mind she'd had a key to mine for over a year already; my studio was closer to the University than her house, and sometimes she liked to study at my place when I wasn't home, so that *just made sense.*

On our two-year anniversary, after making me an elaborate French dinner à la Julia Child, Maddie had presented me with a tiny jewelry box that bore the logo of my father's store. When I'd opened it to find not a ring but a single key lying inside, I'd thought for a brief moment she was suggesting I move in with her. But then I remembered her roommates, and I stared into the jewelry box while short-lived images of commitment rings and shared furniture faded away.

At last I'd looked up at her. "Seriously?" I said. "The key to your house? That's what you got me?"

Maddie's face closed up before I even finished, her lips pursing in the snotty French girl impression she had perfected during her junior year abroad at the Sorbonne, a look she usually reserved for her French 101 students.

"I mean," I'd added quickly, "it's fine. It's great."

But it was too late. I had crossed the invisible boundary Maddie had drawn between us at some point when I wasn't looking, the one that didn't allow me to express displeasure with anything she said or did. Didn't I understand how *busy* she was? Didn't I understand how little *room* she had in her life for drama? She was trying so hard to balance our relationship with her studies, and sometimes it was just *so difficult* for her.

She kicked me out a little while later, and I walked the mile home alone, the ring box tucked into a pocket of my cargo shorts. Later, I'd called Dez and met her at Lucky's, pouring out my bruised heart to my supposed best friend, not finding it unusual in the least that her eyes remained fixed on the crowd of eerily illuminated women on the dance floor, never suspecting that she and Maddie had started hooking up only a few days before.

Looking back from the vantage point I occupied now, I could sigh a breath of relief at my close call with Maddie. And feel sorry for Dez, too. As soon as the honeymoon ended, she would probably find herself just as rigidly controlled as I had. Or maybe not. Maybe Maddie would treat her differently. I'd always thought they had more in common— Dez was an East Coaster too, originally from Massachusetts, and was currently working on her Master's in Geography at the U. It was possible that Maddie would respect my former friend more than she had me, a lowly barista slash glorified weed puller. Possible that Dez wouldn't put up with the crap I had taken to be with the woman I'd decided I wanted to be with forever without actually getting to know first.

After the break-up, I foundered a bit at ordering my days and nights without Maddie's penchant for schedules to fall back on. But once I'd gotten over the initial nausea-inducing loneliness, I'd begun to discover a new sense of freedom. My Friday nights were my own again, along with my Saturday days and nights. I could stay up past midnight if I wanted! I could stay in bed reading past nine a.m. on a Sunday, should the urge strike! I would never, ever have to sleep on her hard, lumpy futon again, or lie awake in her tiny, dark bedroom mentally reciting the names of plants native to Michigan while she snored softly beside me. I hadn't been allowed to read because it would keep her up, and she needed her sleep, which meant that I had lain beside her countless nights practically holding my breath—Maddie was a light sleeper, dontcha know—and trying not to think about what fun my friends might be getting up to without me.

Not being in a relationship definitely had its advantages. Now I could smoke up whenever I liked—Maddie didn't like the way pot made her feel or the way it made me act—and get tipsy enough to dance and sing if I felt like it. No more girlfriend to frown at my *exuberance* or get up and wash the taste and smell of me off her as soon as we had both come. No more girlfriend, just a pair of sexy, interchangeable college students whose names I sometimes mixed up in my head, who claimed not to want more from me than I was prepared to give.

But as the trip drew closer, Caitlyn, the cheerleader, began to call more frequently. She wanted to stay overnight, too, and to go for breakfast together on the weekends and hang out afterward. At first, I didn't mind. It was nice to be sought after by someone cute and smart and attractive to others. But then my friend Alex, a college buddy who had picked me in the divorce, told me that Caitlyn had confronted Steph at Boadicea one morning while I was at the Arboretum.

It was a Thursday night in early April, ten days before my dad and I were scheduled to leave, and Alex and I were checking out Karaoke night at Ives, a gay bar that offered Women's Night once a month. This was our night, and the only gay boys in the house were dyke-friendly, which wasn't always the case. In the old days, Dez and Alex and I would get our drag on and crash Ives, much to the dismay of the boys who flirted with us. But tonight, Alex and I were in lesbo gear—

tight-fitting tees and cargo pants—instead of chest wraps, fake soul patches, and collared shirts. Alex's hair was pulled back in a ponytail, and she wore her ever-present visor, which Dez and I had been after her for years to lose along with the ponytail. We'd all played rugby at Michigan, a club sport, and had been like the Three Musketeers since sophomore year—until Dez'd had to go and mess everything up.

"And then Caitlyn practically tackled her," Alex said as a gay guy up on stage sang yet another song from *Glee*.

"She did not." I groaned into my bottle of beer, wondering why it was always the petite lesbians who were so feisty.

"Actually, she did. Did you not see this coming, even a little?"

To be honest, I may have noticed that Caitlyn had recently developed a tendency to pout if a call or text from Steph came up in her presence. But I had ignored it, choosing to wait for it to pass rather than deal with the unpleasantness of a formal discussion. If Caitlyn was having a problem with our agreed-upon rules of engagement, she was fully capable of raising her concerns. She was an adult. Legally, at least.

"Come on, Alex," I said. "You know I hate dyke drama."

"Which is probably why you're always mired in it. That which you ignore only grows stronger. Unless we're talking house plants or pets. They pretty much just die."

I rolled my eyes. "I am not worthy of your wisdom, oh captain my captain."

Alex had been chosen player-coach of the rugby team our senior year, and Dez and I had never let her forget it. Mostly because we were jealous, Alex always maintained. Maybe. Okay, probably.

As we sat at a table in the corner of the room, far enough from the Karaoke set-up to hear each other speak, Alex filled me in on the apparent scene between my two non-girlfriends at Boadicea. Steph had been there with her best friend, an artsy, hipster type like her who was "more into men than women." Steph was one of those not uncommon girls at the U who didn't believe in labels. I had made sure at the outset that she was disease-free and not currently diddling with a dude, and that was about as far as my expectations went. Other than a liking for each other's bodies, it had been evident from the start that Steph and I didn't have that much in common.

Caitlyn, on the other hand, apparently believed we were soul mates because we were both Dutch Michiganders whose families ran small businesses. Oh, and her father had basically disowned her, too, when a teacher caught her making out with another girl in a bathroom at her high school. Clearly we were meant to be together.

"So Caitlyn gets all up in Steph's face," Alex reported, "and says, 'If you don't really care about Junior, then why don't you stop throwing yourself at her?' And Steph says, all calm-like, 'Who said I didn't care about her? Besides, *I'm* not the one throwing myself at Junior.'"

At that moment, I dearly wished I had thought to smuggle in a joint—a couple of hits would have made what Alex was telling me seem hilarious instead of borderline catastrophic. Why couldn't they have scheduled their little run-in someplace where I didn't work, or better yet, in another state or even country? Canada wasn't that far away. Really, was a little discretion too much to ask?

"You can see the rest for yourself," Alex said, holding up her phone. "I caught it on video."

Suddenly there they were, my two most recent bedmates acting out in hazy color the scene Alex had described, with an even blurrier crowd of a dozen or so looking on. Fascinated despite myself, I watched as Steph told Caitlyn not to play with the grown-ups if she couldn't handle it, patted her on the head, and turned away, laughing to her friend. Oh, no, she didn't. Even before movie-version Caitlyn pulled her arm back, I knew what was coming: The juice she'd been clutching, her favorite tropical Boa blend by the looks of it, made a lovely orange splatter all over Steph's wool cardigan.

Managing to overcome my rubbernecking proclivities, I reached out and hit the pause button, leaving the video frozen on Steph's shocked face.

"It didn't come to blows, did it?" I asked.

"No. I think Caitlyn realized Steph has a good six inches on her because she pretty much sprinted for the door. That, or she saw me and half the crowd with our phones pointed at her."

"Perfect," I muttered, leaning my forehead onto my folded hands. "It's all over Twitter and Facebook already, isn't it?"

"Um, yeah. I'm surprised you haven't been tagged yet. There's even a hashtag—#StephlynshowdownA2."

She started to pull up her Twitter feed, but I put my hand on her wrist.

"Don't. I mean it, Alex. This is exactly why I don't have a smartphone."

"I thought it was because you couldn't afford a data plan."

"Why can't you just let me hold on to my illusions?"

"I did once, remember? And look how that turned out."

Just like that, the Stephlyn face-off didn't seem quite so bad. Like Toby, Alex had confessed in the wake of my defunct relationship that she had never liked the way Maddie treated me. That was why she'd rarely hung out with us as a couple, accepting invitations only when Dez or another friend was guaranteed to be present. I'd been so busy trying to fit myself into Maddie's life that I hadn't noticed my friends pulling away. Or maybe I'd just pretended not to notice, even to myself.

"Hey, I'm sorry," Alex said, her fingers creasing the worn edge of her visor. "I didn't mean it like that."

"I know," I said, even though we both knew she did.

Dez and I used to tease Alex about her Asperger's, but sometimes I wasn't entirely convinced she didn't suffer from a form of high-functioning autism. Her, and half the researchers who worked in her lab at the University Medical Center.

The conversation moved on to my upcoming European adventure and Alex's imminent trip home to Chicago for her mother's wedding. Her parents had been divorced since she was six, but had lived on different floors in the same Chi-Town skyscraper ever since splitting up, determined to maintain a semblance of family unity for her and her little brother, Trevor. The custody agreement dictated that they would be free to live elsewhere once both kids were out of college. Trevor had graduated from Carleton the previous spring, so their mother was finally marrying her longtime "partner," one of Alex's father's golf buddies.

Alex always said she hadn't realized her version of normal wasn't typical or even average until she got to college and saw how other divorced families behaved. She knew she was lucky, and not just because her mom and dad had stayed on such good terms. Her parents had accepted her pronouncement that she was gay without even blinking, and her mother was still always asking if she had met anyone, when she was going to settle down, when there would be grandkids. And in fact, Alex had been in love with the same girl for years: Ariel, an assistant in a neighboring lab. But she had never so much as asked Ariel out for a drink, claiming that she didn't want reality to ruin the fantasy. Dez had called her chicken, but I sort of knew what she meant. Sometimes the idea of what something could be was so much better than what it actually turned out to be. Although she was kind of a chicken.

But a good friend, nonetheless—she asked me about my travel plans, and didn't bring up the Stephlyn debacle again that night or reference Maddie and Dez in any way, shape, or form. She just bought me beer and sang Pink songs with me, even though she was more of a Dixie Chicks girl herself—Ariel looked a bit like their lead singer, though Alex claimed to like the band for the music, not the eye candy.

That night, back at my quiet apartment, I smoked a fat joint, watched a *Friends* episode, and managed to go to bed without even being tempted to check email or Facebook—almost. Then I lay alone in the dark, wide awake and dreaming about Amsterdam, where the spring buds were already beginning to open and where it was all but guaranteed that no one knew my name.

CHAPTER FOUR

The next day, after my shift at the Gardens, I caught the bus home and hid out at my apartment, ignoring my cell and staying off email. Feeling sorry for myself, I got high again and watched old movies on Netflix and tried not to think about the fact that somewhere in the city it was date night once again. Had Maddie and Dez seen the Stephlyn video? Did Dez wish she could tease me about the embarrassing public display of affection made on my behalf? And had the fact that two attractive women were fighting over me caused Maddie any belated regret, however momentarily? This last question made me bite my lip. I knew Maddie had been, at best, a mediocre girlfriend, and I wanted to be over her, to get beyond the break-up and move on with my life. But wanting something didn't magically make it happen.

Saturday dawned cool, the sun threatening to break through fast-moving clouds. Awakened by the light poking through a gap in my blinds, I got up and dressed in old jeans and a paint-stained sweatshirt decorated with my high school mascot and varsity basketball number. A little while later, I rode my bike to Boadicea and peered through the window to make sure the coast was clear. It was, so I helped myself to a mocha and a blueberry muffin before pointing my bike away from the

University District.

Ever since I'd known Fitzy, she'd lived in a blue-gray Tudor on a quiet cul-de-sac in a northeast Ann Arbor neighborhood that offered easy access to main campus and the Arboretum. I'd spent a lot of time at her house over the years, and not just as a variously paid and unpaid laborer. For a private person, Fitzy enjoyed entertaining. She hosted volunteer appreciation dinners in the spring, summer, and fall, planning luncheons each winter, and spontaneous get-togethers with Arboretum staff and volunteers every month or so. She also regularly housed foreign students, particularly botany students struggling to come up with the money for room and board.

Occasionally when I was in college, she'd foisted these foreigners on me and the other interns, an awkward social exercise that usually resulted in a brief dinner at Bilbo's Pizza or some other affordable spot, followed by a quick getaway for all parties involved. Although on a couple of occasions, this babysitting duty had led to friendship. Once, my sophomore year, it had even led to more with a Japanese girl named Tomiko, a hottie who had kissed her share of girls back home and was only too happy to make me her American conquest. Fitzy had never commented on my increased presence at her house that semester, or on Tomiko's overnight absences from the upstairs room reserved for exchange students. Every once in a while, I still wondered what she'd really thought about me dating her boarder. Not that I would ever ask.

As I pedaled through the quiet streets east of campus, lined with tall old trees, wide yards, and classic older homes, I thought of Fitzy's increasing shortness of breath. She had left work early the day before for a check-up, and I simultaneously wanted and didn't want to know what her doctor had told her. By now I'd read and reread the Mayo Clinic website pages on chronic obstructive pulmonary disease, and I knew there was no cure. For some people, the disease progressed faster than for others. Fitzy had been diagnosed two years earlier with a fairly aggressive form, but she had kept working. I'd overheard some of the volunteers discussing her illness, and they'd all agreed that she would probably work as long as she could. Until she died, I knew they meant. In truth, I feared that one day I would show up at the center and find Fitzy collapsed over her desk, blue-lipped and unseeing.

I wasn't a complete stranger to death—a girl I'd known my entire life had been killed our sophomore year of high school when the car she was riding in hit a patch of ice and struck a tree. A year after that, my grandfather, a commanding force in our family's life, died from heart failure, and a few years later, one of my dad's older sisters was killed during a ski trip to the Upper Peninsula. I had experienced the loss of a friend and more than one family member, but I still hadn't been able to wrap my head around what it would be like to lose Fitzy.

I couldn't imagine the Botanical Gardens without her overly competent, often droll presence, couldn't conceive of more than a week passing without riding my bike or catching a bus to Fitzy's house. I loved working with her in her garden, and I always looked forward to her semi-annual dinner parties, with professors from all walks of university life seated about the table in her colorfully decorated formal dining room, one wall of which overflowed with packed, built-in bookshelves. I was almost always the youngest at these dinners, and would sit back and listen to the sometimes heated discussions of politics, religion, art, music, literature. At the Starreveld dining table, conversation centered mainly on work, family, and school. But at Fitzy's, I soaked up Culture. Straight White Culture, for the most part, but college-town intellectualism of a sort I had not previously encountered despite growing up in said college town.

Without Fitzy to spearhead these get-togethers, would they still happen? Would I want to attend if they did?

Soon I was gliding up her long driveway, bordered by the gently sloping front lawn populated with plants Fitzy had added when she first moved in a decade and a half earlier. A fan of natural landscaping before it was popular, she had transformed her property into a biologically diverse woodland park setting that required less water and maintenance than a traditional turf lawn. But when she'd replaced the existing grass with native plants and a retaining bank made up of stones from a nearby farm, her neighbors had accused her of lowering their property values. One man had allegedly dared to call her plantings a "bunch of ugly weeds" to her face. Having been on the receiving end of a handful of Fitzy's glacial stares over the years, I could only pity the fool. But the neighborhood crowd had gradually come around. Now hers wasn't the only lawn on the block to offer raised flower beds and layered plantings in place of a wide expanse of water-guzzling turf.

The driveway wrapped around to the garage, and I leaned my bike against the corner of the house, just like I always did, expecting to find Fitzy in the backyard as usual on a weekend morning, tending to her spring garden or perhaps working in the greenhouse she'd had built years before. But there was no sign of her in either place, so I headed across the brick patio and up the back stairs. I started to push the screen door open, thought better of it, and knocked.

Nothing. I waited a minute or two, then knocked again, louder, and called, "Fitzy? It's me."

Still no answer.

I waited another few seconds, suddenly aware of the cold sweat from my bike ride pooling at my neck; of a sluggish ant crawling up the side of the back door; of the breeze wafting my helmet-flattened hair against my forehead. Before the fear rising in my gut could form fully, I opened the screen and pushed through Fitzy's unlocked back door. When in doubt, take action, she always said. Worked for me.

Just inside the door was a landing. Straight ahead, a steep stairwell descended into the damp basement that always seemed to smell of laundry detergent. To the right, a handful of steps led up into the kitchen. I took them two at a time, my breath coming faster as I called her name again. Where was she?

I found her in the dining room off the kitchen, seated in a chair, eyes narrowed, oxygen mask over her face. She held up a hand when she saw me, fingers fluttering a vague greeting, or perhaps an admonishment. I stopped in the doorway, unsure how to proceed.

"You didn't answer," I said. "I was worried."

Tiredly, she waved to a chair on the opposite side of the table. I dropped into it, suddenly aware that I must stink of sweat and the cold outdoors, a malodorous combination of which Fitzy was not fond. "I prefer the scent of lilies," she would say when I appeared on her doorstep reeking from my crosstown bike ride. It had become a tradition of sorts, me fresh from my bike grinning mischievously at her while she shooed me from the interior of her house, which usually smelled of sage, her favorite indoor plant, and the pungent scent of less easily identifiable herbs.

Now she only closed her eyes and fought to breathe while I sat uncomfortably on one of the wooden dining chairs, its spokes hard against my back. I tried not to look at her, tried to focus instead on the wall of books on one side of the room, on the framed art and family photos decorating the walls. In one picture, Fitzy was standing on a dirt lane in the middle of a green field, fedora-bedecked head thrown back in laughter. This was my favorite photo of her, from what she called her "golden years" as a flower jockey, when she'd been in high demand on the lecture circuit for her work in plant genetics. It was her favorite photo of herself, too, I knew, from a time when her husband and daughter were still alive and well. Now only she remained, and just barely, from the sound of her breathing.

My eyes returned to her face, tracing the wrinkles carved initially by sun and smiles and weather, but made deeper recently by illness. Her hair had been gray since I'd known her, unruly curls that she kept short, but it seemed listless now, thinner. Even her eyes, a rich brown that reminded me of cedar mulch, seemed paler these days. Under the table, my hands gripped the edges of the shorts I wore over leggings, tugging silently on the nylon edges as I prayed to a deity in whose existence I wasn't sure I believed. Until finally Fitzy's eyes flicked open again and she pulled the mask away from her mouth and uttered a single word: "Lilies."

After a moment, I shook my head. "Guess you'll just have to suck it up."

Reaching across the table, I took her free hand and held it in my sweaty one, ignoring the exaggerated rolled-eye look she cast me. Shrugging, she held the mask back up to her face, and there we sat, the minutes ticking past on the clock in the living room, the only other sound besides her labored breathing the slight hiss and whir of the oxygen tank dispelling its measured contents into her scarred lungs.

When she took the mask down a second time, she gave my hand a squeeze and relinquished it, turning away to hang the mask on its hook atop the olive green canister adorned with a large, bright "DANGER: No Smoking" decal. When I dropped by the previous weekend, I'd caught her out on the covered portion of her patio watching the rain fall and smoking a forbidden cigar, the oxygen tank not far away.

"What are you doing?" I'd demanded, rushing to wheel the tank further from the fiery tip of her cigar. "Are you trying to kill yourself?"

She'd looked up at me and shrugged, her eyes glowing. "It'd only be a small explosion."

Now she nodded at me and pointed at a pile of books on the corner of the nearest bookshelf.

"For you," she said. "Bring them."

She moved ahead of me into the living room, an airy room with wood floors, hand-woven Persian rugs, and French doors that opened out onto a front deck that she had designed herself. The cedar planks were constructed in a large arc around the base of a tall elm tree that kept the house cool all summer long. In the summer, a hammock swung lazily between the elm and a post sunk into the ground at the edge of the deck, only a few paces from the French doors. I was pretty sure I had used the hammock over the years more than Fitzy had, resting after assorted lawn and garden projects while she made us lunch or kept on working without me.

With a sigh, she lowered herself onto a cream-colored couch, all wood and angles and not, in my opinion, very comfortable. When she patted the space beside her, I hesitated.

"You sure? I still stink, you know."

"It's fine. I'm not smelling much of anything these days, anyway."

Fitzy was losing her renowned sense of smell? I gripped the pile of books more tightly and sat down beside her, noting almost automatically the thinness of her thigh compared to mine.

"I'm glad you're here," she said, and patted my hand. Then she reached for the top book: *Keukenhof, Lisse-Holland, 1949-1999: 50 Years of Flowers.* "I've decided to show you why you cannot be allowed to miss out on the best spring garden in the world, my girl."

For the next hour, instead of working outside laying mulch or raking dead leaves, I sat with Fitzy and listened as she described the wonders of Keukenhof, reminiscing about her visits to the renowned gardens. The first time she'd visited Holland had been on her honeymoon in 1968. Twenty years later, she had taken her daughter, Amanda, on a pre-college mother-daughter trip to Europe that had included a stop at Keukenhof. One of the pictures on her desk at the Botanical Gardens featured the two of them posing arm in arm on the deck of an enormous windmill, colorful fields of blooms visible behind them. And the last time she'd visited had been in 1999, for the fifty-year anniversary celebration.

As Fitzy leafed through the commemorative photo book, I wondered what had happened to Amanda Fitzgerald. No one at school seemed to know, or if they did, they weren't talking. I had the sense that her death had been sudden, perhaps an accident of some sort, but Fitzy had never shared the story with me or anyone else, as far as I knew. I wasn't about to ask, either—Fitzy's boundaries were firmly established, and one did not cross them lightly. If she wanted me to know how her daughter died, she would tell me. Still, I couldn't help but wonder about the brown-eyed girl in the Chicago Cubs baseball cap smiling into the sunshine on the deck of a Dutch windmill, her arm held tightly, protectively in her mother's.

Toward the end of the book, Fitzy smoothed her palm across a page that showed the tulip fields around Keukenhof from the air—perfect rectangles of deep color lining the Dutch earth. I would be there, in only a matter of days. Too wild.

"You know," she said, "I've been meaning to ask you something."

"Go ahead."

"All right, then. What are you still doing here, Junior?"

I looked at her, wondering if the lack of oxygen had affected her brain. "Um, it's my day off and I thought you might want some company?"

She shook her head impatiently. "Not at this moment. In general. When I offered you the job at the Arboretum, I thought you'd be there maybe a year, two at the most. But five years later, you're still here and not much has changed."

"I *was* waiting for Maddie to finish grad school, and then we were going to move wherever she got a job."

"And now?"

"I don't know," I admitted. "I like what I'm doing, and the University has good benefits. Besides, Ann Arbor is my home."

Her frown clearly communicated, *Bull honkey*. But her words were somewhat more tactful: "From where I'm sitting, kiddo, you look stuck."

I hunched my shoulders and picked at the ivory flowers stitched into a throw pillow.

"Everyone stumbles sometime," she told me. "The trick is to get back up while you still can. Let me ask you this: If you could go anywhere, where would it be?"

"Keukenhof Gardens, of course."

She rolled her eyes and waited.

I thought for a moment. "I don't know. Seattle, maybe."

Two of my best friends from college had moved to the aptly named Emerald City after graduation, and I had visited them a few times, always in the warm summer months. I loved the greenness of the city, the water and the mountains, the gay-friendly culture. Washington State reminded me a little bit of Michigan, only more progressive and without the humidity. Each time I visited, I'd toyed with the idea of not coming home. But there had always been Maddie and my family and friends to think of.

Fitzy nodded, her smile distant. "Seattle is a wonderful place to grow flowers."

"Have you been there?" I asked. Not that this surprised me. Fitzy had been everywhere.

"My daughter was born there." She rose and stretched her arms above her head, grimacing at the effort. "It pains me to say it, my girl, but I think I need a nap."

"Oh," I said, and tried to hide my surprise as I stood up. "Okay."

"These books are for you. Perhaps you can use them to convince your father of the importance of a day trip to Lisse."

"I'll do my best," I promised, slipping the books into my backpack. I rarely visited Fitzy's house without a bag of some sort, as she was always loading me up with books or CDs or DVDs that I absolutely *had* to experience. Or food—typically something plant-based and exceedingly healthy that would provide me with dinner for a few days.

"I thought I'd do some raking," I said as she guided me toward the back of the house, a hand on the small of my back. "Or maybe spread some mulch. Is there anything else you need? I'm not much of a cook, but I could always bring you some food from the café, if you wanted."

"That's kind of you," she said, sounding as if she actually meant it, "but my sister and her daughter are coming down from Traverse City to visit. I will have all the hangers-on I'll need for the next couple of weeks."

"I didn't know they were coming." Hesitating, I cast her a sideways glance. "Is everything all right?"

For a moment I felt her hand press harder against my back. Then she shook her head. "No, it isn't."

I stopped. We were in her familiar kitchen now, morning light streaming in the picture window over a built-in table that overlooked the backyard. "The doctor?"

"Indeed."

"What did he say?"

"Nothing good, my girl."

Her voice was gentle, and for some reason, that hurt more than what she was telling me without really telling me. Tears stung my eyes, and I bit my lip.

"I don't have to go with my father," I said, my voice low. "I could stay and help out. I could stay here."

"No, you can't," she said, but her voice was still soothing somehow, and her fingers, though shaky, were almost tender as she reached to brush my hair off my forehead. "I'm not going anywhere just yet, and besides, you need to be with your father while you still have the chance."

Her bluntness, though customary, could still be startling: My father wasn't going to be around forever either, she was reminding me none-too-gently. Quickly I blinked away the thought of my father's mortality. Not gonna go there. Not gonna do it.

"Are you sure you don't want me to stay? I wouldn't mind, really."

"Positive," she said with a short nod. "Now get. You can work in the yard if you like. It's a beautiful day, and I know how you like getting your hands dirty. But don't you even think about cancelling your trip, you hear me?"

I nodded reluctantly. "Yes, ma'am."

But of course, I did think about it as I pulled a sweatshirt on over my biking clothes and gathered various tools from the greenhouse. *Nothing good*—what did that really mean? How much time did she have left? She'd said she wasn't going anywhere, but maybe she was only saying that to keep me from ditching my father. Would I come home from Europe to find her gone, just like that?

A man from a local agricultural supplies store had recently dropped off his annual free pickup load of mulch, his generous—though illegal, Fitzy always chided him—thanks for his store's University contract. My mind whirring almost audibly, I loaded up a wheelbarrow with mulch from a tarp on the driveway and carted it to the flower bed near the brick patio. Usually working in the garden, any garden, affected me like meditation, calming my mind as nothing else quite managed to do. But not this morning. I couldn't seem to make myself focus on the fresh scent of shredded bark or the brightness of the clear Michigan sky overhead. I just kept hearing Fitzy's voice, all tired and mild and not like her at all; kept feeling her hand bracing my back as if to prepare me for what was coming. I didn't want to be prepared. I didn't want to face the inevitable, not now or ever—as if by refusing to accept it, I could alter the outcome. It was silly, and irrational, and ultimately doomed to fail, but I couldn't force my feelings to align with what I understood to be true. Honestly, I wasn't even sure I wanted to try.

I was on my third wheelbarrow load when I heard the back door open. Fitzy, zipped into her down North Face jacket—her Michelin Man coat, as she called it—made her way down the back steps and came toward me, stopping at the edge of the patio. I kept working, shoveling load after load of fresh mulch onto the previous year's dregs.

"Patrick is on his way, so you'll have some help soon," she announced.

I nodded. Patrick was another former student who lived in Ann Arbor and liked to help out. Like me and half a dozen other people—colleagues, students, friends, neighbors—he had been dropping by

Fitzy's house more and more lately.

Fitzy remained where she was, shivering despite the morning's warmth.

"That wasn't fair of me, was it?" she asked finally.

I leaned against the shovel and looked at her, blinking back tears for the second time that morning. And here I'd thought Maddie and Dez's treachery had permanently damaged my tear ducts.

"No, it wasn't."

"I don't want you to worry, that's all."

"But I do anyway."

She nodded. "I know, and I'm sorry for that."

"It's not like you can help it."

"No, it isn't, is it."

One half of her face was lit by the sun, the other in shadow as she gazed out across the property I knew she loved.

I took a deep breath, steeled myself to ask the question hammering at my brain: "How much time?"

She turned slightly and lifted her face skyward, closing her eyes against the bright sunshine. "A couple of months, maybe. At the current rate of deterioration, I should be spared another Independence Day, at least."

Fitzy had always hated the Fourth of July, not for what it represented, she maintained, but for the irksome antics of her fellow citizens who insisted on experimenting with deafening pyrotechnics for a full week before and after the anniversary of American independence.

"It's not funny," I said, my voice gravelly.

She moved closer, touched my arm. "It's just my time, you understand? I've had a full life, blessed beyond reason some would argue. The fact that my time is coming to a close doesn't have to be a negative."

This declaration was similar to one she'd offered up the previous fall when Curly, at age twelve, was diagnosed with a malignant growth on her liver. But still, as she'd held Curly in her arms for the last time, she'd cried. We both had, before, during, and after I lay Curly to rest at the bottom of the hole I'd dug here in this very yard, not far from the goofy mutt's favorite shady summertime nap spot. Just because it was time for a life to end didn't mean it wasn't hard to say goodbye.

I swallowed. "I know. You're right."

She squeezed my arm. "That's the spirit. Now, I'm going to go in and send some emails. Come in when you get hungry. I have a quinoa salad all made for you. Patrick is on his own—I don't feel like roasting an entire chicken for that boy."

I nodded and forced a smile as she turned away. For some reason, she seemed to need me to act as if her illness wasn't difficult for me— maybe so that she could maintain a sense of control over the situation? It wasn't asking all that much. I could even understand the impulse. For years I had attended family dinners and celebrations and events, all the while pretending that the fact my parents no longer seemed to love me as much as they once had didn't matter. But it did, just as it mattered that Fitzy, who along with Dez and Alex and Toby and Sheila had become my other family, the one that loved me no matter what, would be dead before summer's end. It mattered that she was dying, and it would always matter to me that she was gone.

I turned back to the wheelbarrow, hiding my face from the kitchen window and lifting my shovel again as the tears slid unchecked over my cheeks. She had given me so much. The least I could do was try to help her maintain a modicum of control over her life. Because at some point, I knew, she would lose even that, and then there would be no more pretending for Fitzy, no more illusions to cling to for those of us who loved her.

For now, she could still putz about her kitchen, the smell of quinoa and parsley in the air, while the sun warmed the earth and awakened the bulbs buried underground, unseen by the human eye. For now, I could attend to the rhythms of the season and prepare the ground for the return of the plant life she and I both loved so much. I wiped my eyes and told myself it was enough as I swung the shovel rhythmically and breathed in the cool, sweet air of another Michigan spring.

CHAPTER FIVE

The week before the trip, I steered clear of Lucky's and even avoided Boadicea when I wasn't working. Steph took the hint when I didn't call her back, and other than an apologetic text for her part in the scene she guessed I'd heard about by now, left me to my own devices. Caitlyn appeared less intuitive. In the days leading up to my trip, she took on near-stalker status, tracking me down at Boa twice—a heads-up from co-workers on both occasions allowed me to slip temporarily out the back door—and camping out on my doorstep once, until Alex, alerted by my incredulous text, "stopped by" and shamed my unwanted guest into leaving a note on my (fortunately) locked door.

When I wasn't dodging infatuated cheerleaders or worrying about Fitzy's prognosis, I whiled away the week browsing gay travel web sites and the University library's collection of guidebooks for Belgium and the Netherlands. I wanted to know where I was going before I got there—history, sights, things the average tourist might not know to look for. Toby, who had lived in Amsterdam briefly in the '90s and returned every couple of years to visit friends, did her part to supplement my reading. A few days before I left, she presented me with a gay and lesbian guidebook, a list of places to see, and the phone number of one of her Dutch friends who had offered to show me around the city.

"Sofie is a total flirt," she warned. "Make sure you don't take her too seriously."

I tucked the list into my wallet. "No worries. I'll only be in Amsterdam a few nights."

"We're talking lesbians here, Junior. Dykes have moved in together after less time."

This comment made me think of Maddie, but the tweak of memory was less painful than I expected.

"Don't worry your pretty little head," I told Toby. "I'm not looking to get involved."

"Why do I feel like I've heard that before?" She reached into the cash register and pulled out a roll of bills. "Take this, too. Consider it your vacation pay."

"Wow—thanks, Toby. Are you sure?"

"Of course. Now get out of here. Dani and I can handle closing tonight, and Lord knows you could use your beauty sleep."

I'd come in at Toby's request to cover a shift, but I had to be at work at the Arboretum in the morning, so I was just as happy to head home early.

"Thanks, dude. You're the best."

"She finally notices."

Clutching the wad of money inside my jacket pocket, I walked the five blocks home to my tiny daylight basement studio with its barred windows and towering willow tree that blocked out any chance the sunlight had of reaching my apartment. I loved that tree, loved to lie on the floor of my studio staring up through its long tresses at blue sky just eking through, listening to music that matched my mood and state of inebriation—drunk/sober + nostalgic usually meant the Indigo Girls; drunk/sober + angry, Pink, Katy Perry, or one of the two Melissas; high + spacey, Sarah McLachlan or Enya. Small as it was, I loved my studio. It was the first place of my own I'd ever had, and seemed more luxurious in its solitude than my parents' house with its antiques, English gardens, and tennis courts.

I'd left the mansion on the hill the summer before my freshman year of college and moved into a shared house just off-campus, readily shedding everything that had come with living with my parents—constant family events, rigid schedule of chores, complete lack of privacy. I hadn't fully comprehended the stifling nature of life in the Starreveld clan until I moved into that first shared house, where the weekly house meetings and discussions of purposeful communal living—shockingly, an all-lesbian household—seemed minor inconveniences compared to what I was used to.

After I left home, I lived as independently of my fellow Starrevelds as I could, given that I resided within twenty miles of most of my nuclear and extended family. I answered my cell phone only after checking caller ID; set up a folder in my email account to automatically filter out messages from family members; and picked shared housing near the University, a part of town most of my family members avoided. I used these tactics to combat filial proximity even as I continued reporting to bi-monthly dinners at the house. This outward show of faith kept my parents and sisters from convening a messy intervention. I knew I had distanced myself from the family; no need for them to know just how far.

Even now that I'd moved into my own place, my family rarely visited, except Jane, who had always looked out for me. I was never sure if their reticence arose more from the fact that I didn't invite them or from the nature of my neighborhood. Surrounding buildings sported rainbow flags and pink triangle banners, while gays and lesbians walked the sidewalks holding hands and otherwise "flaunting" their sexuality. Whatever it was keeping them away, Jane was the only Starreveld who had ventured onto my street since they'd helped me move into my apartment the previous summer.

That was probably why, when I came home from a pre-trip breakfast date with Alex and a couple of other friends the Sunday before my European adventure and discovered my mother waiting on the stoop to my building, I nearly tripped and impaled myself on the cast iron railing. I stopped on the sidewalk before her and folded my arms strategically over the large red "Lesbian Avengers" slogan scrawled across the front of my favorite ever thrift store T-shirt.

"Mom," I said, mentally cataloging the potential disasters awaiting in my apartment: dirty laundry sitting out in heaps; empty beer bottles and half-full coffee cups littering the kitchen counter; and assorted queer paraphernalia I'd been known to tone down for scheduled familial visits. "What are you doing here?"

"I was in the neighborhood," she said, "and thought we might have a chat. Do you have a few minutes?"

"I actually have to be at work pretty soon," I lied.

"That's okay, honey. This won't take long." She waited on the steps.

What else could I do? I fished my keys from my jeans pocket and escorted her inside.

"I had forgotten how dark this apartment is," my mother remarked, pausing in the doorway.

"You get used to it," I said, and dashed about corralling dirty socks and sports bras. "Anyway, with the growth lights on, it's nice." I had infrared lights rigged along one entire wall of the studio to supplement the paltry sunlight my jungle of indoor plants received. Sometimes when I came in, the torpid, tropical smell of plants reminded me of the Arboretum's conservatory, one of my favorite places. Maddie used to say my apartment smelled like spring—on the rare nights she deigned to stay over.

"Ah, yes," my mother said. "The growth lights."

My father, who was allergic to anything borne of seed, had sneezed prolifically the night he helped move my queen-sized bed in. Another reason my parents rarely visited?

I shoved my laundry behind the Asian screen that separated my rumpled bed from the rest of the apartment, and glanced around, looking for other areas of concern. While the door to the walk-in closet was open, a false back fortunately hid my weed plants. I didn't grow enough to sell, only to consume and share with friends, though I had been tempted to deal on more than one occasion. But while my conservative upbringing might have been what led me to grow marijuana in order to avoid paying street prices—we Dutch-Americans are notorious Scrooges—it also gave me pause on matters of felony criminal conduct.

"Have a seat," I said, waving at the futon couch, a vestige of Jane's grad school days, in one corner of the living area. As I did so, I noticed lace peeking out from under a pillow on the nearby papasan chair. Caitlyn's bra; we'd wondered where it had gotten to. Could I actually have Alex deliver it to her while I was gone, or would I have to face her again? More than likely, the latter. The whole head-in-the-sand approach had proven dysfunctional too many times in the past, a fact that Jane and Toby had tried—separately—for years to drive into my resistant brain.

Fortunately, my mother appeared to be busy selecting a clean spot for her Coach purse on the battered black military-issue trunk that passed for a coffee table, so I quickly stuffed the bra in my back pocket and removed a couple of beer bottles from the trunk.

"Let me get these," I said. "Would you like something to drink?"

"No, but thank you, dear."

I stowed the bottles under the kitchen sink and returned to drop into the papasan, wondering what could possibly have convinced my mother to leave her safe, comfortable existence for my not-so-safe world. Perched on the edge of the futon couch in dress pants and a pale blue V-neck sweater, a string of pearls cinched at her pale throat, she looked efficient and professional, and thus grossly out of place in my ghetto studio. She always appeared well put together, even first thing in the morning. It was one of those mysterious feminine qualities that I alone among my sisters had failed to inherit.

"Okay. Well." I tried not to stare at the Botticelli print behind her head, overflowing with voluptuous fifteenth century beauties. All naked. "It's, um, kind of surprising to see you here, Mom."

"I suppose I don't get here as often as I might," she admitted, sounding genuinely disappointed by this circumstance. Killing others with kindness wasn't just her favorite adage; it was a way of life.

Sighing inwardly, I waited for her to proceed. The guilt fest would begin momentarily, no doubt. Five-four-three-two…

"I'll come to the point, honey. It's no secret that you and your father have enjoyed a somewhat strained relationship in recent years. I'm just hoping you'll be able to set aside your resentment during the trip."

"*My* resentment?"

Her head tilted as if I had spoken in Russian, or perhaps Mandarin.

"He's the one who refuses to accept me for who I am," I insisted. Her maternal instincts were usually more accurate. Had she somehow missed the fact that he rarely looked me in the eye?

"Correct me if I'm wrong," she said with a motherly smile, "but I believe it was you who said, 'Suck it up and deal, old man.'"

I frowned. "Yeah, but only after he made it clear he wasn't interested in having a lesbian daughter."

"And wasn't it you who said, 'I'm here, I'm queer, get used to it,' shortly after sharing your sexual orientation for the first time?"

That did sound familiar.

"I think the point is," I said, "and I'll agree to this, Dad and I haven't been on the best terms in recent years."

"That's why I'm here. I could use your help, Elizabeth."

"What kind of help?"

"I'm hoping you can be kind to your father while you're overseas together," she said. "He's under a great deal of pressure at work right now."

I blinked, trying to remember if my mother had ever approached me with such a request. My parents nearly always presented a unified front, working out any potential differences behind closed doors. He couldn't possibly know she was here now, which made me wonder— what kind of pressure at work was my father under?

"Um, yeah, okay," I said, nodding.

"I knew you would, Elizabeth," she said, bestowing another of her pleasant smiles before guiding the conversation elsewhere. She didn't ask about my personal life, which was just as well, given its current chaotic state of lesbodrama. Jane was the only member of my family who knew about Maddie and Dez; everyone else appeared to believe wholeheartedly in the Don't Ask, Don't Tell approach, which could also be known as putting your head in the sand. I wasn't sure where Jane had come by her assertiveness. Perhaps it had skipped a couple of generations.

After another quarter hour of conversation about work and assorted relatives—my father and I would be missing one cousin's birthday and another's christening while we were gone—my mother announced that she had to be going.

At the door, she turned. "We'll see you for dinner tonight, won't we?"

"Actually," I said, "I have to pack."

Our flight was scheduled to leave at four thirty the next afternoon. My father had asked me to be ready by one o'clock so that we could get through security and be at our gate at least two hours early. I couldn't remember the last time I'd been more than half an hour early for a flight. Not that I flew all that often.

"Oh?" my mother intoned, again with easily discernible disappointment.

"I have to work today and tomorrow," I told her, ignoring the familiar tug of guilt. "Tonight's my only chance to pack. I was going to call you later."

"You work too hard, sweetie," she said, kissing my forehead. "Just like your father. But I'm glad I got to see you before you go. Have a safe trip. Enjoy Europe—and take care of Dad for me, will you?"

"Of course," I said, kissing her back.

"I love you."

"Love you, too."

With that, she hugged me again and withdrew, closing the door softly behind her. The maternal ambush was over.

I released a breath and turned back to my apartment, gazing upon WWII-era women's recruitment posters, shelves full of GLBT books, counters and windowsills overflowing with plants. Judging by my family's standards, I could see it wasn't much. But it was mine.

My mother's elegance, at least, was mostly assumed. She was a typical Euro-American mutt, sprung from poor, Irish-German roots with nothing particularly extraordinary or memorable to boast about in her ancestry. All the prestige and history, not to mention money, came from my father's side of the family. Sometimes, okay, usually, I wished my mom could be more like her sister, my Aunt Barbara, who lived with her husband and kids on an organic farm near Kalamazoo. Six years younger than my mother, Barb had always seemed as if she came from an entirely different generation. Whereas my mom had dutifully married and bore children, Barb had demonstrated against the Vietnam War and spent two years with the Peace Corps teaching African villagers sustainable farming practices. She and her husband, Mark, had traveled the world for almost a year after they got married in Senegal. Unlike a lot of Baby Boomers, they'd remained idealists as they grew older, rather than selling out for a Volvo and a McMansion.

More than anything, I wished my mother would follow Barb's lead when it came to my "sexual orientation." When I was sixteen, my high school girlfriend Kelly and I used to escape as often as possible to Saugatuck, a gay-friendly art colony on Lake Michigan. One Saturday afternoon the summer before our junior year, Kelly and I were wandering the shops, hand in hand. I had just purchased my first set of freedom rings and was wearing them proudly on a chain around my neck when we turned a corner and ran, literally, into my Aunt Barb.

I let go of Kelly's hand. "Barb! What are you doing here?"

"My friend Martha has a gallery opening today," she said, and enveloped me in one of her customary bear hugs. She smelled like patchouli. "What a wonderful surprise to run into you." She held her hand out to Kelly. "I'm Lizzie's aunt. And you are?"

"Kelly," she murmured, and shook Barb's hand.

"We play softball together," I said lamely, even though I knew my aunt would not have missed the fact that Kelly and I had been holding hands. She was too quick.

"Softball," she repeated. "How nice for you both."

She asked after my mother, whom she hadn't seen in a while even though they only lived an hour and a half apart. We chatted briefly, weather and summer plans and family, and then Barb said she had to get to that opening.

"Lovely to see you, Lizzie, and wonderful to meet you, Kelly. You girls have yourselves a fabulous day." And with a sweep of her African print sari, she strode off down the sidewalk.

I caught up to her halfway down the block. "Barb, wait."

"What is it, sweetie?"

"I just wanted, well, could you not tell my mom you saw me today?"

She tilted her head sideways. "Can I ask why?"

"She doesn't know I'm here." I gestured back at Kelly, who was pretending to be engrossed in window-shopping at a store that specialized in crystals and animal totems. "She doesn't know we're here."

"Oh, I see. Don't worry, your secret is safe with me." She squeezed my forearm.

"Um, thanks." But which secret?

She didn't keep me wondering long. "I like your freedom rings," she added. "Martha and her girlfriend have theirs hanging from their fridge."

With that, I knew my secret really was safe. I wasn't ready for anyone else in my family to know about my sexuality yet. I wanted to be away from them all, beyond the reach of their constrictive presence, before I officially acknowledged the part of myself they had always appeared to want most to change.

When I did finally feel secure enough to come out to my family a couple of summers later, and it didn't go so well—my sisters exchanged money, my father walked out, and my mother cried—it seemed only natural to borrow Jane's car and drive out to Barb's farm in Paw Paw for the non-judgmental acceptance I knew awaited me.

To be fair, once the furor over my pronouncement died down, my mother had emulated her sister's approach and made a concerted effort to accept me for who I was. Though it took her close to a year to work back up to her usual motherly displays of affection, she never stopped telling me she loved me. I knew I had it pretty good, comparatively. Other friends' coming out stories featured forbidden contact with younger family members, college tuition left unpaid, even outright physical violence in a couple of cases. My story was mild in comparison, pairing as it did an almost undistinguishable change in affection with a more obvious refusal to openly acknowledge or condone my *chosen lifestyle*. Things had gotten better, yes. But someday, I hoped they wouldn't have to.

After my mother left, I still had nearly an hour to kill before work. I flopped on the futon couch and turned on my flat screen television, another hand-me-down from Jane. Strange to think that soon I would be in the country my father's ancestors had left behind to seek their fortunes in America. I wondered if visiting the Netherlands would feel like coming home somehow. But then, if I didn't fully belong in Ann Arbor, where I had lived my entire life, how would I ever feel at home anywhere else?

WKBD was showing a replay of the Bulls at the Pistons in a late season match-up. I turned up the volume. The waiting was almost over now. The following night, my father and I would be on our way to Antwerp, the diamond capital of the world, far from the Palace of Auburn Hills. It was like time travel, in a way, only far less likely to create a potentially deadly space-time conundrum.

"I'm going to Europe," I said to the wall of plants watching TV over my shoulder. "Can you effing believe it?"

I'm pretty sure they couldn't.

CHAPTER SIX

"What are you reading?" my father asked.

We were sitting knee to knee on the plane, which had reached its cruising altitude of 37,000 feet a little while before. The captain had turned off the seat belt sign, my day hikers were off, and I'd just started an Emma Donoghue novel Toby had loaned me about a flight attendant and passenger who meet and become involved after the passenger's seatmate expires in-flight. Not even ten pages in, and I was already questioning Toby's judgment when it came to suitable reading material for traveling. Ruminating on death and flying usually leads me to the specter of 9/11, an event I suspect many twenty-first century Americans can't help but recall each time we board a plane. Reading was supposed to distract me from fears of international terrorism, not reinforce them.

"It's a novel," I said, showing my father the paperback cover and hoping he wouldn't ask for details. I didn't mind the L word, but he definitely did.

"Ah," he said, and turned back to his own book.

I hesitated. If we'd had a nice, simple relationship rather than one fraught with Freudian complexes and congenital enmity, I would inquire after his reading material in return. We didn't, but I did remember the promise I had made my mother only twenty-four hours before.

"What about you?" I asked.

He held up a library book: *The Nature of Diamonds*. "It's a companion volume to the American Museum of Natural History's diamond exhibit. Fascinating stuff—all about the history and dual value, both scientific and symbolic, of the diamond."

"Gotcha."

I smiled politely and hit play on my iPod. "Fascinating" seemed a bit of a stretch. Had my father been born loving gemstones, or was it learned behavior? What about my love of all things green and my ennui toward precious stones? That pesky nature vs. nurture argument— always a mystery.

In DC, the sky was dark when we changed planes and boarded a jet bound for Brussels. The first fifteen minutes in the air, I crossed my fingers and watched intently for cockpit attacks that didn't come, images of the falling towers and burning Pentagon still vivid in my memory even after a decade. But soon we were out over open water, and my vigilance eased. As we crossed the Atlantic, a seemingly endless expanse of black water from one arced horizon to the other, I took a break from fiction for light-hearted lesbian gossip in *Curve* magazine and, later, some sobering news from the *Advocate*. My father didn't ask after my reading material again.

After a meal, a movie, and several hours of uneasy sleep, all accompanied by the monotonous drone of the engines keeping the jet and its human cargo miraculously, to my mind, airborne, the sky lightened and land finally appeared below us again. Europe! We had crossed the ocean, reversing the journey my great-great grandfather had taken a hundred and fifty years earlier when he immigrated to America, uncertain what awaited him on the other side of the sea. Only in our case, the crossing from one continent to another took seven hours instead of seven weeks.

Yawning—it was still the middle of the night according to my body—I checked the in-flight map on the tiny television screen built into the back of the seat in front of me. We were over France now, its green land mass hidden beneath an inexorable layer of clouds. Our route would take us near Paris, I noted, and closed my eyes against a rush of memories. Maddie and I had planned to take a romantic trip to the French capital to celebrate the successful completion of her oral exams, scheduled for the following spring. She would take me to her favorite spots in the city, she told me—coffee and crepes along a quiet street not far from the Bastille; long walks on the Left Bank and the Champs-Élysées; sun-filled mornings of lazy sex and lavish breakfasts in bed. In short, the vacation from real life we never seemed to have time to take.

Now I was in Europe without her, and she was at home with Dez, of all people. I still wasn't sure how we'd gotten from where we started to where we were now. We had planned so many things—marriage, children, a home of our own. First off, Maddie would finish her degree and find a faculty position at whatever educational institution would have her. I was only too happy to go along, assuming it wasn't to Boise or Birmingham or Texas. We both wanted kids eventually, but Maddie would carry the babies, since I couldn't quite imagine being The Bio Mom myself. I'd watched my sisters go through their pregnancies, and could honestly say I had no interest in following suit. Maddie had always wanted to have a baby, though, so that seemed perfect.

When had she stopped wanting our future? But I knew when,

thanks to Dez's big mouth: day four of the previous summer's Michigan Womyn's Music Fest, mere hours after I caught a ride back to Ann Arbor to visit the hospital bedside of a cousin who had been badly injured in a car accident. Classy, my ex-girlfriend and former best friend, you must admit. Was Maddie now planning to be Dez's baby mama, Dez the lesbian dad to Maddie's future offspring? Whatever. They deserved each other, I assured myself, switching the tiny TV screen back to Comedy Central. Why mope about a ruined future when you could watch weeks-old episodes of *The Daily Show with Jon Stewart*?

A short time later the plane slowed as we descended through multiple cloud layers above the gray city of Brussels. I watched out the window as we floated downward over orange tile roofs and brown brick buildings awash in a sea of green countryside and pale morning light, the colorful image distorted by the beveled window pane. Seasonally, Michigan was a few weeks behind Belgium, and nowhere near as green. Which meant, I hoped, that the spring flower season here would be further along. Spring bulbs were my favorite. Fitzy's, too. She'd asked me to take copious amounts of photos, and I damn well intended to try.

As we deplaned, passports stowed safely in my father's briefcase, two thoughts occurred to me: I was in Europe! And, twelve hours down, roughly 150 more to go with my father. Just the two of us. Traveling together in a foreign land.

Piece of cake.

The first famed European sight I saw was not a gold-gilded, Michelangelo-adorned cathedral. Nor was it a quaint cobblestone square bordered by picturesque buildings. Rather, it was a seemingly innocuous fountain that contained a tiny statue of a boy peeing. In his left hand he held his miniature penis, a steady stream of water pouring from it. Tourists, laden with chocolate cell phones and Tintin postcards from shops on the nearby alley, giggled and snapped shot after shot on their cameras. Meanwhile, beside me, my father tapped his foot in staccato rhythm against the stone street.

The Mannekin Pis had been my idea. One of the most famous Belgian attractions, the statue was supposedly better known to tourists than any other point of interest in Brussels. The inspiration for the statue had long since been lost. Prevailing theories now ascribed the boy's fame to different exploits: He was a nobleman's son who had gotten lost and been found while relieving himself; he'd patriotically peed on a Spanish soldier who passed beneath his window; or, most popular on the tourist circuit, he'd saved Town Hall during an unspecified war by extinguishing a sputtering bomb with the only liquid available.

My father, however, showed no interest in this particular sight. We only had two hours in Brussels before we had to catch our train to Antwerp, and he wanted to visit the Grand-Place square on the way to the Stock Exchange and Royal Palace. But I pointed out that the Mannekin Pis was only a few blocks from the train station, and as my father had refused to even consider visiting the Brewery Museum, reputed home of the Knights of the Mash Staff, I was putting my foot down. He begrudged me the stop but declined to pose for my pocket-sized digital camera in front of the fountain.

Was it impatience making him avert his eyes from the peeing stone boy, or was his Dutch Reformed upbringing (and adulthood) getting to him? I wanted to tell him to relax, that bodies were no big deal. Even before I came out, I'd never understood why my parents had to be so uptight. But as I stood on the crowded street in front of Belgium's best-known fountain, I again remembered I had promised my mother I would take it easy on him. Besides, my dad had picked *me* to bring to Europe, when he could have chosen pretty much anyone. A fake smile fastened to my lips, I posed solo and followed him down a narrow, tourist-infested street toward the city center.

The Grand-Place, I decided later, in all its Gothic absurdity, was my favorite sight in Brussels. According to my guidebook, the sculptures on the facade of the square's ornate Town Hall included a group of drinking monks, a sampling of medieval torture devices, and a sleeping Moor with his harem. Belgians, apparently, knew how to have a good time. Or some of them did, anyway. We poked around the Royal Palace and the Stock Exchange—*yawn*—picked up croissants and juice from a bakery whose scent lured us in from a block away, and headed back to the train station through a maze of gaudy restaurant-bedecked alleys that bordered the Grand-Place.

I was going to like this Europe thing, I decided as we collected our luggage from storage lockers at the station.

From Brussels, we continued by train to Antwerp, me with my traveler's backpack on loan from Toby, my father with his wheeled suitcase. As we rolled past the Belgian countryside and small towns composed of seemingly identical red-roofed stone cottages and central town squares, I studied my guidebook. At one time, Belgium and the Netherlands were known collectively as the Low Countries. Now, however, the two nations are staunchly independent and somewhat competitive, like many other neighboring countries across Europe.

This inter-nation rivalry reminded me of the tension between states back home. Michiganders hate Ohioans for mostly forgotten historical transgressions (not counting various Wolverine-Buckeye grid iron battles); Minnesotans resent the Cheeseheads of Wisconsin one would assume for the mascot's tackiness, although Minnesota *is* home to the Mall of America, so perhaps the hostility isn't based on taste; and most western states have little patience for California's self-obsession. Apparently regional rivalry is a universal human trait.

I let my eye wander across the map at the back of the book, taking in the layout of Northern Europe. While I knew little about Belgium and couldn't manufacture more than an average interest in the tiny country sandwiched between France and the Netherlands, I was bummed that I'd missed the Brewery Museum. I'd wanted to experience Belgium's passion for beer firsthand. One of my guidebooks said that in the sixteenth century, when plague ran rampant throughout the Low Countries and water was unfit for consumption, commoners drank beer instead. My kind of people.

The Dutch, however, were literally my people. I'd been hearing stories of my ancestors' homeland since before I was old enough to understand the concept of emigration. On the map, I zeroed in on Rotterdam, where my great-great grandfather Wilhelm Starreveld had set sail for America in the mid-1800s, leaving his homeland for the new Dutch Colony in southern Michigan. The tale was as familiar to me as the legendary battle cry at Bunker Hill: "Don't fire until you see the whites of their eyes!" Until college, I had believed that everyone knew the story of their forbears' landfall in America. Now, however, I understood that we were more of an exception for knowing, not the rule.

I didn't need to read the guidebook to know some things about the Netherlands. I already knew, for example, that almost half its land mass is below sea level; that its system of dikes—one of the more ironic homonyms in the English language, in my opinion—and canals evolved over a thousand years to prevent unruly rivers and seas from flooding the lower-lying regions; that the Dutch like to say, "God made the earth, and the Dutch made Holland." But I knew informal history, mostly. The guidebooks would supplement my Netherlands experience with formal data.

We weren't going to the Netherlands yet, though. For the next two and a half days, we would attend the IAJ convention in Antwerp, Belgium, diamond capital of the world. I pictured it again—hotel conference rooms filled with so many clones of my father, well-dressed, mild-mannered men all inexplicably obsessed with gemstones.

Two days of boredom wasn't such a bad price to pay for four days in Amsterdam. Besides, maybe I could sneak away at some point to experience the renowned Belgian knack for brewing, preferably without my father at my side.

We arrived in the middle of the day at our hotel, a comfortable establishment near Antwerp's central train station in the heart of the diamond quarter. While he went by the convention center to check in and pick up our registration packets, I gorged myself on a fresh cheese sandwich from the hotel dining room and then promptly fell asleep, remaining dead to the world until my father woke me up for dinner three hours later.

The extended nap was perhaps a bad idea, I realized as I lay in bed that night unable to sleep. It was only dinnertime back in Michigan, so I left the television on in the background and thumbed through Frommer's. Antwerp sounded like a cool place, and I didn't particularly want to spend my entire time here cooped up at the convention while a vibrant European city hummed unseen around me. First order of business the next day would be to figure out how to get some time to myself away from the convention.

But in the hotel dining room the next morning, as I faced my father across a mahogany table covered in a white lace tablecloth that reminded me of home, I couldn't bring myself to mention my agenda. He seemed so animated as he leafed through the convention guide, unintentionally hip in wire-rimmed glasses that kept slipping down his nose.

"I thought we could both attend the morning seminar on e-commerce for retail stores," he said, "and then after lunch you could attend the GIA lecture on stone-cutting research while I go to the symposium on conflict diamonds. That is, if you're willing."

"Of course," I forced myself to say.

Even I recognized that it would be exceedingly ungrateful of me to bail on the convention, but I was torn. While I had endured years of dinner conversation about ways to boost sales figures and the encroachment of big-box retailers on independent jewelers, I had never been to Europe. I'd only left the United States for brief trips to Canada and a lone spring break in Mexico my senior year of college, and besides kilometers-per-hour speed limits and other metric-based road signs, Ontario was nearly indistinguishable from Michigan. I couldn't help wanting to play tourist—to poke around the Antwerp Zoo, explore the Rubens House, visit the Steen Castle on the banks of the River Scheldt.

My father studied me over the top of his glasses, perhaps attuned to my less than authentic enthusiasm.

I smiled. "It sounds really interesting. When do we get going?"

"After breakfast," he said. "Are you planning to wear that?"

I glanced down at my faded jeans and U of M Athletics T-shirt. "No," I lied. "I have khakis upstairs."

I actually did, assuming cargo pants counted.

"Good," he said, and went back to perusing the twenty-page color guide to the convention.

At first, things went better than I'd expected. The e-commerce seminar was interesting, though perhaps somewhat simplistic. I thought the presenter could have gone a bit more in depth into the specific types of inventory database programs and business software packages he would recommend for independently-owned shops. But as it was, I had to explain much of the largely generalized material to my father over a buffet luncheon at the convention hotel, one of Antwerp's most exclusive.

After I finished describing the difference between open-source and proprietary software, my father sat back in his chair.

"I wasn't aware you knew so much about computers."

"I took a bunch of computer science classes in college," I told him. "The first one was required, and then I ended up really liking it. I designed Boadicea's website, actually."

"You designed a website?" He seemed amazed.

"It isn't hard once you know how. Toby wanted something simple, more of an online brochure with directions and a PDF menu. It isn't fancy, by any means. Any high school kid with half a brain could probably do better."

"I doubt that," my father said. "I would have been lost in that seminar without you, and I like to think of myself as possessing more than half a brain."

"You know what I mean—anyone who knows something about computers, or even just how to tweak a free template. You don't have to know HTML to design websites anymore."

"Do you think I might be able to see it sometime?"

"It's public, Dad. Anyone who wants to can see it online."

I had never mentioned the website to my parents because it reflected Boa's bohemian, mostly queer clientele. But they could deal with a few lines from a Sappho poem, the story of Boadicea and her armies, and some tasteful graphics created by one of Toby's artist friends.

After lunch, unfortunately, the convention went downhill. I hadn't slept much the night before, and despite fortifying myself with excellent Italian roast coffee at lunch, food coma set in. I had a hard time keeping my eyes open at the afternoon lecture, "Update on Gem Cutting Research at the Gemology Institute of America," which I attended alone while my father checked out a different seminar on diamond acquisition in the twenty-first century.

My sisters and I had all obtained a gemology certificate via a GIA correspondence course before we went to work part-time in our father's store. But it had been nearly a decade since I'd taken the course, and the lecture at the convention was intended for people like my father or his manager: highly experienced—and greatly interested—in working with precious stones. I tried to take notes as the GIA researchers described assorted laser techniques and the use of computer modeling, but the language was far beyond my basic level of understanding. I ended up simply recording Power Point bullets in a notebook while struggling to stay awake, projection screen blurring in my vision.

After the lecture, my father and I met in the hotel's ballroom for a stroll through the vendor booths in the exhibition hall. My head soon ached from the bright lights accentuating the wares of diamond distributors (DeBeers, the largest distributor in the world, maintained the largest booth); makers of CAD/ CAM jewelry design software; laser manufacturers; repair equipment retailers; technical schools;

wholesale suppliers; torch and drill makers; and a dozen other types of vendors and suppliers of the gemstone industry.

I'd never been much of a fan of shopping, and usually became overwhelmed after fifteen minutes at a mall or megastore. Roaming crowded convention display booths on an empty stomach while jet-lagged in a foreign city was, I soon discovered, worse than overwhelming.

Perhaps if my blood sugar hadn't been so low, I could have soldiered on through dinner, feigning interest in the seminar my father had attended on minimizing the effects of conflict diamonds—stones obtained on the black market from war-strewn African countries—on sales. The next morning, I might have dozed on and off through the seminars he wanted us to attend on laser refraction, computer modeling, and jewelry as luxury goods. I might even have muddled through the afternoon symposium on keeping the business in the family, though the last thing any of my sisters or I wanted was to join the family business. My father and I might have caught the train to Amsterdam still on good terms, Dad pleased that I hadn't flaked out on him, me disappointed I hadn't seen much of Antwerp but satisfied that I'd played the dutiful daughter. If I hadn't needed to eat so badly, the rest of the trip might have gone completely differently, which may have meant worse or better, hard to say which for sure.

But I was sugar crashing from the Belgian chocolate I'd smuggled into the GIA lecture, and my head hurt, and I was tired, and the classy decor of the restaurant my father selected, the Sir Anthony Van Dyck (with zero apparent sense of irony), did little to quell my growing impatience with all things gemology-related. When my father said he was looking forward to hearing what I thought of the following day's events, I said exactly what I was thinking and feeling at that moment:

"About that, Dad. I'm not sure it makes sense for me to spend the whole day at the convention tomorrow."

"Excuse me?" My father frowned at me across the table's floral centerpiece.

This restaurant, with flagstone floors and old Flemish paintings, was considerably fancier than where we were staying. Dining here was like eating in a museum, my father, the experienced Antwerp traveler, had said. I didn't quite see this as a winning endorsement.

I fiddled with the edge of the lace tablecloth. "I was just thinking that my lack of experience is preventing me from being much professional help. I barely understood what the speaker was talking about this afternoon."

"I see." My father slowly unfolded his napkin and laid it across his lap, even though we had only just ordered. "And what might you do instead?"

"I don't know. I thought maybe I could spend part of the day walking around town."

I edged my chair back from the table slightly, not trusting the apparent calm in my father's demeanor. He was a slow-cooker when it came to anger. If and when he exploded, it did not pay to be nearby.

"Elizabeth, I brought you here to be a second set of eyes and ears at the convention. You know that."

"But you just said you wanted us to attend the same seminars tomorrow, lectures that I can't possibly understand the way you will. The way Keith would."

"Well, yes, but..." He paused and pushed his glasses up momentarily, rubbing the bridge of his nose. Then he exhaled noisily. "Fine. I can go without you. Which would you rather attend, the morning or afternoon session?"

I could tell from his squint, the slight tilt of his head that there was a right and a wrong answer to this question. He'd adopted the same head tilt when he'd asked me if I really wanted to take a year off before college, as I'd haltingly suggested the summer after my senior year of high school; the same squint when he'd asked me when I was younger if I would rather miss a family member's birthday party or one of my many youth sporting events. Those times, I had known which answer he wanted. But sitting at the table in the fancy Belgian restaurant, the smell of food from neighboring tables nearly overpowering, I couldn't remember which time slot he'd said the family business workshop was scheduled for.

"The morning?" I guessed.

His nostrils flared. Wrong answer.

"Or the afternoon. Whichever one you want," I said quickly. "It doesn't matter to me."

"Of course it doesn't." He shook his head and looked away. "You know what? Take the whole day if that's what you'd rather do."

"I didn't say that. I just said—"

"I know what you said, Elizabeth, and I'm not particularly surprised that you'd rather play tourist than fulfill your responsibilities. I only wish I were."

My mother's face wavered before my eyes—*he's under a lot of pressure right now*—and I gritted my teeth. Still, I couldn't entirely resist saying, "That's not fair."

"Isn't it? Tell me, what is it exactly that you're planning to do with your life, Elizabeth? You can't serve coffee and dig in the dirt forever."

"Easy for you to say." I scooted my chair back another inch. "There aren't exactly jobs growing on trees for people my age."

"You have a job at the store anytime you want it. But you're not interested, you've made that abundantly clear. With your sisters, it makes sense. They're driven to pursue other paths that don't involve the store. But I haven't a clue what drives you, what it is you love. The frightening thing is, I'm not sure you do, either. Am I wrong?"

I clenched my fists beneath the tablecloth and didn't answer. The restaurant's entrance wasn't far away. I could be out the door and halfway down the block in under a minute.

"You're twenty-six years old," my father continued, "and you're one of the smartest people I know. You can't actually be thinking of working at your friend's restaurant indefinitely, can you?"

"Of course not." Which wasn't entirely true. I liked Boadicea. But he had asked the question in such a way as to predetermine my answer, blast him. Of course, he'd also called me one of the smartest people he knew.

"Then why not give the store a chance? It's not like there's something else calling you. Not like your sisters."

"That's why you brought me on this trip, isn't it? To try to convince me to come work at the store?"

"Not directly." He leaned away from the table. "Everything was already paid for, and I figured you had the least amount of commitments. Besides..." He trailed off, frowned, glanced at his watch, looked around for the waiter.

"What?"

He fiddled with a fork. "You and I haven't had much time together in recent years. I suppose I thought this might give us some."

I wasn't sure what to say. Ever since I had moved out of their house, my father and I had treated each other like polite acquaintances. It was hard to imagine him even noticing my absence, let alone being bothered by it.

"Well, thanks," I said finally. "But you probably should have just brought someone from the shop. I'm not like you, Dad. I'm sorry, but I don't want to work in the shop. I thought you knew that."

The waiter appeared then with our salads, seemingly oblivious to familial strife. By the time he left, I'd decided that I might as well stay put for now. For one thing, I wasn't sure I could find my way back to the hotel.

We ate silently until our entrées came, and then my father asked me what I had in mind to see the following day. I mentioned a few tourist attractions and we chatted in stilted fashion about Antwerp's history the rest of the meal. My father didn't bring up the convention or my lack of an approved career plan again. After he paid the bill, we walked back to the hotel in a light drizzle, where he retired to his room for the night with a brief, weary, "Goodnight, Elizabeth."

Back in my room alone, I checked the convention guide, confirming my error: By electing to miss the afternoon session, I had inadvertently chosen playing tourist over the family business planning seminar. Except I couldn't be sure my mistake had been entirely unintentional. Some part of me had wanted him to admit he'd brought me on this trip to try to coerce me into joining the family business. Why else ask me to attend the planning seminar? And yet, when I'd pressed, he'd said he wanted to spend time with me. That, along with his stated belief in my native intelligence, was news to me. Welcome or unwelcome, I couldn't yet say.

I undressed and turned out the light, listening for any sound of my father moving around in the next room. It was quiet, and I wondered if he were lying in bed awake, too, and if he were, what besides jet lag might be keeping him up. Was he even now listing the multitude of ways I had disappointed him—short hair, tattoos and piercings, lack of interest in the opposite sex, unwillingness to assume familial responsibilities? Was he picturing me as a small child riding on his shoulders at the annual Tulip Festival in Holland, Michigan, and wondering what had happened to turn me into the genderqueer lesbian I now purported to be? As a little kid, I'd looked up to him, and for a while, I'd actually believed I was the favorite among "his girls," as he referred to my sisters and me. But then, as adolescence accentuated my androgynous tendencies, my tomboy qualities had stopped being cute. He'd stopped adoring me, even before I defied his religion and his moral code by defiantly, proudly declaring myself queer.

That was the word I had used the night I came out to my family. Not the gentler "gay" or "lesbian," but *queer*. I had guessed my father saw me as abnormal, peculiar, odd compared to the rest of his daughters. And in the moment before he called me a string of unkind names and slammed out of the house, leaving the rest of us arrayed about the antique dining table in momentary silence, in that brief instant when he stared at me, his mouth twisted in rage or disgust or some other uncharacteristically volatile emotion, I saw a look in his eyes that confirmed my guess. He hated that I was different. Hated it, and was even, maybe, a little scared of it.

Since that night, instead of admitting to me and everyone else that he wasn't comfortable with my sexuality, he'd steadily nitpicked other aspects of my life, and not only my career path. He questioned my housing decisions, political views, wardrobe, and even, on occasion, my choice of friends. In college, he had let it be known in his subtle, indirect way that he considered Dez to be a negative presence in my life. Later, when I went to work at Boadicea, he'd asked about Toby in a way that let me know he didn't approve of her outward appearance, her penchant for Harleys, her unapologetically butch façade.

Maybe he hadn't been so wrong about Dez, after all.

Tonight, at dinner, we'd been more honest with each other than in years. Or *he* had been honest, anyway. When he asked if I knew what I loved, I could have told him: Women, my friends, Mom and Jane and Mary and the grandkids, all manner of green, leafy things that practiced photosynthesis, one of the most amazing phenomena around. But as an adult, I had never spoken to my father about what I loved. He had closed himself off from me for so long, and anyway, I didn't want to have to see myself through his eyes. The plant thing would seem inexplicable to him, or possibly just inane—"digging in the dirt" sounded like an insult coming from him. And frankly, I didn't want to talk to him about my love of women any more than he wanted me to.

When you're gay, somehow your sex life and who you love becomes open fodder for the rest of the world to dissect, discuss, judge. Talk about unfair—I didn't look at my parents and think of sex, despite the fact that I and my sisters were proof that our mother and father were heterosexual fornicators. And yet when they looked at me, all they seemed to see was a homosexual. Not me, their daughter who was mourning the betrayal of one friend and the coming loss of another, but a mannish lesbian. When people like me could just be ourselves without having to worry that other people were obsessing over our sex lives, that was when the gay rights movement would no longer be needed.

Fitzy had asked me a couple of times about graduate school in botany or a related field, since I clearly loved mucking about in the dirt—so different the way she said it—as much as she did. I'd told her I didn't think I wanted to teach or work in a lab. I liked being outdoors too much. She didn't press. She seemed to accept me for who I was, not for whom I had been or who I might be in the future. Sure, she called me on my bullshit, like any good friend and mentor should do, but she wasn't continually challenging me the way my father had done in recent years.

An image of the photo of Fitzy and her daughter, Amanda, from their visit to Keukenhof popped into my mind, and I wondered if she had been as nonjudgmental and accepting with her own daughter. Maybe it was simply easier to allow other people's children to be whomever they might choose to be. Except that Jody, my childhood friend with the certifiably hippy parents, had seemed just as encouraged to be himself within his family fold as I, the visitor, had been. No wonder I used to wish Jody's parents were mine. My father may think I was smart, but when it came to the four of us, his progeny, I had always seemed to come up lacking. These days the reasons were obvious: I didn't have a notable career he could brag about to friends and customers, I didn't and wouldn't ever happily inhabit a house down the street with my husband and children, I didn't look or act the way he thought a woman should.

If I ever had kids, I told myself, closing my eyes against the streetlights angling through the blinds, I would love them no matter what. Unless they became born-again bigots. That would definitely require an intervention of some sort. But probably, in reality, they would be more embarrassed or ashamed of me, their brazenly genderqueer mom, than I would ever have cause to be of them.

Lucky kids.

When I rose the next morning, the scent of rain wafting in through my third-story window, I found a note with a wad of Belgian currency my father had slipped under my door sometime earlier:

Elizabeth, please take the day to enjoy Antwerp. It is a lovely city, impossible to take in all in one day, but I know you will do well trying. We need to check out by 1 p.m., so please pack up and leave your suitcase at the front desk. I'll meet you back here at 5 p.m. Have a good day.

Love, Dad.

P.S. Here's some spending money. Also, please take a hotel card with you so that you have the phone number here in case you need it.

I knocked on his door, but he must have already left for the convention. Looked like I was on my own for the day. It was what I'd wanted, so why didn't I feel better about the turn of events?

Forget him, I told myself, and set about packing. I would enjoy the day, damn it. Disappointing my father was nothing new, but being in Europe was. The family thing could wait. For now, I only had twelve more hours in Belgium.

Time to get cracking.

CHAPTER SEVEN

I breakfasted alone in the hotel dining room, fortifying myself with coffee as I studied the guidebook and planned my day in Antwerp. I'd never played tourist alone in a strange city, or even in a familiar one. While I'd ventured out to other American cities and geographical regions, New York and DC among them, I'd always traveled with friends or family. Today I could pick the stops that interested me alone. No planning around other people, no working anyone else's needs into my day. To be honest, I wasn't sure where to start.

Fortunately, one of the front desk clerks paused beside my table while I was working on my second cup of coffee.

"Are you sightseeing Antwerp today?" she asked in an accent I couldn't quite place.

"Yes, I am."

I checked her nametag: Michelle. I'd noticed her when we'd first arrived, even though she'd been helping another guest. With brown curly hair, dark eyes, and hipster glasses, she was totally my type. Then again, most cute twenty-something women were.

"I could describe to you some good places to go," she offered.

"That would be fantastic. I'm Elizabeth, by the way."

"Michelle. If you stop by the front desk before you go out, Elizabeth, I will tell you what I know."

I watched her walk away, appreciating the sway of her hips and the way she filled out the nondescript hotel uniform. Gathering my books together, I retreated upstairs to finish packing, humming as I went. All at once I felt more awake than I had since I'd arrived in Europe. Probably it was just the coffee.

Back downstairs a little while later, clad in jeans and a Boadicea T-shirt—free advertising for Toby, provided in exchange for the use of her backpack—I stopped at the front desk and caught Michelle's eye.

She headed my way with a smile. "Hello again."

"Hi," I said, returning the smile. Yep, definitely my type.

"Who is that on your shirt?" she asked.

"Boadicea, a Celtic warrior. A friend of mine back home owns a café named after her."

"This is the woman who drove the Romans from London."

"Exactly."

She knew about Boadicea? Perhaps I would have to correct my low gadar reading on the lovely Michelle.

"So, today you play the tourist?"

"Yeah. My father's at a convention, so I'm on my own."

"What does your father do?"

"He owns a jewelry shop back home in Michigan."

"Ah, Detroit, the motor city." Only she pronounced it *Deh-twah*.

"What about you? Where are you from?"

Michelle Martineau, it turned out, was a Parisian taking time off from her studies to travel and work her way across Western Europe. She'd already spent two months in Edinburgh, three in London, and another two in Antwerp. In a couple of weeks she was planning to move to Amsterdam. Her uncle owned a canal house there and had said she could stay for as long as she liked.

"Sweet," I said. "My dad and I are taking the train to Amsterdam tonight."

"And how long will you be there?"

"Four days."

"Ah," she said. "Then I suppose we will miss one another."

Too bad we wouldn't be there at the same time. If she didn't already like to kiss girls, marijuana, legally available in Amsterdam's coffee houses, had been known to loosen many an inhibition.

"What about today? What time do you get off work?"

"Not until evening," she said. "Otherwise I would offer to introduce you to Antwerp myself."

Was I imagining the slightly sultry tone, the lowering of her lids? Or was it simply that all French women were terrible flirts? Maddie used to complain that her junior year abroad had been frequently frustrating, as French women did not seem to know how to turn off their carefully cultivated sensuality.

Just then, the hotel manager, a portly Belgian with thinning hair and a fixed polite smile, drifted over to us. "And how are you this morning, Miss Starreveld?"

"Fine, thank you. Michelle was just giving me some recommendations on what to see in Antwerp."

"Starreveld?" Michelle echoed. "Your name is Flemish, no?"

"Yes," I said. "Or Dutch, anyway."

Her manager hovering at her left elbow, Michelle pulled a map from under the counter and drew a line through the maze of city streets between the hotel and the River Scheldt. "Now, as I was saying," she resumed in her professional hotel clerk's voice, "the Rubenshuis and the

Steen should not be missed, especially on a rainy day like today. What else would you like to see? What is it you like to do?"

"I work at a botanical garden back home, so plants and gardens are always good."

"But of course. I know just where to send you."

Ten minutes later, armed with Michelle's doctored map and a small backpack containing my guidebook, a bottle of water, and a handful of Power Bars, I set out to explore Antwerp.

As I paused before the Central Station to read about its neo-baroque design, I pictured my father sitting in a folding chair surrounded by stuffy jewelers. For a moment, just a moment, I considered joining him at the convention. How would he react if I strolled in? Would he be happy, surprised, indifferent?

I set the idea aside and returned my attention to Frommer's. I didn't even care that I looked like an American tourist with my backpack slung over one shoulder, a lightweight jacket and faded U of M baseball cap shielding me from the Belgian rain.

My day of exploration passed far too quickly as I struggled to cram the sights of Antwerp into an eight-hour block. Michelle's selections were perfectly suited to someone our age, a mix of museums, history, and pop culture. And for me, flowers. My favorite morning stop, other than the two hundred year old Antwerp Botanic Garden with its disappearing heads and other sculptures, was a shop called the Science of Plant Essence. I wandered its neat aisles packed with bottled emulsions, stopping to inhale my favorite scents: tulips, of course, of which there were many; hyacinths, lilacs, daffodils, all the blooms of spring, along with peppermint, rosemary, assorted herbal blends. Before I left, I purchased a tiny vial of lavender emulsion for Fitzy. She would have loved the place.

The rest of the morning I spent investigating Rubenshuis, the private-house-turned-art-museum of Antwerp's most famous artist, and the Museum Plantin-Moretus, the former site of one of the great publishing houses of Renaissance Europe. Each had its own courtyard with impressive gardens, blooming with the requisite crocuses, hyacinths, and tulips. At the Museum Plantin-Moretus, after wandering rooms filled with old books, wooden printing presses, and portraits of the Moretus and Plantin families, many of which bore Rubens' signature, I wandered into the cloistered courtyard gardens.

There, I parked myself on a bench next to a yellow-flamed forsythia bush and pulled out the postcards I'd picked up at the Rubenshuis gift shop. I wrote one to my mother, one to Fitzy, one to Aunt Barbara, one to Toby and Sheila, and one to Alex. In my head, I'd been having a conversation with Dez on and off all morning concerning the dearth of Biebians—lesbians who look like Justin Bieber—I'd so far observed in Europe. Disappointing, of course, but more upsetting was my apparent relationship relapse. Maybe it was the jet lag interfering, but as I wandered Antwerp, I couldn't seem to convince my brain that my friendship with Dez was truly over. Habits were hard to break, and Dezi and I had been buds for a long time. Did she miss me? I hoped so. No way she was getting a postcard, though.

Later, I picked up a brie sandwich and a bottle of Orangina at a coffee shop along Meir Street and headed to a private garden nearby for another break. The sun peeked out from behind enormous cumulus clouds occasionally, just enough to keep the chill out of the air, as I sat on a bench to eat and looked around the garden, mentally cataloging the flowers I knew and jotting notes on the ones I didn't. On the train to Amsterdam tonight, I would use Fitzy's worn *Field Guide to the*

Plants of Western Europe, on loan for the trip, to look up the unknowns. I had kept a journal of sorts since I'd first started interning at the Gardens, recording the common names of the plants I observed, along with Latin names, descriptions, favored environments, and historical data. So far I had 246 entries. I was hoping this trip would add at least a dozen new varieties to my life list.

Thinking about my plant journal reminded me of the question my father had posed the night before: "Do you even know what is it you love?" Honestly, he had some nerve accusing me of not knowing when he was the one who had refused to accept what—and who—I loved.

Six months into my relationship with Maddie, a record for me since Kelly, my high school girlfriend, left Ann Arbor to go to college on the West Coast, I called my mother and asked if I could bring a friend to Sunday dinner.

"What kind of friend?" she'd asked.

"A romantic friend."

"You know the rules, Elizabeth—only serious, um, romantic friends may be invited to Sunday dinner."

I didn't fail to notice how she stumbled over the terminology. When we were younger, the rule had always been that only friends and serious boyfriends were invited to dinner, which was how Kelly had slipped under the radar. Then I came out and made the language my family had always used "politically incorrect all of a sudden," as Cat, the lone social conservative of the younger Starreveld generation, had once complained.

"I know, Mom. That's why I'm asking. Maddie's important to me. I'd like her to meet my family, and for you to meet her, too."

"Okay, sweetie. But I'll have to speak to your father about it, all right?"

"Sure," I'd said, confident that my dad had had enough time—more than half a decade—to get to the point where he could stand to have dinner with my girlfriend. When Maddie asked me how the phone call had gone, I told her my parents were discussing the matter, but it was just a formality. She'd already met Jane, Mike, and the kids when my favorite big sister had invited us over for dinner; soon she would meet the rest of my family, too.

"Is this really something I want to do?" Maddie had asked, chewing her lower lip in the way that had endeared her to me when we'd first met at the Michigan Womyn's Music Fest the previous August, waiting in line outside the Tantric massage workshop. We'd quickly ditched the friends we'd come with and paired up for the workshop—and the rest of the festival. Who says that relationships that start under intense circumstances don't last?

Oh, wait, that's right. Here I was two and a half years later, a lesbian singleton lunching alone in Antwerp. Maddie had never made it to a Starreveld family dinner, though it wasn't her fault. A few days after our initial phone call, my mother had informed me that she and my father didn't think such a "display" would be appropriate or comfortable for the rest of the family, given there would be children present. Outwardly, she had projected solidarity with my father on this decision, but less than a week later, she'd stopped by Boadicea to invite Maddie and me to lunch at the house on a weekday at a time when my father would be at work. Apparently there were things my mother and father didn't agree on, after all.

Given how badly things had ended, I was sort of glad now that my "serious romantic friend" had never received the official Starreveld stamp of approval. Glad, too, that no one other than Jane knew all the details. Well, that wasn't entirely true. There were hundreds of women who were arguably fortunate enough to witness both the start of Maddie and me *and* the commencement of Maddie and Dez's affair in non-consecutive years of the Michigan Womyn's Music Fest.

"Good times," I muttered out loud and stood up, crumpling my sandwich wrapper into a ball. This train of thought was why it was better to keep moving than to sit around contemplating the past. Or, at least, my own past.

Antwerp's history offered considerably less personal angst, and as I resumed my wandering, I tried to push away thoughts of Ann Arbor and focus on the city in which I somehow, incredibly, found myself. Next on the itinerary drawn up by the lovely Michelle was the Steen, a medieval fortress located on the banks of the River Scheldt. According to Frommer's, the Steen was built in the ninth century, and is Antwerp's oldest building. Some claim it was once home to the famed giant Druon Antigoon, who was supposedly responsible for Antwerp's name. According to legend, Druon cut off the hand of any boatman who neglected to pay a toll for passing the castle, and threw the severed appendage into the River Scheldt. Then along came Brabo, a Roman centurion. Brabo avenged the giant's victims by slaying him, cutting off his hand, and throwing it into the river. The Flemish word for "throwing of the hand," *handwerpen*, eventually became Antwerpen, the city's Flemish name.

Even if he'd existed, the giant couldn't have lived in the castle— Brabo, his slayer, would have lived in the area long before the Steen was built. But I liked the story and the castle, too, anyway. We don't have many non-Disney-related castles in America, or legends of Roman centurions, or anything that dates back to the ninth century. The Steen had been around for nearly a millennium already when Europeans first began to settle in the New World. To me, frontier cabins built on the edge of hostile American Indian territory were historic, while to my European ancestors, centuries-old churches, town halls, and market squares stretched back across generation after generation. I couldn't quite fit my mind around the difference. I wondered if Europeans visiting my country could, either. No wonder they seemed so condescending toward America—our paved strip malls must appear ridiculous to people raised in towns with squares whose cobblestones date back to the Middle Ages.

With only a few hours left to enjoy the city, I didn't linger long in the National Maritime Museum housed in the Steen. I hurried through the maze of little rooms inside the large stone castle, creaked over wooden floorboards to observe haphazardly displayed collections of ship models, figureheads, charts, and instruments. The basement contained an excavated cesspit, but I opted to skip that exhibit. Some things even history couldn't romanticize.

From the Steen, I followed Michelle's instructions and went underground to the pedestrian tunnel that connected the city center to the left bank of the River Scheldt. Built in the early 1930s, the tunnel had been preserved in all of its original technological simplicity. I jogged across, unnerved by the thought of the river coursing overhead. On the far bank, I was rewarded with the promised view of Our Lady's Cathedral, the largest church in Belgium or Holland, looming above the city center. Definitely worth risking life and limb for, I decided, snapping a few quick shots.

Back on the city side, I wandered the wide promenade at water's edge, trying to imagine the conflagration of boats that had once jammed the port of Antwerp, in its heyday the Manhattan of sixteenth-century Europe. It was still one of the largest and busiest ports in the world, but at some point in the city's long history, the main docks had moved a few miles north. My view from the waterfront promenade featured only a few tourist cruises.

As I looked out across the city, which probably hadn't changed much over the centuries, I wondered if, on a day like today two hundred years earlier, some past-life sister had taken this very path to the bakery, butcher shop, grocer's. What would a lesbian's life have been like back then? Likely she would have been married with half a dozen kids already, for what option would a nineteenth century gay chick have had? Would she even have known she was gay?

Probably, I knew, a woman who'd looked and felt like me back then would have ignored her deviant feelings and prayed to God for mercy. Or maybe she would have gotten herself a little on the side. At least sex with a member of the same gender couldn't possibly lead to a baby. One of the benefits of the homosexual lifestyle, to be sure. But would my fictitious lesbian have been able to live openly with the woman she loved? Not likely. Even now, there are still plenty of nations where homosexuality is outlawed.

I lingered on the promenade for a bit in threatening sunshine, trying to conjure previous eras, then consulted my guidebook and map again. Michelle's route took me to the Grote Markt, Antwerp's main square, next. When I got there, I discovered that it wasn't quite on the same scale of the Grand-Place of Brussels, but I liked the Grote Markt's cafés, guild houses, and town buildings better. They were less imposing and more approachable somehow than the buildings lining the Grand-Place. In the center, an enormous fountain depicted Silvius Brabo, the Roman centurion, holding the giant's severed hand aloft.

From Grote Markt, I moved on to the Cathedral of Our Lady. I wandered the exterior first, taking in its several Gothic tiers and hundred-plus pillars. It was immense, and not only on the outside.

Inside, the cathedral boasted a multitude of religious-themed statues and paintings, including three Rubens altarpieces. The layout reminded me of the plant conservatory at the Botanical Gardens at home. Alden B. Dow, the architect who had designed the U of M conservatory, had drawn on ecclesiastical design for the building's layout—a central alley like the knave of a church; small break-outs on either side that functioned like chapels with different climactic and regional focuses; and, at the end of the walkway, a fern pool that served as the altar. As I soaked up the rarefied hush of the cathedral, I couldn't help picturing the conservatory and wondering how Fitzy's health was treating her. She wasn't going anywhere yet, I reminded myself. She would still be there when I got back. She had better be, or—or what? Wasn't it the dead who did the haunting? I shivered a little and rose from the pew I rested on, pacing back down the central aisle.

It was nearly time to meet my father, so I headed back toward the diamond quarter, pleased with my day of tourist travels. I had definitely made the right decision, even if my father wasn't exactly pleased with me. Antwerp was like no place else I had ever been. I still had a hard time comprehending that the buildings were centuries old, and had likely been occupied continuously over those centuries; that multiple generations of families and their businesses had been born and died in these very neighborhoods. Nothing in my American travels, not even a sojourn to New York City and Ellis Island where my great-great grandfather had first made landfall a century and a half earlier, had exposed me to this much history. I was used to mini-malls and restaurant chains, new housing developments that bordered orderly farm fields, paved roads lined with brick school buildings and ranch-style, single family homes.

This Europe thing, I decided, was awesome—in both the

traditional and the uniquely American sense of the word.

My father was waiting in the hotel lobby when I returned from my solitary adventures, his briefcase propped on his lap, a manila folder open inside. He closed the case quickly when he saw me, glanced at his watch as if he couldn't resist, and nodded.

"Elizabeth."

"Hi." I was only ten minutes late. For me, that was practically on time.

"How was your day?"

"Good. How was yours?"

"Fine." He looked at his watch again. "We'd better get a table for dinner here before we leave for the train station. We're running a little behind."

I started to follow him into the dining room when I noticed Michelle at the desk.

"I'll be there in a second, Dad," I said, ignoring his frown.

Apparently my predisposition to spontaneity didn't come from his side of the family. But then, I'd already known that, hadn't I?

"*Bonjour*, Michelle," I said as I paused at the desk. "Or *bon soir*, I suppose I should say."

"*Bon soir* to you, Elizabeth. How was your day?" she asked, her smile alive and well even after a long shift.

"Awesome. The route you gave me was perfect." I smiled back, checking her out subtly. Yep—she still looked as good as she had that morning.

"I am glad to hear it. And was the city more fun than your father's jewelry convention?"

"Immeasurably. And better than working, too, no doubt. How was your day?"

"Good," she said. "Although not all of our guests are as nice as you. I have only fifteen minutes more, though, and then I am done for the day."

"I have an idea," I said, glancing over my shoulder. My father was waiting in the doorway to the dining room, watching us. "We're about to grab a quick dinner before we catch the train to Amsterdam. Why don't you join us when you're done? I'd love to hear about your travels."

"I would like this, too, but we are not allowed to socialize with guests."

"Technically, my father and I are no longer your guests. As of now, we're merely passing through."

"That is true." She hesitated and glanced over her shoulder, but the officious hotel manager was nowhere to be seen. "All right, then, I will join you. Thank you for the invitation."

"My pleasure." I went to join my father, trying not to smile too widely.

At my father's request, the waiter came to take our order immediately—a salad and sandwich for my dad, the pasta special and half a carafe of wine for me.

"How was the convention?" I asked when we were alone again.

"Very informative," he said. "As always."

"Good."

After a moment, he added, "And how did you find Antwerp?"

"It was fantastic," I said, and launched into a detailed description of the sights I'd seen, not about to let his lack of enthusiasm discourage me.

Just as I was finishing a description of the fountain at Grote Markt, Michelle appeared in the dining room doorway.

"I hope you don't mind," I told my father, "but I invited the girl from the front desk to join us."

My father stared at me. "You do know we have a train to catch, don't you?"

"Chill, Dad. We still have to finish dinner, don't we?"

Michelle's arrival thwarted whatever response he might have had. Instead, he stood up and shook her hand as I made the introduction.

"*Enchanté*," he said with a little bow. "How delightful that you could join us."

I couldn't tell if he was being sarcastic. As Michelle squeezed my hand and smiled intimately at me, I decided I didn't really care, anyway.

The waiter brought another glass, and Michelle helped us polish off the rest of the wine. An experienced traveler, she amused us with anecdotes from her journeys—odd encounters, language difficulties, missed connections. My father behaved beautifully, and even offered up some stories of his own travels. The jewelry business had kept him on the road quite a bit. Not that he'd minded, he assured us.

Finally he glanced at his watch again. "I'm sorry, Mademoiselle Martineau, but I am afraid Elizabeth and I must catch our train."

"Ah, yes, the train to Amsterdam. I hope that you enjoy your time in the Netherlands, Monsieur and Mademoiselle Starreveld."

"You, too," I said, and touched her hand where it lay on the white lace tablecloth. "Thanks for the map—though it would have been an even better day if you had been able to show me the sights yourself."

"It is a pity I did not have today off," she agreed, and turned her hand palm up to squeeze mine.

My father rose suddenly. "I should take care of the bill."

Michelle and I stood up, too, and she shook his hand again.

"Goodbye, Monsieur Starreveld. It was a pleasure to meet you."

As he strode from the dining room, I shouldered my daypack and followed more slowly, Michelle at my side. "I wish we were going to be in Amsterdam at the same time."

"So do I," she said. "It isn't often that I meet someone like you, Elizabeth."

She was smiling again, and I decided that she did, in fact, like to kiss girls. And maybe, even, would have liked kissing me.

"Listen," I said, pulling a card from my wallet. "This is my father's store in Michigan. If you ever get to the States, come look us up."

"I will do so," she said, pocketing the card. "And now, *adieu*, Elizabeth. Your father is waiting."

He was standing near the door to the street, suitcase and briefcase in hand, poised to leave. I hugged Michelle and she kissed each of my cheeks, her lips lingering familiarly on my skin.

"Goodbye," I said, my hands on her shoulders. Then I kissed her cheeks too, borrowing the custom. My lips came close to hers, and we looked into each other's eyes for a long moment. Until, in my peripheral vision, I saw my dad check his watch.

"Goodbye," I said again.

"*Bon voyage*, Elizabeth."

I retrieved Toby's backpack from the front desk and followed my father from the hotel, pausing once in the doorway to wave to Michelle. She waved back, and then my father and I were out on the street, lugging our bags toward the train station.

He didn't say anything, and I didn't feel the need to speak, either. I was still thinking about Michelle, the subtle scent of her perfume as she'd kissed me. Too bad my father had made a reservation at the hotel in Amsterdam for tonight; otherwise we could have stayed, and I might have been able to convince Michelle to show me Antwerp at night. Among other things.

I sighed, adjusting the pack on my shoulders.

"What's wrong now?" my father asked.

"Nothing," I said. "Not a thing."

We were in plenty of time for our train, early enough even to find comfy seats in a mostly empty compartment. Before we settled our luggage in the overhead rack, I pulled out Fitzy's European flower guide and my well-worn plant journal. Then I sat down and began to leaf through the guide. Beside me, my father looked up from his book—still *The Nature of Diamonds*—and watched me make a notation in my journal.

"What are you doing?" he asked.

"Looking up the flowers I saw today. Michelle sent me to a few gardens, and I saw some varieties I didn't recognize."

"But what are you writing?"

I explained about the journal I'd kept for years, the life list of plants I'd been tracking under Fitzy's tutelage.

"Why didn't I know about this?" he asked.

"I think I told you guys."

"Well, if you did, I don't remember." He paused, watching me record the characteristics of a Golden Apeldoorn Darwin hybrid tulip in my journal. "If you like plants so much, why didn't you study them in college?"

"I did, Dad. Remember? I have a minor in botany," I said, as surprised as he looked that he hadn't retained this fact. After all, he'd paid my tuition bills. "I didn't want to spend my college years hidden away in a lab, so I decided to major in history instead."

"You do know, don't you, that your Grandma Edith was an avid gardener?"

Edith Starreveld, my father's mother, had died when I was in elementary school. "No way."

"She designed the gardens at the house shortly after they moved in. She used to say that she and my sisters had green thumbs and my father and I had glass thumbs."

"I didn't know that."

My love of plants and the outdoors, which had always seemed out of place in my family of jewelers, lawyers, orthodontists, had intractable genetic roots, after all.

"You were so young when she died. Her favorite thing in the world was Tulip Time." He shook his head, smiling a little. "She went right up until the end."

That part I'd known—Grandma Edith's love of the Tulip Time Festival that took place each year in the small town of Holland on the eastern shore of Lake Michigan was legendary among the Starreveld clan. Each May, even after Grandma Edith died, my family celebrated Mother's Day by wandering the craft booths at the festival, stuffing our faces with Dutch cheeses and pastries, and watching the Klompen Dancers, folk dancers attired in traditional Dutch costumes complete with noisy wooden shoes. I remembered my father's mother as a slightly loopy, shrunken old woman who had suffered a stroke that necessitated nursing home care when I was little. Now I would have to reshape her in my memory.

My father went back to reading, and I finished recording the new varieties in my journal before we reached Brussels. We changed trains there, and after getting settled on our new train, I opened the novel Toby had loaned me and fell into the queer world it depicted. While the train raced through the darkening countryside, my father and I read quietly in our separate seats. I wasn't sure when we passed from Belgium into Holland; I didn't notice a border marker. Only when the conductor announced the next stop as The Hague did I realize that we weren't in Belgium anymore.

The train slowed to a stop at The Hague, and I glanced through my window at the people milling about the station platform. These were genuine Dutch natives, born and bred and living in the Netherlands. I'd lived among Dutch Americans for so long that it was hard to remember that, culturally speaking, we were practically a separate species from our counterparts here. As the train picked up speed again and continued on through the night, I tried to imagine the lives of the people on the platform. Did teenagers here text and hang out at malls like American teenagers? Did Dutch parents feed their children Cheerios and frozen pizza? What kind of work did they do? They were so foreign to me, and yet I was the foreigner, trespassing on their turf. The realization made me a little homesick, and as the train chugged along, I wondered how refugees and ex-patriots managed.

How, for that matter, had my grandfather's grandfather done it? A hundred and fifty years before, at age twenty, Wilhelm had left the Netherlands with only a trunk and a satchel, bound for Michigan. He'd planned to join the new Dutch settlement on the shore of Lake Michigan, but his timing was lousy—smallpox and the son of a rival jeweler had preceded him to the west side of the state. He made it as far as Ann Arbor, where the innkeeper's daughter was enough to hold him. We Starrevelds had been born, lived, and died in Ann Arbor ever since.

The train slowed again when we reached the outskirts of Amsterdam. As the station materialized out of the dark night, I imagined my great-great grandfather leaving his stone cottage early one morning, saying goodbye to his family and traveling on a carriage under gray broiling skies to his ship, then venturing out across the cold, dark Atlantic to where an entirely new world awaited him. What courage it must have required to give up everything familiar for nothing known. In the nineteenth century, there was no option of returning by airplane, no annual holiday visit, no Google Earth to allow you a glimpse of your hometown from above. A move to the United States was usually a permanent, one-way trip.

As the fourth and youngest son of a Rotterdam jeweler, my great-great grandfather must have believed there was nothing for him in his homeland. Or maybe he was simply adventurous. Either way, America had beckoned. And now we Starrevelds were back in the homeland—for business, for adventure, for whatever came our way.

The train coasted to another stop.

"We're here," my father announced.

I gathered my bags and followed him from the train.

CHAPTER EIGHT

"Stay close to me," my father said as we waited in line at Immigration. "This station is one of the most dangerous in the world."

I rolled my eyes to myself—I was hardly a child. But a few minutes later, as we walked down the long corridor into the crowded main terminal of the station, I was only too happy to follow my father's advice. Gangs of sketchy-looking men wandered about, eyeing passengers boldly. American college kids weighed down by backpacks nearly as tall as they were lurched about the cavernous room, staring at the flickering schedule board that occupied most of one wall. Drug addicts and prostitutes trolled for customers, eyes empty as they wandered about mumbling to themselves. I had never seen so many people chemically altered in public before.

Ew, was my first thought. How could Toby like this place? I stuck to my father's side as he maneuvered us through the crowds to the main entrance. Outside, I exhaled in relief and paused to take in the nighttime view of the city. Across a canal lined with parked bicycles two and three thick, the lights of Amsterdam spread out before us. The neon of the Red Light district in the distance reminded me of a scaled-down version of Times Square in New York, which I had visited several times with a college classmate from Brooklyn.

We boarded a tram waiting at a stop just outside the station and took a seat at the back. I watched as several people (actual Dutch folk—the thought fascinated me once again) followed us aboard and inserted a small slip of paper in a machine near the door. The machine dinged each time.

I leaned closer to my father and said, softly so that my fellow passengers wouldn't be forced to think *Dumb American* just yet, "Shouldn't we buy a ticket, too?"

My father appeared to examine his fingernails. "No, the number five rarely has a rear conductor."

I gave him the same look I would have given him had an alien suddenly burst from his chest, shrieking and bloody. Eugene Starreveld, sneaking aboard public transportation? Beside me, he sat back and folded his arms over his chest as the tram we had boarded illegally pulled away from Central Station.

Leaning back beside him, I watched Amsterdam pass beyond my window. As we rumbled down neon-lit streets past hotel after restaurant after hotel, alongside canals flanked by chained-up bicycles and tiny cars barely larger than their motorless counterparts, it occurred to me that this trip might alter the view I had previously held of my father. Like, in a big way.

That first night, we retired to adjoining rooms in a hotel located just around the corner from the Van Gogh Museum and the Museumpleine, the wide green that bordered the Stedelijk Modern Art Museum and the Rijksmuseum. The hotel walls were thin enough that as I lay in my narrow twin bed trying to sleep, I could hear my father snoring in the next room. Listening to him sleep struck me as somehow intimate, and as I drifted off myself, I pondered again the incongruity of my father illicitly hitching a ride on the tram, the apparent lone renegade among a car full of paying customers.

He rose ridiculously early the following morning and knocked on my door, cheerfully calling out something about combating jet lag. I rolled over and muttered curses into my pillow, but the damage was done. Still grumbling, I got up and accompanied him downstairs for breakfast in the hotel's dining room. As soon as we were seated, he pulled out Frommer's *Guide to the Netherlands* and began to leaf through it.

"So. What's on your list of must-sees here in Holland?" he asked, gazing at me over the top of his reading glasses.

"Not before coffee," I mumbled, looking around for a waiter. For some reason, I was more tired today than I'd been since we'd arrived in Europe.

"Pardon me?"

"I don't talk before coffee," I said succinctly.

He tried not to smile. "Duly noted."

Jackass. I hate people who don't require caffeine to function. At that moment, I wanted nothing more than to be home sleeping peacefully in my own bed. I did the math in my head—in Michigan, it was still the middle of the night. The streets of Ann Arbor would be silent, stoplights flashing yellow against the dark sky. My apartment would be warm and cozy and quiet, and maybe I would have gone out the night before and met someone fun who was neither a former gymnast nor a stalker, and that someone might be sleeping beside me on my lovely bed right at this moment, her body warm next to mine, streetlights casting bar-shaped shadows across the comforter cover. If only I were in Ann Arbor instead of eating breakfast with my uptight father in the stodgy dining room of our Amsterdam hotel, half a day's journey from home.

Then the waiter brought coffee, the same rich, lovely Italian roast we'd had in Antwerp, and my homesickness dissipated.

"What did you want to talk about?" I asked my father midway through my first cup.

"Sightseeing. I'll have more time to spend with you here. Any spots in particular you wanted to visit?"

I thought for a moment, nibbling on jam-smothered bread. "The Anne Frank House and the Van Gogh Museum."

"Excellent choices. I've been to see Van Gogh many times, but Anne Frank will be new to me. Anyplace else?"

"Yes," I said, deciding I was suitably fortified with caffeine. "Keukenhof Gardens in Lisse. Oh, and the Homomonument."

My father swallowed his mouthful of tea and set his cup in its saucer. "The what?"

"The Homomonument."

"I heard you the first time. What is it?"

"A monument to all the gay people killed in World War II and by AIDS."

Toby had mentioned this particular attraction, so I'd read up on it in the Damron *Women's Travel* guide Toby had loaned me for the trip. The book contained a map to LGBT venues in Amsterdam, including queer-friendly coffee shops and taverns.

"I was going to call a friend of friend while we're here, too," I added. "You know, maybe get the skinny on the city from the locals."

I had no intention of sharing with my father exactly where I would be spending my nights in Amsterdam. What he didn't know wouldn't hurt him—or freak him out, more to the point.

He wiped his mouth with his linen napkin. "Of course, you're welcome to do as you like. I was just hoping that we might spend some time together when I'm not in meetings."

I nodded, hoping it didn't seem grudging. "Me, too. I mean, that's partly why we're here, isn't it?"

"Sure. Exactly." But he didn't quite meet my eyes.

It turned out that he didn't have a meeting until the afternoon, so after breakfast, we decided to check out the nearby Van Gogh Museum. It was only a short walk from our hotel, and as we crossed the green to the museum entrance, my well-dressed father didn't, for once, make a snarky comment about my casual ensemble: cargo pants, a retro Izod shirt, and Converse sneakers. He just paid our entrance fee and waved me ahead of him into the central hall where an atrium arched high overhead, allowing daylight to flood the lower floors.

In another surprising move, given that Dutch-Americans are well-known for our spendthrift tendencies, Dad splurged for the audio tour, a cell phone-like device that played sound bites for numbered selections. As we wandered the lower galleries, I surprised myself—and him, probably—by listening to every available recorded exposition, which offered details of Van Gogh's heartbreaking life and excerpts from his letters. How impressive that he'd managed to produce such a prodigious amount of work in such a short time while battling mental illness, and with little professional recognition or support. I had seen most of his better known pieces, but his lesser known works wooed me as I wandered the gallery, audio handset glued to my ear.

"Did you hear the part about how he started painting?" I asked my father when we stopped for lunch in the museum café, which looked out across the Museumpleine. "Can you believe he didn't even start painting until he was twenty-seven? That would be like me deciding now that I wanted to be a painter, and then becoming one of the most famous artists in the world. After I died ten years later, I mean."

My father winced. "Fortunately, you likely have more time ahead of you than he did. Anyway, it's a top-notch museum. I'm glad you wanted to come here. Every time I visit, I learn something new. For instance, I didn't realize Vincent planned to be a minister."

"Like his father."

"Except that being a minister would have made him miserable."

"Exactly," I said. "Miserable."

We looked at each other across the table, recognition (I hoped) flickering between us. Why was it so difficult for him to accept that none of his children wanted to follow in his footsteps?

"What's your favorite piece so far?" he asked finally, his hands barely able to contain his plump mozzarella tomato sandwich. We'd been eating mountains of fresh cheese ever since we'd stepped off the plane.

I looked out over the bright green grass of the park beyond the window, considering. "They were all amazing, but I think I liked his town shots the best, the way he always painted a place when he first arrived. And then there's the painting of his bedroom in Arles, with the two pillows on the bed. He wanted to be with someone, to settle down, but he just never found the right person."

"That one impressed me, too," my father said. "It could have been lonely, but it seemed so hopeful. His life was tragic, but his art doesn't necessarily reflect that. He saw such light and beauty in the world."

"I know. His letters were full of it. I loved hearing the excerpts."

"Me, too," my father said. "I first became interested in Van Gogh in college when I saw a play called *Vincent's Letters to Theo*. Vincent Price read aloud from the brothers' collected letters. It was beautiful."

As he spoke, I seemed to float out of my body and hover overhead, watching the two of us there in the museum café discussing Deep Thoughts. I wasn't used to talking to my father much at all, let alone sharing ideas on art.

I snapped back into my body. "I also liked the one of the all-night tavern in Arles," I said, and munched on my brie sandwich, watching my father out of the corner of one eye.

"So did I," he said, and popped a tomato slice into his mouth.

After lunch, we wandered the gift shop, browsing the books, prints, and post cards of just about every Van Gogh painting held by the museum. I bought cards of Vincent's bedroom in Arles; the all-night tavern with the billiard table; and one of the last paintings before his death, a landscape of a wheat field against an indigo sky, black crows above the field harbingers of gloom. Despite its bleakness, the painting seemed oddly imbued with hope to me, like my dad had said. I was no art critic; I couldn't have explained my own reasoning. I just knew what I liked.

My father shopped separately. As we left the museum, he reached into his brown paper bag and pulled out a book.

"This is for you," he said almost shyly, holding it out to me.

I held the hard cover book in both hands: *The Collected Letters of Vincent and Theo Van Gogh*. I had leafed through this book at the gift shop, considered blowing some of the money Toby had given me on it, and finally decided it was too expensive. After all, who knew what I might need money for here in Amsterdam?

"Thank you," I said after a moment, glancing up at my father.

"You're welcome," he said, and grasped my shoulder as if he meant to hug me. But then he stopped, turned away, lowered his head.

"And thanks for bringing me to the Netherlands," I added. "I'm really glad you invited me, Dad."

"So am I," he said, smiling sideways at me as we crossed the Museumpleine.

When I was little, I used to walk between my parents holding onto their hands, swinging as high as I could, laughing all the way. But ever since I'd hit puberty, my father had grown more and more awkward around me. After I came out, he'd stopped touching me at all. I'd assured myself his reticence didn't bother me, but now I wasn't so sure.

We walked back to the hotel in silence, but it was a nice walk. A little later my father left for a meeting—just networking, he said vaguely when I asked about it. I didn't actually know what kind of work he had in Amsterdam, I realized as he walked off down the hallway. Not like I could have been any help if I had. My mother's words came back to me, about how he was under a lot of pressure, and just for a moment an idea flickered in the recesses of my brain, something to do with the store and my father's age and the lack of blood relatives clamoring to take over where he would eventually leave off... But the idea remained inchoate, unformed, just off the tip of my tongue.

Alone in my hotel room, I leafed through the book my father had given me, but my attention wandered determinedly after only a few minutes. I did want to read the brothers' letters in detail someday, but right now I was feeling a bit arted-out. I dug through my bag until I found the cell number Toby had given me for her friend Sofie, the flirty redhead, and punched it into the bedside phone.

"Allo?" a lilting voice answered.

"Hi, is this Sofie?"

"Yes, it is. Is this Toby's friend Junior?"

"Yeah. Hi."

She laughed a little. "And how are you finding my city, Toby's friend Junior?"

"It's nice. I mean, beautiful. Anyway, Toby said I should give you a call."

"She was right. What have you been up to since you arrived, Junior?"

"Museums."

"Of course. Well, that won't do. Toby said I am to introduce you to the real Amsterdam. Does this interest you?"

Did it ever. By the time I hung up the phone, I had plans for the night: Sofie would pick me up at the hotel around nine and take me out for drinks and dancing. I lay back on the bed, smiling, and fell asleep almost immediately.

A little before nine, I knocked on my father's partially open door.

"Come in," he said, peering at me over his bifocals. He was stretched out on the bed in shirtsleeves and dress pants, his jacket and tie hanging on the nearby chair. A briefcase lay open on the bed beside him, a manila folder on his lap.

"I just wanted to tell you I'm heading out to meet a friend."

"Fine."

"You probably shouldn't wait up."

"I won't."

"Okay." I hesitated, but he only eyed me expressionlessly. "Well, I'm going downstairs now."

"Have a good time," he said, and returned to his papers.

On the way down to the lobby in the hotel's tiny elevator, I ran through the day in my mind. Everything had seemed fine, better between us than usual, in fact. But then he'd returned from his mysterious meetings all distant and moody. Dinner had been, frankly, painful. The only interesting moment came when the host of the Indian restaurant had welcomed my father by name, and I'd realized again just how often he'd visited the Netherlands.

The restaurant itself had been beautiful: soothing fountains, gold-threaded tapestries, and stone gardens; the food, awesome. But my father had sat quietly, distracted, marching through his entrée on auto pilot. When I asked about his afternoon, he replied in monosyllables. He didn't ask about my day, and I didn't mention I'd started the book he gave me. Dinner had been over in record time, and he'd returned afterward to his room and his briefcase. So much for bonding.

Whatever, I told myself as the elevator reached the ground floor. If he wanted to work, or sulk, or whatever it was he was currently doing, that was his prerogative. I, however, was going to have some fun. It wasn't every day I found myself in the sex and drug capital of the Western world.

Downstairs, I checked my outfit in the hall mirror: hair pomaded into place; dark brown twill pants cinched with a thick black belt; black V-neck T-shirt accompanied by a shiny hematite necklace on a leather strap; and black leather jacket and Doc Marten wingtips to complete the outfit. I grinned at myself in the mirror, pleased with the effect: all-American dyke, ready to check out the Dutch scene.

My father's eyebrows had lifted when he'd seen me thus attired for dinner, but he had said only, "You look nice." And by some Dutch standards, he was probably right. I'd seen the same amount of green hair, dread locks, and piercings in Amsterdam as I had in Seattle the previous summer. At least *I* looked freshly showered.

I nodded at the desk clerk—a plump woman in her fifties this time—and went outside to wait, wondering what sort of trouble Toby's friend would get me into. I hoped there would be some weed involved.

This was the longest I'd gone without smoking up in a while. Not that that was a bad thing. Probably I'd been relying on pot to take the edge off a bit too much recently. I'd never been a wake-and-baker, and didn't intend to start now. Still, I would be happy to sample some Dutch ganja, seeing as it was legal and all.

As I waited for my mystery date to appear, I pictured my father working quietly upstairs, my room next door empty. What had gone on this afternoon to leave him so troubled? For once, I didn't think it had anything to do with me, other than the fact I wasn't much help with the business part of the trip. If Keith had come along as planned, my father would have had someone to share today's meeting with, and maybe he wouldn't be sitting alone in his hotel room looking somehow defeated. The unformed idea about the store and my father's future returned, dancing tantalizingly about the periphery of my subconscious. It seemed important, whatever it was. But important enough to call Sofie and cancel?

I was warming to the idea of arm-wrestling my father to come out with me for a beer when an adorable redhead approached on the sidewalk, smiling quizzically at me. This was Sofie? No wonder Toby had felt hard-pressed to warn me about her. She was lovely, with short hair and an elfin face that reminded me somehow of pixies and fairy dust. One look, and I was already setting thoughts of my father aside.

There would always be breakfast to find out what was on his mind, I told myself, stepping out of the hotel's shadow. Assuming I made it back in time for breakfast.

CHAPTER NINE

"You must be Junior," the vision in freckles said, coming right up to me and kissing me lightly on either cheek.

"And you must be Sofie."

"Naturally. Now, let us go. I have an evening of Amsterdam's best planned for you, my American friend."

Her English was excellent, her slight accent as charming as the rest of her. We caught a tram in front of the Van Gogh Museum and took it toward the Jordaan, Amsterdam's gay and lesbian neighborhood. The name Jordaan came from the French word for garden, Sofie told me, and was based on the area's prior incarnation as a flower-strewn meadow.

Flowers, I thought. Perfect.

As the tram rumbled and jolted across town, Sofie asked if my father and I were enjoying our trip.

"It's okay. He can get kind of moody sometimes. You know how parents are."

She frowned. "Mine do not get moody."

"Oh." Culture gap. Speaking of... "Your English is amazing."

"Thank you. We learn to speak it at a very young age here. You will not meet many people in the city who do not at the least understand you."

Sofie went on to reveal that she spoke five languages in total. Born in The Hague, she had moved to Amsterdam a decade earlier to attend university. Since college, she had worked in video production for an independent film production company, specializing in documentaries about the local educational system.

"And what is it you do?" she asked.

I slouched down in my seat. "Um, I work at the local university."

"I was thinking you work for Toby?"

"Only part-time. The rest of the time, I work at the University of Michigan."

"That is fantastic. What department?"

"Botany. The Arboretum, actually," I amended. "I'm on the grounds crew."

"Ah. I see."

I felt a familiar flash of inferiority, ingrained from years of mingling with PhD students at Michigan. Not to mention, with my family. "The truth is, I'm still looking for what I really want to do with my life."

"For what it is that moves you?"

"Exactly."

When we reached our stop, I recognized the large bell tower I'd seen from other parts of the city.

"This is Westerkerk," Sofie said as we approached on foot.

At the top of the bell tower hung a banner that read, "XXX." I had seen these banners all over the city, and while Amsterdam did have a certain reputation, I couldn't believe that triple X meant the same thing here as it did at home. I asked Sofie what the acronym stood for.

"It is a symbol of local pride and quality," she said, "taken from

Emperor Maximillian's official seal. He received safe harbor and medical treatment here in the 16th century."

"Oh." Five hundred years later, and they were still flying the banner?

"Did you think it was something sexual?" she asked, pausing in front of the church.

"Of course not."

"You Americans always do. Look, just there on the sidewalk, it is part of the Homomonument. The other parts are there"—she pointed to a matching granite triangle that extended into the nearest canal— "and there."

I couldn't see the third part, but I knew she was pointing to another pink triangle built into the ground at street level. Pink granite bricks connected the individual triangles, forming a larger one that measured almost 120 feet on each side. From above, I imagined the memorial would be impressive. But up close, it was a bit disappointing. I had expected something dramatic, but the nearest section was only a triangular slab of granite that extended a few feet above the surrounding stone tiles. Still, any monument to homos was better than none.

Sofie led me away from the Westerkerk through an impressive maze of narrow angled streets and canal-side roadways. Night cloaked the city streets, and she had to keep pulling me out of the path of bicycles that hurtled past at breakneck speed. After the fourth near-miss, I laughed and apologized yet again.

"It is not your fault," she told me. "It is a matter of pride to frighten a tourist. If you live here long enough, you develop a sense about it."

To be honest, I didn't mind too much. I kind of liked Sofie's hands tugging me out of the way of careening cyclists. For a moment, Toby's warning sounded in the back of my mind. But like I'd told her, I wouldn't be here long enough to get attached, just enough time, I hoped, to get my official groove back. The Stephlyn debacle, though it had eased me through the roughest spots, didn't count.

Soon we turned down a street intersected by several other waterless avenues. At a non-descript intersection, Sofie led me toward what looked like an old-fashioned tavern on one of the corners. *Zeemeermin*, the wooden sign over the door read.

"This is where my friends and I like to go," Sofie said. "The name means 'mermaid.'"

Inside, my eyes adjusted quickly to the smoky, dimly lit bar. The smoke was a surprise—I was so accustomed to American bars, where smoking was rarely allowed anymore. The tavern had three levels— straight ahead was a long bar; to the right, a few steps led down to a lower level with a pool table commanded by several old-school butches; and another rickety-looking set of stairs to the right led up to a balcony littered with tables and chairs. Everything in the place was made of dark wood, except the mounted stuffed deer head—as in Gund, not taxidermist—above the door.

The bartender and two women at the bar, attractive in varying lesbian fashions, greeted Sofie with kisses and me with curious looks. Sofie introduced me as Junior, her American friend. Juliana, the bartender, was Dutch, but the other two, Ann and Jackie, were Australian. Juliana poured a beer and set it before me on a coaster adorned with a picture of a buxom blonde. I sipped the beer and felt its warmth in my sternum. Yum.

"Now you know why Belgians are known for their breweries," Juliana said, smiling at the look on my face.

The alcohol flowed rapidly, like the conversation: history, travel, work, women. All five of us had visited the American gay Meccas of San Francisco and New York, and three of us had even been in Chicago at the same time a few years earlier for the Gay Games, the international gay and lesbian Olympics. Talk about a party—after a week in Chicago with my people, I hadn't wanted to return to Michigan. But the Starreveld pull was strong, like The Force. Only without the gravity-defying capabilities.

"You were what age at the Gay Games, sixteen?" Juliana asked me.

"This must be why you are called Junior," Sofie added.

"Hey, now," I said, but I laughed along with the rest of them. I was used to the age jokes. When you came out at fifteen, you ended up spending a lot of time with older people who weren't always as comfortable with your sexuality as you were. Besides, I'd always looked more like a teenage boy than a grown woman.

We stayed at Zeemeermin for a couple of hours, drinking and talking. Sofie introduced me to more and more people as her American friend, her arm warm about my neck. I basked in the attention, joking and laughing with these beautiful foreign people. This has always been one of the things I appreciate most about being gay—the friendliness and instant affinity you can find with people you've never met. The gay and lesbian international community is small. Everyone goes to the same events and the same bars in the same cities. This commonality lends a feeling of camaraderie to being gay, I've always thought, providing an automatic ice-breaker that allows strangers to seem less strange.

But the really great part about going out in a foreign city, I soon realized, the beauty of doing typical scene things with people who belonged to a community far removed from my own, was that I didn't have to contend with dyke drama. If there were currents of jealousy, resentment, unrequited passion lapping at my feet here, I didn't notice. If Sofie's ex-girlfriend had been playing pool with her new girlfriend, who happened to be Sofie's former best friend, just as an example, I had no idea. It was freeing to be above all the romantic wrecks no doubt strewn throughout the bar. No matter where I went tonight, I wouldn't have to worry about running into anyone I didn't want to.

A little after eleven, Sofie announced that it was time to hit the Getto, a mixed gay and straight dance club that held women-only nights a couple of times a week. As we walked along a canal in the Jordaan headed toward the Red Light District, Jackie pulled me away from the others. I hoped she wasn't about to hit on me. With her bleached blonde hair and toothy grin, she was definitely not my type. Sofie, on the other hand...

"Want a magic pill?" Jackie asked, holding out a small capsule.

"What is it?" I asked, eyeing the offering warily.

"Pure magic. It'll make you fly, mate."

"Huh." I thought about what might happen if I did take the pill being proffered, imagined the headline on Yahoo! were something to go wrong: "American woman overdoses in the drug capital of the world; Michigan native accepted unknown substance from virtual stranger." I could see my father telling my mother and sisters in his calm, deliberate way, voice tinged with sadness, "I never thought she would take drugs from someone she didn't know."

But to refuse the pill, I decided in that split moment, headlines and lectures rotating through my brain, would be rude. And as a Midwesterner, the last thing I wanted to do was offend my new friends. I took the tiny pill, popped it into my mouth, and swallowed it before I could imagine any further calamities.

"That's the spirit," Jackie said, slipping her arm around my shoulders in a friendly manner as we rejoined Sofie and Ann. "Now we'll really have some fun."

As we walked through the Red Light District, the several blocks of sex shops and other businesses surrounding the Central Station, I forgot about the chemical substance working its way through my bloodstream, both fascinated and disturbed by what I was witnessing. Prostitutes stood nearly naked on display in shop windows alongside sex clubs with doors opened wide, topless women on stage visible from the narrow, neon-lit alley where we walked. Sex shop after sex shop beckoned customers inside with gaudy displays of lingerie, dildos, and sex toys, some of whose nature I couldn't imagine.

Small groups of men of all ages and nationalities roamed the district, looking on the scantily-clad window women with apparent delight. The eyes they turned on us were aglow with the same amazed boldness, despite our boyish haircuts and androgynous figures. It made me nervous to be female and walking among all these testosterone-drunk men in this strange, glittering part of the city where S&M implements and human beings were for sale in adjoining windows. Feeling personally at risk was not at all what I'd expected of the famed Red Light District.

My father, I thought, would be horrified if he knew where I was. Had he witnessed this part of Amsterdam himself? He must—he'd been coming to this city for business for thirty-odd years, since well before he took over the store from his father. But I couldn't imagine him here, didn't want to picture him in his neat suit and wire-rimmed glasses wandering this section of the city. He seemed too good for this, too wholesome or kind. Too upstanding, I hoped. And if he wasn't? Well, I would rather not know.

For just a moment, I wondered if that was how he felt about me being gay. Did homosexuality equate in his mind with the sex being hawked here in the Red Light district? The thought made me slightly ill. I was hardly a prostitute for hire. And yet, undeniably, sex was what differentiated me from the heterosexual majority, some of whom rented the bodies of other people in order to fulfill their "normal" desires.

As we walked on, Amsterdam, which until then had seemed mostly picturesque with its museums and bicycle-lined canals, began to take on a less shiny, more sinister tone. America had never felt like this. Not even Vegas, where I'd gone one weekend with college friends, could match this depth of visual debauchery. Suddenly home, with its Puritanistic laws and suburbs lined with cut-out houses and neat lawns, seemed a lot more attractive. Safe, ordered, in control.

A group of American college boys, easily identifiable in fraternity baseball caps, rugby shirts, and Nike cross-trainers, walked just ahead of us through the neon noise. We passed a sex club, open doors leaking music and glimpses of flesh, and a man out front zeroed in on the group of boys.

"Come in, come in now," he appealed in accented English. "Come see the women! Do you like girls? Do you like pussy?" When the four just slouched quietly past, ignoring him, the doorman cast after them, "What are you, gays? Faggots?"

Sofie rolled her eyes at me. "Don't worry, we are almost there."

Her smile cooled a little of the rage suddenly bubbling in me, but not much. How could she stand this part of the city? It didn't seem possible that only a few blocks away, cute cafés and historic brick buildings lined similar stone streets.

Soon we stopped before a bar whose windows were painted black. "Voila," Sofie said, waving me ahead of her into the darkness. I felt her hand on my shoulder, guiding me. Her gentle touch eased any remaining anger inside me, and I was sorry when she released me as we emerged into the crowd of women occupying the lighted interior. Dutch women, I reminded myself, taking in the colorful dye jobs and assorted black leather get-ups around me. In Amsterdam, the punk Euro thing was still happening. Or maybe it was happening all over again.

We ordered drinks at the bar and took them upstairs, where a spinning disco ball, a DJ, and huge bass speakers turned a small room into a killer dance space. The pill Jackie had given me kicked in shortly after we arrived, and she dragged me onto the dance floor, grinning at me and twirling me through space. The chemical compound whirling through my blood soon made it hard to focus, but not in a bad way. Later I remembered trying to interpret distorted images while I danced with a variety of strangers who seemed to exude visible energy, their bodies edged by shimmering auras. Shiny white smiles, beads of water, the bass pulsing inside me—I seemed to circle for hours around that creaky wooden dance floor, joy and sweat slipping from my skin, a slick amalgam created by the combination of chemicals and exertion.

At one point I noted with interest that if I turned my head sharply in any direction, the lights in my sight would streak just like they did in time-lapse photography. I occupied myself with this trick for what seemed to my addled brain to be a long time—in reality, it might have been ten minutes, or one, or fifty. Thanks to the magic pill, it did not occur to me in that unknowable stretch of time how I might appear to others as I experimented with my brain's startling new ability. My past wasn't important, or the future. Only this moment, right now, right here.

I had never been happier, I was certain that night, spinning about the back of a Dutch bar surrounded by friendly foreign lesbians.

Wherever I went, I would always know to find my people out in the night, dancing in cramped spaces where you couldn't escape the pound of the bass in your gut, in your head, in your blood. That was another thing I loved about being a lesbian—you never had to be alone if you didn't want to. There would always be enclaves of gay people twirling the nights away. You only had to know where to look.

Between the three of them, Jackie, Ann, and Sofie appeared to be friends with an entire gaggle of cute young lesbians, the kind who dressed in American clothes and played soccer in the Gay Games every four years no matter where the event was held. This group spilled out from the downstairs bar up and across the dance floor and back down again, recognizable by the usual pouts, laughter, and stolen kisses of incestuous twenty-something lesbians everywhere.

Some of these women drifted nearer, eyeing me with a familiar look of possibility. But Sofie stayed close, her eyes on mine and her hand sometimes lingering at the back of my neck, the base of my throat, the curve of my hip. She, I understood, was making a play. Seduced by the foreignness of it all, I encouraged her with my own look, touch, smile. Here I was, an American tripping on an unknown drug, dancing with Dutch and Australian and God-knew-what strangers in a darkened gay bar in Amsterdam, and a beautiful woman who was the friend of a friend seemed to want me. Sweet.

We stayed at the club until it closed at four a.m., and then we caught a cab back to the Museum District. The magic pill was beginning to down-shift into another gear, one in which everything around me appeared rapturously clear. I could see each ray of lamplight cutting through the thick city air, slicing through car exhaust and damp spring nighttime; feel each drop of water gurgling below us as the cab traversed one bridge after another over winding canals; sense each urban boat anchored in the darkened Amsterdam waterways moving gently on wave tops, brushing against mossy stones and cracked wooden docks.

I leaned my head on Sofie's shoulder and looked up through the half-open backseat window, watching small city trees wave overhead in the night's breeze. Finally, something that was younger than in Ann Arbor. Back home, maples and oaks towered over houses, businesses, streets; in Ann Arbor the trees were wild and the buildings weren't. Just the opposite of Amsterdam, where the trees looked tame and orderly beside ancient, hulking edifices.

The cab stopped at my hotel first. Sofie stepped out of the car with me and kissed each of my hot cheeks.

"It has been a good night, Junior," she said, smiling.

"Yes, it has. Too bad it has to end."

"It does not have to yet," she said, and tilted her head sideways. "Does it?"

I looked around the quiet Museum District, where neon restaurant signs and hotel lights had been dimmed for hours already. "It doesn't?"

"I feel like a walk. Would you like to join me?"

"Oh. Well, sure." I leaned into the cab and waved at the two Aussies. "Bye, guys. Thanks for an awesome time."

"You're welcome," Jackie said, wiggling her eyebrows at me.

"Hasta luego," Ann added.

"See you later, girls," Sofie said from behind me. Jackie waved, but Ann looked away and told the driver to continue on. Drama? Possibly. But I didn't know for sure, and I liked it that way.

"Do you like parks?" Sofie asked as the cab sped away.

"Love 'em."

"Then follow me."

I nearly had to run to keep up as she set off down the sidewalk. She led me into the dimly lit edges of a nearby park, where we walked a paved trail lined by generously spaced lamp posts at the edge of a lake, twisting and turning alongside benches, trees, patches of spring flowers. If you listened closely, you could hear people giggling and moaning in the dark bushes. I was glad the night masked my pink cheeks. I didn't want Sofie thinking I was too provincial even if, perhaps, I was.

She stopped finally, dropping onto a bench near a lamp post in the middle of a garden, and patted the narrow space beside her. "Join me?"

"Okay," I said, and settled myself between her warmth and the bench's wrought iron handrail.

We sat quietly under the low Dutch clouds for a bit, looking around. To quell my nervousness, I pointed out flowers near us and told her their Latin names.

"You are showing off," Sofie said, laughing. "You did not mention you knew so much about flowers."

I confessed that I had studied botany in college; told her how long I'd been working at the Arboretum; described Fitzy, the varied offerings at the Botanical Gardens, the staff and volunteers I'd worked with for years.

"It sounds like you love what you do," Sofie said.

"I do. I love the seasons, planning ahead and then waiting to see what each new week brings. In the summer, my days take on this rhythm that depends on the moon and the sun and where the earth is in its orbit. We have plants, like chickweed, that actually sleep when the sun goes down, folding in to protect new growth. Sometimes I go in early just to watch the chickweed open again at sunrise."

"And yet you say you are still looking for what moves you. How can this be?"

"My job at the Arboretum is fine for where I'm at now. But if I ever want to own a house or support a family, I would have to go back to school and become an instructor, or at least a grad assistant. And honestly, I'm not sure I'm the teaching type."

"Surely there must be something else you could do, something similar, other than becoming a teacher?"

I looked up at the clouds racing low and gray overhead. "Sometimes I think I might like to study landscape architecture. Do you know what that is?" She shook her head. "It's the design and construction of gardens and outdoor spaces. I think I might really like that kind of work."

The idea had first occurred to me—or rather, been suggested to me—the previous summer during my third trip in five years to the Pacific Northwest, where my college buddies Lesley and Steven lived. One afternoon while walking around Capitol Hill, the gay section of Seattle, I stopped to watch a landscaping crew put the final touches on the outdoor space at a new house. The home was a contemporary Craftsman design with rustic timbers, deep overhangs, and large windows. A wrap-around cedar deck provided a transition to the terraced lawn, where the designer had added a slate path, rock walls, native plantings, and a decorative gate with a cedar arbor.

Over dinner that night, I'd waxed so enthusiastically about the property that Lesley had asked if I'd ever considered a career in landscape design. With my botany minor and Botanical Gardens experience, he'd pointed out, I shouldn't have a problem getting into a graduate program. One of their friends had earned his master's degree at the University of Oregon, where the Landscape Architecture department focused on environmentally sustainable design. Even with the recession, Lesley said, their friend had more work than he could handle.

"That sounds perfect for you," Sofie said. "Why don't you do it?"

"Maybe," I said, tracing the cold iron handrail with my fingertips.

The previous summer, when I was in Seattle, I wasn't looking for a new plan. I'd been content to work at Boadicea and the Gardens, wake up to Maddie on the weekends, and hang out with Dez and Alex and our other friends while I waited to see where Maddie's career path would take us. But my future no longer depended on how high Maddie scored on her oral exams.

Everyone stumbles sometime, Fitzy had said. She was right. Maybe it was time I started getting myself unstuck.

Dawn was beginning to cast the buildings at the edge of the park into serrated relief against the lightening sky when Sofie slipped her arm behind my shoulders and kissed me. Her mouth tasted of cloves. The thought that drifted lazily into my mind caught me off guard—*I wouldn't mind exploring Sofie's nether lands*—and I giggled.

"What?" she asked against my mouth. Her hand dipped down from my shoulder to trace my collarbone lightly.

"Nothing."

She kissed me again, deeply, and I let myself get a little lost in the feel of her tongue against mine, the scent of spring flowers, the damp night air heavy on my skin. Until she drew away and began to kiss her way delicately along the edge of my chin and down my neck—then I became aware of muffled sounds from the bushes, footsteps on the paved paths of the park, the passage of buses and taxis on nearby streets. I may have been in a foreign country, but I was still a Michigan girl who had never had sex with a virtual stranger in a public place. Even at the Womyn's Music Fest, there are tents for that sort of thing.

"Um, Sofie," I said, and leaned away, "I think I should get going.

I'm exhausted—you know, jet lag?"

She pulled back and squinted at me. Then she smiled, shrugged, gave me a chaste peck on the cheek.

"Okay," she said. "We will get you home."

Back at the hotel, she kissed me again on both cheeks. "Call me later, Junior, if you like," she said as I pressed the hotel's door bell.

The front desk clerk buzzed the door open. I paused and looked back at Sofie, the night's events swirling through my memory.

"You got it," I said, and leaned in to kiss her squarely on the lips. Like an American. "I'll call you later."

"Good."

And with a genuine smile, Sofie walked off down the street, her jaunty step uninfluenced by intoxicants. I watched for a moment, noting that the lights in my line of vision were behaving normally.

The magic, it appeared, had worn off.

CHAPTER TEN

My father's knock two hours later brought me swimming up from a dream of Sofie's red hair and pink lips. I had unwisely agreed the previous day to have breakfast this morning with my dad before his early meeting. Swearing mildly, dreams rapidly receding, I staggered from my side of the suite, groggy and rumpled in men's pajamas and a sweatshirt.

He frowned. "Are you going downstairs like that?"

"Oh, right," I said, and retreated to my room to grab a baseball cap. When I rejoined him, he merely lifted an eyebrow in ever-so-familiar disapproval and waved me ahead of him into the elevator.

I managed to stay awake through eggs, toast, and juice, and dazedly approved a plan for the afternoon: a visit to the Anne Frank House, a walking tour of the Jordaan—which I suspected my father did *not* know was the gay part of town—and dinner at a Tapas bar. Then he rushed off to his still-unspecified meeting and I went back upstairs to bed, where a full stomach deposited me in a most satisfying food coma.

I slept until noon and awoke to pale spring sunshine fluttering through the gauzy curtains at my window. Looked like decent weather. Maybe I would go outside and read among the flowers and trees of the park I'd visited with Sofie the night before. Assuming I could find it again.

And speaking of Sofie... I lay in bed a few minutes longer, remembering the previous night's events. Then I dug out my address book and found her cell number. This was beginning to feel familiar, staring up at the hotel's gray tile ceiling listening for Sofie's lilting English in the telephone receiver: "Allo?"

"You sound wide awake this morning."

Her voice dropped to match the warm intimacy of mine. "You do not, my friend. Are you only now waking up?"

"Kind of." I related the morning's events, ending with my singularly pleasant nap. "I thought I might go read in the park for a little bit. Any interest in joining me?"

"Ah, I wish, Junior. But I will be in the editing booth all day."

"But it's Saturday."

"I know this. However, we are working on a deadline, so the day of the week does not matter."

"Sounds fun."

"It is," she said, missing my sarcasm. She told me in more detail about her project, a documentary on a small private school in a town thirty miles from Amsterdam. The cameras had followed the students through their daily lives over the course of a school year, and now it was up to Sofie and her team to uncover the narratives hidden in the voluminous raw material.

"Of course, there are many stories," she said. "Our challenge is to select only a few. But look at me—I ramble. I will let you go enjoy the beautiful day in the park."

I'd liked listening to her talk about her work, but the sunshine was calling. "Only one thing. Which park did you take me to last night?"

Turned out we'd been wandering Vondelpark, a popular recreational area between Leidseplein and Museumplein where, I had read, even adults should not take candy from strangers unless they were prepared to trip the day away. Sofie gave me directions, and then she added, "Would you like to do something tonight, after your dinner with your father?"

"You mean, something with you?" I teased.

"Junior..."

"I would love to meet up with you later. How about I call you when I get back to the hotel?"

"Okay. If I go anywhere, I will leave you a message."

"It's a date," I said, the smile on my face as goofy as my sentiments. Toby's warnings about Sofie's congenital flirtation drifted into my mind, but I pushed them aside once again. Just because I'd be going home in a few days didn't mean I couldn't have some fun.

After we hung up, I was tempted to lie in bed revisiting my memories of the previous night, both reality and dream world. But a sunny spring day was not to be ignored, and so, hotel towel and the book my father had given me in hand, I headed out to nearby Vondelpark. There, I relaxed in the sun at the edge of a patch of tulips near the spot where Sofie and I had sat the night before.

Our conversation returned to me, and I cradled my head on my arms and considered again the possibility of a future career in landscape architecture—in Ann Arbor or in the Pacific Northwest, that was the question. Lesley and Steven were forever hounding me to pack up and move west. They had a spare bedroom where I could stay if I wanted, they reminded me whenever we chatted. I always refused, but that didn't mean I had to keep saying no. Ann Arbor was home, but it was also full of the living, breathing ghosts of people no longer in my life.

As I'd discovered the night before, in a new city I wouldn't have to worry about running into Maddie or Dez or any other ex, for that matter. Drama-free fun could be a permanent occurrence, as long as I kept myself out of new trouble.

I closed my eyes to the Dutch sunshine and inhaled one of my favorite scents, damp dirt and newly bloomed flowers, picturing the Arboretum and all the work being done there without me to get the Gardens ready for the spring flower season. But even that couldn't keep my mind from wandering back to the topic of my suddenly wide open future. Assuming Seattle or someplace else was in my cards, how would I tell my family? Before, I'd assumed I would have Maddie's job as my excuse to exit the Ann Arbor city limits. Now, though, it would just be me by myself swimming against the current of family tradition.

For generations, Starrevelds had dutifully attended the University of Michigan—State was only if you messed around in high school like a couple of my meathead cousins, and good luck trying to flourish as a Spartan in a family of Wolverines—married a suitable partner, and settled down within a few miles of the family home. My father and his sisters had all done this, as had their parents' generation. As had my own sisters. Telling my family I was moving to the West Coast would be harder than it had been to tell them I was a lesbian. At least they hadn't been able to argue with that one.

Still, blood ties weren't my only consideration. Fitzy was too important a presence in my life. No matter what, I couldn't just pick up and leave Michigan now, not when she had so little time left. I couldn't set out blithely in search of my future while hers continued to slip away.

Apparently, if I wanted to live my life and not the one set out before me by virtue of being born a Starreveld, there were to be no easy answers. Family history, Fitzy's prognosis, and Steven and Lesley's open invitation all roiling through my mind, I dozed off, the book of Vincent Van Gogh's letters serving as my pillow among the tulips of Vondelpark.

While the morning nap, a brie sandwich, and a long hot shower restored my energy, the same could not be said of my father's morning meeting. If anything, he returned to the hotel after lunch crankier than he had the day before. When I heard him stomping around in his room, I knocked on the adjoining door.

"Come in," he grunted, and I poked my head around the door. As I watched, he loosened his tie and threw it on the neatly made bed. "What?"

"Um, just checking to see if you still wanted to play tourist today."

He hesitated, looking toward the small table near the window where his briefcase lay. Then he glanced back at me. "Sure. Of course."

"How was your meeting?"

Grimacing, he turned away and stripped off his suit jacket. "I don't want to talk about it, okay?"

"Fine," I said. "Knock when you're ready." And I ducked back into my room.

Something was clearly up. Was Starreveld & Sons in financial difficulty? I pictured its quiet elegance, the beautiful displays my father took such pride in. If the store were in trouble, what could I do? My knowledge of precious gems would fit on an index card. Maybe. And even if I had possessed the means to help, would I have wanted to sacrifice my dreams, amorphous as they might still be, to save the family business? I knew the answer to that question. It was the same for me as it was for my sisters.

My poor dad. Not only had he ended up without a son to carry on the business name, he'd raised four daughters who had no interest in his life's work. It was no one's fault, but it was a tough position for him to be in. Even I could recognize that.

A little later, as we descended to the ground floor in the tiny hotel elevator, my father resolute beside me, I tried to regain my former good mood. After all, who knew when I would be back in this part of the world again? On the tram on the way to the Jordaan, I ignored his silence and focused instead on the cadence of nearby conversations. To me, the rhythm of the Dutch language sounded suspiciously like the Swedish Chef from the Muppets, and it was all I could do to refrain from blurting out a stream of imitative gobbledy-gook. To do so, I suspected, would not endear me to my fellow tram passengers. I could never mention this to Sofie, either. As good-natured as she appeared to be, I doubted she would look kindly on such mockery.

Meanwhile, an American family of four—the perfect proportion, a pre-adolescent boy and a younger girl—clad in REI jackets and boots, spoke loudly and snapped shots of each other on the tram, the Amsterdam cityscape a smear in the background. The young black man next to me with dyed blonde hair and multiple piercings frowned at the spectacle and returned to his Dutch newspaper.

What is it about Americans that causes us to behave so badly abroad? Is it a genetic flaw that makes us speak loudly and simplistically, shrinks our attention spans, leads us to self-consciously do and say things we would have sworn at home before the trip we would never do or say? Back home we might be quiet, polite, secretly annoyed by flamboyant Texans (especially true for mild-mannered Midwesterners); but get us overseas and suddenly we take on Minnie Pearl-esque characteristics, guffawing on trams and trains, taking photos indiscriminately and inappropriately, speaking English increasingly loudly to people who don't speak or understand English.

Like me, I was certain that the family on the tram—well, the parents, anyway—were somehow powerless to prevent their own crassness. And, like me, I imagined they contented themselves with the knowledge that they would never see any of these people ever again. Except maybe on the streets of an American city, where the currently supercilious Europeans would be the foreigners, staggering along skyscraper-lined blocks with their backpacks bowing them over, eyes filled with traveler's bemusement.

My father and I took the tram to the Westerkerk church stop where Sofie and I had debarked the night before, and walked around the corner and down the block to where the tour book said the Anne Frank House would be. There we found the museum housed in an unassuming brownstone, just another in a long row of four-story townhouses on the banks of a typical Amsterdam canal. We waited in line for a few minutes, standing in the warm afternoon sun with the usual bicycles, Mini Cars that looked like they should be overflowing with clowns and zooming about a circus big top, and Smart Cars—a motorcycle/ Mini Car combo—whizzing past along the narrow road.

At the ticket counter, a middle-aged woman barely glanced at us and asked, "One adult and one child?"

"Um," my father said. "Two adults, actually."

The woman looked up, startled, and squinted at me. With my short hair and baseball cap, I was guessing she hadn't mistaken me for a girl-child. She laughed nervously, said, "Oh, I am sorry. I am not wearing my glasses," and quickly handed us our tickets and change.

As we walked away, I elbowed my father. "Why didn't you just go with it? I could have gotten in half price."

"But she thought you were a boy."

"It's not the first time. If people are going to make assumptions, you might as well use it to your advantage."

"But that's dishonest."

"This from the man who rides trams for free all over the city?"

"That's different."

"How, exactly?"

"It just is." I started to retort, but he held up a hand. "I don't want to argue, Elizabeth. Let's just enjoy the museum, all right?"

But enjoyment is hardly what one looks for—or finds—at the Anne Frank House. Once inside, I headed determinedly away from my father, trying to escape his potentially contagious bad mood. As I wandered the downstairs exhibits on my own, I soon found myself forgetting about my father altogether as I became swept up in the saga of a family that had lived—and died—forty years before I was born.

It had been a while since I'd read the diary of the girl who, with her family, spent more than two years hiding from the Nazis in a secret annex of this, her father's business building. On the lower level, I moved from display to display, pausing to read quotes from Anne's journal and other documents in the office building, to read about and gaze upon pictures of the people who had hidden the Franks and four others in the annex, to watch video clips of an interview with Miep Gies, the woman who had delivered food to those in hiding. Then I ventured up a narrow set of stairs to a hidden passageway closed off by a bookcase on hinges, into the secret annex itself.

Along with a steady stream of other visitors, I walked slowly through the rooms of the annex. The walls of the room Anne had shared with another young Dutch Jew in hiding, Fritz Pfeffer, still bore the remains of her yellowing magazine cut-outs, photos, postcards. Here, Anne had spent her days reading, writing, and dreaming of a time when she might lead a normal life out in the open again. I couldn't imagine how she had maintained hope, but she had. It was here in the record of the life she'd lived.

As I stood in the small room, people from all over the world moving about me speaking in hushed tones, I tried to picture what 1940s Amsterdam might have been like. German soldiers patrolling the streets, signs barring Jews from public places, Gentiles spitting on their Jewish neighbors and turning them in to be transported to concentration camps where they would be starved to death or gassed. We always said it couldn't happen again, but to me the mystery was how it had happened in the first place. How had so many people developed so much hatred for their fellow human beings?

I wasn't a complete stranger to hatred. Homosexuality triggers extreme responses in various quarters of the globe, including parts of my own country. In my Queer Studies introductory class in college, we learned that eighty-five member nations of the UN still have laws against homosexuality that prescribe jail time for offenders. Even more frightening, seven UN nations have the death penalty for homosexual acts. As an American, it's difficult for me to imagine living in a place where government agents have the legal power to put citizens to death for the gender of the person they love. In the US, the government may have the legal right to deny me my civil rights, but I can't be arrested for being gay. At least, not anymore. The Stonewall Riots in June 1969, when a bunch of drag queens and manly dykes stood up to the bullies of the NYPD, changed that decades before I even knew what the word *gay* meant, let alone what it would end up meaning to me.

In Anne Frank's time, the government of Nazi-occupied Holland had relied on average citizens to enforce its policies. That was one of the many facts I couldn't wrap my mind around. In August of 1944 someone, their identity still to this day a mystery, had betrayed the Frank family to the police. A local Dutchman (or woman) had phoned the Nazi authorities to tell them about the Jewish families hiding at Prinsengracht 267. As a result of this treachery, Anne, her family, and the others hiding in this nondescript building had been rounded up and sent to Auschwitz-Birkenau in Poland. A fellow Dutch citizen, perhaps even a neighbor who had watched the Frank children grow up, had sent Anne and her family to the camps. And for what? That was the question that, to my mind, could never properly be answered.

The display led through the annex and back downstairs into a wide room, where separate video stations offered information about each of the eight people who had hidden upstairs for those two years. The residents of the secret annex had been dispersed across Nazi-occupied Europe. Anne and her sister Margot, their stations explained, had eventually been sent to Bergen-Belsen in northwest Germany, where both had died of typhus in March 1945, only weeks before the camp's liberation. Otto and Edith Frank, Anne's father and mother, remained behind in Auschwitz. Edith Frank died in January of 1945, twenty-two days before the Russians liberated the camp. Otto Frank, I learned, was the only resident of the secret annex to survive the camps and return to Amsterdam.

I stood before the monitors alongside strangers, tears blurring my vision. The material included concentration camp documents and clips from the liberation of the camps, when Allied soldiers had walked the rows of barracks recording images of skeletal inmates, many of whom wouldn't live to see their homes again. The black and white reels revealed the mountains of bodies amassed at the camps, unburied victims who had died of starvation and illness. I had seen similar footage before, but it still packed the same sickening, jarring punch.

How anyone could have participated in such cruelty to other living beings, let alone members of the same species, I would never be able to fathom.

I'd first become interested in World War II in high school, back when I used to watch TV after I finished my homework, alone in the den downstairs at night, cathode rays flickering on the walls around me. One evening I stumbled across a documentary on World War II, and perched at the edge of my easy chair, staring in horrified fascination at film footage taken during the liberation of the camps. My parents, I suspected, wouldn't have allowed me to watch the documentary had they known it was on. But I watched anyway, sensing that I was witnessing something vital to my evolving awareness of the world and my own place in it. I knew I would never forget the images, burned as they were in my mind that night—Jews, Gypsies, political dissidents, gay men, all declared subhuman by the Germans, rounded up, and tortured to death.

Already aware of what it was that made me different from my sisters and the other girls at school, this was the first I had heard of an organized and systematic attack mounted against people like me. I already knew that some individuals—mostly devout Christians, which even then struck me as ironic—hated gays with a disturbing intensity. But this was the first evidence I'd come across that large groups of people might not only want homosexuals (particularly, in the case of the Nazis, gay men) dead, but would be willing to see to our deaths personally.

As I paused at Anne's station wiping away tears, my father caught up to me. I'd nearly forgotten he was here, but as he slid an arm across my shoulder, his touch warm and somehow soothing, I leaned into his side gladly. I couldn't remember the last time he'd put his arm around me. But then, my family had never been particularly demonstrative. Fortunately my friends and girlfriends usually more than made up for my family's coolness.

I've long believed that one reason queer people are so affectionate with our own kind—our families of choice, as many of us refer to our circle of friends—is that we often come to each other starved for physical contact. Once the straight people in your life know you're gay, it's like they worry that you might be contagious or something. Or maybe they see your sexuality every time they look at you, so that they can't touch you without thinking about sex. Whatever the cause, straight people in my experience often treat gays and lesbians as if we're untouchable. Sometimes even our closest relatives treat us like lepers. The psychic effect of this can be devastating—to other people, I had always told myself. Not to me. And yet here I was leaning gratefully into my father's side as if I had longed for his embrace all these years.

Loser, I castigated myself, even as I stayed right where I was.

Eventually my dad and I continued on through the museum together, stopping to read letter and journal excerpts. In early 1945, Otto Frank, sole annex survivor, had returned to Amsterdam to await word of Anne and Margot's whereabouts. The news of the girls' deaths finally reached him that summer. A year later, he finished editing Anne's wartime journal and began the search for a publisher. Now, sixty-five years later, there are nearly thirty million copies of the journal in print, and it has been translated into more than fifty languages. The words of one ordinary Dutch girl have managed to reach millions of readers across the world. Anne, the would-be journalist, would have been thrilled.

My father and I wandered past a glass case that held various editions of the journal, pausing on the other side to read Otto's letters to inquiring relatives. The first was written in early summer 1945, when he still held hope that "his girls" were alive. That hope, he said, was the only thing keeping him going. The second letter he had written after hearing news of both girls' deaths; in it, there was more loneliness than I had ever observed in any piece of writing. Standing in the building where he had once worked and lived with his wife and two daughters, I wondered how he had survived the first years after the war. But he had, somehow. By the time the journal was published and on its way to international acclaim, he might even have gotten back into the habit of living, which, I thought, must have been much harder to relearn than that of dying.

From the manuscript room, we wandered through a series of displays charting current developments in racism, neo-Fascism, and anti-Semitism. Then we passed through a gift shop with wide sun-filled windows, crossed the threshold, and moved back outside into the spring afternoon.

In unspoken agreement, my father and I headed toward an empty bench not far from the museum exit. Once seated, I crossed my legs and looked up and down the Prinsengracht canal, trying to imagine what the neighborhood had looked like in the 1940s. Judging from the pictures and film footage we'd seen, this part of the city hadn't changed much since Anne Frank and her family had hidden here. In fact, it may have looked almost exactly the same, with only the cars and bikes offering testimony to the contrary.

"So," my father finally said after a few minutes of contemplative silence, "what did you think?"

"Amazing. What about you?"

"Incredibly moving."

I didn't think I'd ever heard him use the word "moving" before. He was usually so practical, the opposite of emotive. But then, I didn't know how anyone could remain untouched by what we had just witnessed. We sat in the sun for a while, budding trees overhead casting weak shadows across our faces, and after a little while, I realized I was glad to be sitting next to my dad as strangers passed us by on the narrow, foreign street.

After a little while, my father pulled out his Frommer's *Guide to the Netherlands* almost apologetically and suggested we get started on our walking tour. We could end at the restaurant he'd proposed for dinner, a Spanish tapas bar our hotel manager had recommended. My head still full of World War II and the secret annex, I rose and followed my dad down Prinsengracht Street, back the way we had come.

The official tour started at the Westerkerk Church. There, my dad pulled his camera from its padded bag and snapped a shot of me next to a small statue of Anne Frank.

Then: "'On the stone plaza at the north end of the church,'" he read aloud from Frommer's, "'stands the Homomonument.' You wanted to see that, didn't you?" he asked, scanning the plaza and focusing in on the granite triangle Sofie had pointed out the night before.

"Actually, I saw it yesterday."

"I didn't," he replied. "Come on, let's get a closer look."

And he headed right for the Homomonument, not even waiting for me. His next move shocked me even further—he asked a passerby to take our photo in front of the monument. We posed together at the edge of the pink stone, my father's arm around me again, the sign that explained the granite triangle visible in the background. While the polite Dutchman caught the moment on film, I faked a smile and tried to convince myself that my father, who had seemed dismayed by my sexual orientation for at least the past decade, had in fact willingly posed for a photo with me beside an international tribute to gays and lesbians. Not just willingly—he had come up with the idea to have our photo taken together there in the first place.

Do people actually change, or do they only appear to? This was a question Fitzy and I had debated the previous summer after a dinner party she'd hosted. As we washed and stacked the dishes the party-goers had left in their wake, I'd maintained at first that no, people don't really change, they only appear to. But eventually Fitzy had won me over with her argument that if the appearance of change was persuasive enough, maybe the reality didn't matter. By extension, then, maybe it didn't matter if my father was comfortable with me being queer, as long as he could pretend convincingly enough that he was. Faked tolerance might even morph into genuine acceptance at some point—the old *fake it till you make it* adage come to life.

The unexpected moment dutifully recorded on film, my father and I continued on through the streets of Amsterdam alongside canals and intricately gabled facades. He read aloud from the guidebook's descriptions of various buildings as we walked: 6 Westermarkt, where Descartes had lived while writing *Treatise on the Passions of the Soul* and carrying on a torrid affair with his maid; the houses at nos. 15-22 Noordermarkt, each adorned with an agricultural figure (cow, sheep, chicken, pig) dating from the time when a livestock market had been held in the nearby square; the House with the Heads, built in the 1620s, at 123 Keizersgracht, which boasted casts of Apollo, Ceres, Mars, Athena, Bacchus, and Diana; the West India House at Herenmarkt, the seventeenth century headquarters of the famed Dutch company that had handled trade with Africa and the Americas; and numerous other flamboyantly-gabled houses overlooking the many canals lining the Jordaan.

While we wandered yet another picturesque canal, my father said, seemingly out of the blue, "So how about that Anne Frank House?"

We had mostly exhausted the topic of today's museum visit, I felt. In fact, I wasn't sure what we had left to talk about in general. Only a couple of more days, I reminded myself. Later tonight I would hang out with Sofie again, tomorrow would be filled with more tourist activities and (according to the weather report) hazy sunshine, and then on Monday we would say our farewells to Amsterdam and hop a plane back to the Motor City.

I frowned at my dad. "What about it?"

"I didn't realize the pink triangle came from World War II. Until this trip, I wasn't even aware that gay people were put to death in Nazi concentration camps."

Whoah. I glanced at him quickly, but he was looking across the bridge-speckled canal, his gaze seemingly fixed on the view. How could he not have known the Nazis included queers on their list of the socially undesirable? But realistically, most people probably don't know that thousands of homosexuals, mostly men, were put to death in the camps, or that some gay men remained imprisoned in Germany long after Jews and other political prisoners had been released. Being gay was a crime in Germany until 1969, which meant that many homosexuals who'd been arrested by the Nazis remained in custody, sometimes up to two and a half decades after the war ended.

How, indeed, would the average person, gay or straight, know any of this? Queer people are even more invisible in mainstream history courses and literature than women and people of color. Which is saying quite a lot.

"What I don't understand," my father added, still staring into the distance, "is why you would want something associated with such evil to be the symbol of a movement."

My dad, asking about the philosophical underpinnings of the gay rights movement? I almost couldn't get over my astonishment to focus on what he was saying, but somehow, I managed. I'd actually asked the same question myself when I first learned of the connection between the symbol of the gay rights movement and Nazi concentration camps. Sometimes I still wasn't sure I fully understood the answer I'd been taught, but I repeated it anyway: "By reclaiming the pink triangle and turning it into a symbol of pride, gay activists have taken away our oppressors' ability to wield it against us. Basically, we decided that it doesn't have the power to hurt us, so therefore it doesn't."

"Oh. Okay." He nodded slowly. "Then why haven't I noticed the Star of David displayed the way pink triangles are?"

"You're talking about two very different symbols. The Star of David predates Nazi Germany. But if you think about it, it is on the flag of Israel. Anyway, Jews have been a recognized group for centuries. Gay people only started organizing in the last hundred years or so."

"Why not before then?"

And before I knew it, I was explaining American homo history 101 to my father: the definition of homosexuality and its accompanying stigmatization in the late nineteenth century; the impact of World War II in bringing large numbers of gay people together in major cities through war work and military service; police crackdowns on gay establishments throughout the '50s and '60s, when it was illegal in America to visit a gay bar; and, finally, the Stonewall Riots, when New York City queers stood together against a police raid and gained a political voice for the first time.

"Some people say Judy Garland's death led to the riots in Greenwich Village," I told my father. "That all the gay men at the

Stonewall Inn that night were in mourning, and the police picked the wrong time to bust up the bar. But I think it was just time to fight back."

"You certainly know a lot about this," my father said.

"My history degree has to be good for something."

"I didn't realize the University offered classes on, well, this kind of thing."

"They probably didn't when you were in school."

"No," he said. "I don't suppose they did."

A cyclist buzzed by just then, nearly clipping my dad. I reached out and tugged him out of the way, steadying him as the bicycle's airstream faded.

"Thanks, honey," he said, and smiled at me.

"No problem. So what's next on this tour of yours?"

He pushed his glasses up his nose and peered down at the guidebook, the page marked with a thin silver chain I recognized from the store. "Let's see. Where are we?"

I watched him trace the page with his index finger, and for a moment I stepped back mentally and saw the two of us in context: a middle-aged father and his queer daughter strolling the streets of the gay quarter of Amsterdam.

"We're almost to the restaurant, I think," he said, and glanced up at the nearest street corner. "Assuming we're on Prinsengracht. Or are we on Keizersgracht?"

I looked around at the colliding blocks of richly ornamented canal houses and narrow stone bridges. "I have no idea."

"Neither do I." He held out his arm. "At least it's still daylight. Shall we wander?"

I slipped my arm through his. "Why not?"

That afternoon, somehow I didn't mind being lost with my dad on unfamiliar streets as lights flicked on over canals and houseboats, on bicycles and Smart Cars, in doorways and windows, illuminating the painted facades and stone arches all around us.

CHAPTER ELEVEN

We eventually found the tapas bar on a street that had a parking strip down its center where a canal should have been. In spite of this flaw, the restaurant was excellent. My father and I ordered sangria, potato tapas, asparagus salad, sautéed mushrooms, and garlic bread. He hadn't ordered red meat once since arriving in Europe, I'd noticed. Was it coincidence, or out of respect for me? I was a pescatarian, a fish and vegetables kind of girl. Not that he ever seemed to remember.

The food came quickly, which was a good thing—I didn't want to sit there too long thinking about how odd it was to be imbibing alcohol with my father. Before this trip, we'd rarely sat at a bar or restaurant together, just the two of us. With six people and their respective spouses and children in the family, we hardly ever caught each other alone.

Shortly after the food arrived, my dad swallowed a large gulp of sangria and inquired, "Can I ask you another question?"

Apparently he was on a roll.

"Of course." I looked at him curiously, but he focused on spearing hot mushrooms and cold asparagus with his fork.

"I hope this doesn't sound ignorant," he said, "but I've heard more about gay people having parades than being persecuted by the Nazis or the police. Why is that?"

My father was asking questions I'd learned to answer for myself my first year of college, but then he had never needed to consider the impact of cultural forces on his own life. He was straight and white and male, and not just a little financially privileged. Why would he need to learn to think critically about a culture that had always compared other people to him, only to find most of the others lacking?

"What you hear and see," I explained carefully, as if he were a U of M student newly freed from a farm near Muskegon or a suburb of Detroit, "is filtered through a media dominated by a majority that isn't always interested in being fair or inclusive. Anyway, what do you expect from a group who organized politically in the '60s and '70s? Once we realized we couldn't stay hidden anymore, we knew we needed to be visible on our own terms."

"Is that why you look like you do?" my father asked, gesturing at my gelled hair, assorted piercings, low-slung jeans.

Really, did the man not watch *Glee*?

"I actually feel like myself like this. But also, it lets other gay people know I'm like them. It's a kind of subcultural cue so that we can find each other."

In my head, I started devising a reading list for him: that book by Ellen's mom, the one by the Boy Scout in Iowa raised by lesbian moms, and maybe someday well down the road, *Heather has Two Mommies*. I pictured a child with elfin features and adorable freckles, but the image was shattered by another, more frightening one—Toby, sporting a disapproving glower.

"I never realized any of that," my dad said. "You've just always seemed so angry, as if you had something to prove."

"In a way, I do. And anyway, it's infuriating, the proclamations that ignorant people come up with. Like the idea that being gay is a choice—who would choose to be hated by so many people? I mean, seriously, who would *choose* to risk being ostracized by their family and community?"

I stopped abruptly. It wasn't so long ago that my dad had expressed his own throwback opinions about the life I had "chosen," spouting the same dogma that my childhood church had spoon-fed its credulous members for years. Swallowing nervously, I looked down at my plate, busying myself with moving bits of food around in aimless circles.

My dad reached across the table and touched my hand. "I never asked how you felt about any of this, did I?"

I looked down at his hand, at the familiar blunt fingers and the gold wedding ring that I knew hid a circle of paler flesh. "No."

"I'm sorry, Elizabeth. I think I'm starting to understand that you're just being the person God intended you to be. Your mom got it right, but all I could think was why you, when I should have been asking what it was like for you."

I glanced up at my father, seeing the genuine regret in his hazel eyes that were so like mine, and Jane's, too. Was my dad actually apologizing for how bad things had gotten between us, or was this just a delayed, drug-induced hallucination? Was the previous night's magic pill creating some sort of bizarre flashback, the opposite of a bad trip? But no, he was watching me anxiously, his hand tense on mine as I tried to process his words.

"It's okay, Dad," I finally said, swallowing hard. "I'm sorry I've been so angry with you."

"You don't have to be sorry. We both know you've had good reason," he said, and grimaced.

To agree would be honest but a tad cruel, and I didn't want to ruin the fragile accord just beginning to take shape between us. I squeezed his hand, hoping he could feel my gratitude. It didn't have to be like this, and yet, it did. *He* had to be the one reaching out, the one apologizing, and not only because he was the parent. Our eyes held for a moment longer, and then, as one, we let go of each other.

We ate and drank in silence for a little while, foreign voices rising and falling around us as I tried to wrap my brain around the idea that my dad had really just apologized for his large-ish part in creating the emotional chasm that had divided us for so long. Secretly, I realized, I had always hoped this day would come, though I hadn't allowed myself to wish for it outwardly. I almost reached for my phone, already writing the text to Maddie and Dez in my head. But then I remembered that not only had I not brought my phone on the trip, but my go-to text buds were the ones who were lost to me now. It was as if some spiteful see-saw were in effect—I couldn't have both my family and the two non-family members I cared about most in my life at the same time. That would have been too much love for any one person, apparently.

Except I still had more than enough people back at home who would be thrilled to hear about my day with my dad in Amsterdam— Fitzy, Toby, Alex, and the rest of my family of choice these last years, the ones who had made my blood family's rejection a little easier to bear.

Somehow I doubt that, Fitzy had said when I told her my dad was only bringing me to Europe to try to talk me into working at the store. Turned out she had been right, but how had she known? I could almost see her shrugging her broad shoulders and chewing on the stump of an unlit cigar. She was always right, wasn't she?

Another memory intruded, the one where Fitzy reminded me that my father wouldn't be around forever, and I was doubly glad for this conversation, this day, this trip that was possibly my dad's way of signifying that he wanted us to bridge the chasm permanently.

As I munched tapas and swigged the best flavored wine I had ever tasted, I realized that I wanted my father to have better from me, too. It wasn't as if a single apology made everything okay, but he was trying so hard. I could meet him halfway, couldn't I?

I took a breath and said carefully, "How did your meeting go this morning?"

He frowned and washed a bite of salad down with sangria. A lot of sangria.

"Do you want another drink?" he asked, standing up abruptly.

"Okay."

I watched him walk to the bar, noticing the thinning hair at the back of his head, the slight hunch of his shoulders beneath his suit jacket. He'd always had a seemingly endless supply of suits. In high school, I used to try his clothes on when no one else was at home. By the time I was a senior, I was almost as tall as he was. I had loved to parade down the upstairs hallway in a pair of dress pants and one of his tailored shirts, a silk tie knotted clumsily at my throat as I half-listened for the sound of a car in the driveway. My parents never caught me cross-dressing, but sometimes I wondered if my father noticed his shirts hanging slightly out of place, his ties out of meticulous order.

He returned to the table with two glasses of fruity sangria, and as he sat down across from me, I took in his wrinkled shirt, gray hair, the creases about his eyes. Somewhere along the way, and I had no idea when, my father had gotten older. He would be sixty this summer. Cat had been busy for months now planning a surprise party, against the better judgment of the rest of the family. He would hate the fuss, Jane and I agreed. Eugene Starreveld would prefer a quiet family celebration without store employees or church friends. But that wasn't Cat's style, so that wasn't what he would be getting.

I waited until he had taken another fortifying drink before I said, "Do you want to tell me about these mysterious meetings, Dad?"

He held up his glass. "Let's have a toast first, and then I'll tell you everything."

"Deal." I lifted my glass and waited.

"To family," he said, "because no matter what you do with your life, no matter what other people think about you, your family will always love you."

I wasn't sure if he meant the general you, as in "one," or if he meant me specifically. Probably it didn't matter. My cheeks warm, I murmured something appropriately vague, clicked his glass with mine, and drank.

He drank, too, and then swirled the wine about in the glass, his gaze fixed on the bits of cherry and peach floating in the purple liquid. "The thing is, Elizabeth," he said, and looked up at me, "I'm not getting any younger."

And all at once, the hazy notion that had floated at the edge of my subconscious for the past few days became clear.

"You're selling the store, aren't you? That's why we're here."

He tilted his head sideways. "Not exactly. Trudy, your mother, and I have decided that it's time to take a partner into the business."

Like me, my dad was the youngest of four siblings. But Trudy was the only one of his sisters who showed any interest in the store these days. Karen had died years before, and Liesel, the next closest in age, was like an older version of Mary. Her sons were the ones who had gone to State and now worked at Radio Shack and a Ford dealership, respectively. Not that I was in a position to throw stones at anyone else's career aspirations. At least they could both afford cars and smartphones.

"You and your sisters are all busy with your own lives," my dad continued, "as are your cousins, and Keith isn't in a position to buy into the business. But there is a family-owned company here in Amsterdam looking to branch out internationally. They've expressed interest in investing in the store, so I've come to discuss the possibility of partnership, face-to-face."

I took a gulp of sangria. "No wonder you've been so crabby."

He raised an eyebrow. "Crabby?"

"You're right, I'm sorry. You've been downright pissy ever since we got here."

After a moment, he smiled a little. "That's probably true." He rubbed his forehead, the smile slipping. "Obviously, I have mixed feelings about this venture. Bringing in an outside partner is not the ideal solution, but I can't work forever."

"Of course you can't. You also can't help that none of your children love the store like you do, any more than we can help it."

He squinted at me. "But how do you know you don't love the store if you don't know what it is you do love?"

"I do know what I love, Dad," I said, thinking back to my conversation with Sofie. "I love making things grow, and creating opportunities for people to connect with the natural world."

He nodded slowly. "Like your grandmother. You know, I still have some of her old gardening things stored in the attic. Maybe we should dig them up when we get back. No pun intended." But he smiled, clearly pleased with his own wit.

I rolled my eyes.

"Show your old man a little respect. I brought you to the Netherlands, didn't I?"

"You did. Thanks, Dad."

"You're welcome, Lizzie. It's been a good trip so far, hasn't it? In spite of everything?"

"It has." I held up my glass. "To the new Starreveld & Sons. May it prosper for many generations to come."

He nodded. "And to plants. May your life list continue to grow."

We clicked our glasses and drank, and it didn't seem strange anymore to be sharing sangria and tapas with my father in a restaurant in Amsterdam, just the two of us.

Later, after we'd finished dinner and made our way back across the city, I had to switch gears—mental and physical—to get ready for my date with Sofie. In my room, I showered and dressed in my favorite faded jeans, a white dress shirt, and a tie my sister Jane had given me for my college graduation. This time when I ducked my freshly re-coiffed head into my father's room to say goodnight, he smiled tiredly and said, "Don't worry, I won't wait up. Be careful, okay?"

"I will," I said, suppressing a flutter of guilt at the memory of the previous night's adventures. Perhaps I would steer clear for the duration from drugs I couldn't readily identify.

"Are we still on for tomorrow?" he asked.

On the way back to the hotel, we had decided to spend part of the following day, our last in the Netherlands, touring Fitzy's favorite European attraction, Keukenhof Gardens and the bulb fields surrounding the nearby village of Lisse.

"Of course," I said. "Wouldn't miss it."

"Good," he said, and surprised me with a hug.

I kissed his cheek quickly, then slugged him in the shoulder. That was more like it.

"Go on now," he added. "I have work to do."

Growing up, I'd heard him say this last bit more than a few times. But now that I knew what sort of work he meant—selling off half the store to foreign investors—I couldn't help associating a bittersweet quality to the familiar pronouncement.

"Don't work too hard," I said.

He nodded, his eyes already focused elsewhere.

It was just after nine when I caught a tram to the Red Light District. Sofie wasn't difficult to pick out of the crowd near the designated stop—she was wearing a tight pink and orange floral tunic and matching flowy pants, funky and ugly to the point of attractiveness. She slipped her arm through mine, and although I was the novice Amsterdammer, I felt fierce as we walked the neon-lit alleyways, masculine attire my armor against the Red Light District.

Everywhere we strolled, arm in arm, people did double-takes. A couple of American guys with long hair and backpacks passed us in front of a sex shop featuring a stunningly wide selection of dildos and vibrators. One of the boys turned to whistle at us. We just smiled coolly and strolled on.

"We are their favorite fantasy," Sofie said.

"I know. My straight guy friends are obsessed with my sex life."

"They like to think all the equation misses is their penis."

"As if." I laughed.

Sofie watched me. "I like when you laugh. You look happy."

"I am happy. This trip has been amazing."

"Is tomorrow really your last day here?"

"Yeah," I said. "Sucks, huh?"

"It is immensely sucky."

She was so cute. And intelligent, and motivated, and a grown-up with a real job in a beautiful, wacky European city. Just then, Ann Arbor felt more remote than ever—in the best possible sense.

We soon reached our destination, a retro Euro coffee shop with slick plastic and leather furniture in muted prime colors, walls draped with psychedelic polyester curtains, and a glass display case that held pastries, joints, and pills.

"This is your first coffee shop, no?" Sofie inquired as we paused before the display case.

I frowned, confused. "Of course not."

"I mean, Junior, your first coffee shop in Holland."

"Oh, that. Well, yeah."

"You are a virgin, then, no?" She tilted her head.

The boy working the counter, with carefully messy hair and a seashell necklace that peeked out from beneath his chartreuse collared shirt, smirked at us.

"If you say so."

Sofie picked out a fat joint, paid for it over my protests—"You cannot pay your first time; it would be like paying for sex"—and led me to a table in the corner.

"Okay," she said once we were seated. "A few ground rules to keep in your mind tonight. Have you smoked the marijuana before?"

"Um, hello, I grow my own weed."

"Toby did not mention this."

"Only a few friends know, and my aunt."

"Your aunt? The sister to one of your parents?"

"My mom's sister, Barb. You would love her."

"You will have to tell me more about her momentarily." She

returned to her list, ticking the points off on her fingers: "One, go slowly; two, remember that Dutch drugs are stronger than American drugs; and three, no mixing with different drugs. No alcohol, either. You would be surprised how many foreigners come here and have a terrible time because they do not follow these rules."

"Guess I'm lucky to have you, then," I said, knowing my sarcasm would likely get lost in translation. I'd first developed an affinity for weed in eighth grade under the influence of my gender-neutral friend Jody, who liked to raid his parents' stash. I was hardly a novice.

Sofie smiled, and just like that, bossy Dutch girl vanished, sexy hot girl returned. "That is sweet, Junior. Now, what is this about your aunt and the marijuana?"

I launched into my favorite Aunt Barb story: "The night I came out to my parents, almost ten years ago now, it didn't go very well. I ended up going to stay with Aunt Barb, who lives on a farm a couple of hours away. My sister Jane had already called to let her know that I was AWOL."

"A-wall?" Sofie lifted the joint to her lips, pulled out a lighter, and inhaled deeply.

I watched her for a moment, and then looked around to see if anyone else was staring. Here we were at a café filled with strangers, the sounds of conversation, laughter, and eating echoing in the cavernous room, and Sofie had just taken a puff on a fat joint. But no one else seemed to find it out of the ordinary.

"Junior?" Sofie was good. Only a tiny bit of smoke escaped with my name.

"Sorry. AWOL means absent without—it means I ran away."

"Ah." She exhaled at last. "It is very good and very strong. Are you ready for your first legal marijuana?"

"You betcha."

I took the joint from her, sucked in a good bit of smoke, tried to hold it in, and immediately coughed most of it out. I grabbed my glass of water and gulped some down, feeling my face flush. Now I realized why Sofie had come on so hard with the rules of engagement. That shit was strong.

"Okay?" she asked, and took another puff.

"Uh-huh," I managed, my voice strangled. I drank more water. My whole body had begun to lighten almost as soon as the smoke hit my lungs, and as my breathing evened out again, I noticed a most pleasant warmth spreading through my limbs. That shit was good.

"Your aunt?" Sofie prompted.

"Oh, yeah, sorry. She took me out to the back porch, handed me a joint, and let me stay the night. By the time I fell asleep, life didn't seem nearly as dire. She actually told me a lot of things about my mother I didn't know. Of course, I could only remember bits and pieces afterward."

"Naturally."

Sofie only let me have one more toke, but I was floating anyway. The coffee shop felt warm and cozy to me for all its imposing furniture, the other patrons interesting and endlessly amusing, although I couldn't have said why exactly. An Asian woman with purple hair and a faux fur-collared vest sat at the next table with a blonde man who sported metal in places even I hadn't known could be pierced, and every time I looked at them, I burst out laughing. Sofie would lean over to shush me, but then she would lose it, too, and we would both collapse in laughter and forget what it was that had gotten us started in the first place.

Eventually, Sofie ground out the unfinished joint to save for later, and we went back up to the counter for snacks. Struck by a small pang of homesickness, though short-lived because after all I would be home in less than forty-eight hours, I chose a chocolate chip cookie, *oliebollen*—one of my favorite Dutch pastries from childhood—and an Orangina. Sofie selected *oliebollen* and a Perrier. I was not impressed with her restraint, but she told me that she had learned a long time ago to resist the munchies. If she hadn't, she said, she would now weigh three hundred pounds. This of course struck me as hilarious, and I had to lean against the counter top to keep from falling down.

Back at our table, we continued to talk over dessert and our non-alcoholic beverages. I wasn't sure later what we talked about; mostly I remembered the hard edge of my chair, my utter inability to stop laughing, the taste of the chocolate chip cookie, and Sofie's shining wit and exceptional attractiveness.

Once I started mellowing out from the pot, though, yawns took the place of my previous mirth.

"Do not do that," she said when I leaned my head on my arms and closed my eyes.

"Just for a minute."

I sighed happily. I felt perfectly relaxed and content, even if I was an ocean away from home. I could have curled up right there on the floor of the café and gone to sleep, lulled by the world music leaking from the speakers mounted in the corners of the room.

"Not even for a minute," she said. "Finish your drink. It is time to go."

I downed the last of my Orangina, pulled on my jacket, and let Sofie guide me toward the exit.

"Where are you taking me?" I giggled. "Take me to your leader."

She smiled indulgently. "We are going back to my place. I live quite close, and you should not be alone right now in your condition."

I recognized a good line when I heard one, but I wasn't arguing. I followed her from the coffee shop, sneaking one last glance at the odd couple who had kept me giggling all evening. They smiled and waved, which surprised me. In Michigan, the Dutch are known for their conservative politics and particularly judgmental brand of Christianity. But apparently only the most unpleasant of my ancestors' countrymen had left to settle the New World. Same with the Puritans. Present generations of Americans are still paying for our nation's early role as safe haven to the Old World's most uptight, intolerant Christians.

I waved back gaily—in both senses of the word—and joined Sofie on the sidewalk. She looped her arm through mine again and we walked through the Amsterdam night under the watchful eyes of gargoyles and other stone creatures.

"What do you think of your family's homeland?" she asked.

"It's lovely," I said. "You're lovely."

"As are you. What do you like best so far?"

I tilted my head back as the bells of Westerkerk echoed dimly from afar. For how many centuries had people walked these streets, those same bells playing accompaniment?

"The history. That, and the canals and the bicycles," I added. "But tomorrow, after my dad and I go to Keukenhof, that'll probably be my favorite."

"You will love Keukenhof," Sofie said, stopping in front of a nondescript townhouse.

I looked up, slightly disappointed—no sculpted animals or Greek gods peered down from the upper facade, nor was the front door brightly painted. Her house reminded me of Anne Frank's, with its block of townhouses facing a narrow canal and one of Amsterdam's ubiquitous stone bridges a few paces away. But then Sofie unlocked the door, and I was following her inside an Actual Dutch Home, and I forgot about the bland exterior. The floor in the entryway was polished stone tile, the molding on the door and window frames intricately carved, the handrail on the stairway heavy and scrolled. The hand-finished interior was redolent of age, even as the shiny metal mailboxes on one wall testified to the building's modernity.

Sofie led me up the narrow stairwell to a door on the first landing.

"This is me," she said as she turned a key in the lock, her inflection almost American. "Please, come in."

I stood just inside the door as she bustled around turning on lights. The apartment was large and almost obsessively neat, its walls painted in muted colors, the dark wood of the molding and built-ins lending a slightly somber feeling to the space. A thin gray tabby jumped down from its perch on a window ledge, stretched lazily, and paced toward me. I knelt down and held out a hand, but the cat remained just out of reach, rubbing against the edge of a bookshelf.

"That's Giles," Sofie said, hanging her jacket over the back of a kitchen chair.

I glanced around, noting the proliferation of books in every room—some shelved or stacked on coffee and end tables in the living room, others arranged on a baker's rack in the attached kitchen, yet others visible in shelves and stacks through the door that led, I guessed, to the bedroom. The living room contained nearly as many DVDs and VHS tapes as books. A media unit filled one wall of the living room, with a wide-screened television and various electronic viewing and recording devices. The cream-colored walls were decorated with framed movie posters, some in Dutch, many in English—*New York Confidential*, *On the Waterfront*, and *Gone with the Wind*, among others.

"Can I get you something to drink?" she asked. "Apple juice, milk, Perrier?"

I always wanted to like Perrier, but I never did. "Juice would be great."

"Make yourself comfortable."

She waved at the couch that faced the media center. It was large, plaid, and seemed somewhat incongruous compared to the rest of the more sophisticated furnishings. But as soon as I sank into its soft welcoming depths, I realized why she kept it. After thirty seconds, I was already in love with her couch.

"I need to get me one of these," I said when she joined me a minute later. I caressed the worn woolen armrest, sinking lower into the cushions. "This is the best couch ever."

She laughed and set our drinks on coasters on the coffee table. "My friends call her 'Mini,' short for *minnares*, our word for, how do you say, mistress? I have thought about buying a new couch many times, as I have had Mini since school. But I cannot bring myself to part with her."

With a low trill, the gray cat jumped onto the couch and walked along the back. He settled down right behind me, purring against my neck.

"Am I in his spot?" I asked.

"No, he's just friendly. Aren't you, my little slut?" she added in a low murmur, leaning over to scratch his ears. The motion brought her closer to me, too. Another smooth move. I reached a hand out and traced the length of her collar bone where it showed beneath the edge of her shirt.

She remained still beneath my touch. I caressed her neck and chin, slid my fingers lightly across her cheek, paused over her freckles. Her

165

eyelashes brushed my fingertips as she leaned into my hand. I wasn't exactly stoned anymore, but my senses were still heightened. The apartment smelled of incense and lemon, the air warm and slightly heavy. The cat's purring seemed to vibrate through me, while Sofie's skin felt soft, her hair silky as I ran my hand over her short curls.

It seemed only natural that she open her eyes and reach for me. We fit together easily as we kissed, limbs entwining. She pressed me down into the endlessly yielding sofa cushions, and I let her, my head spinning a little with the pot, jet lag, her delicate perfume. This was the best European trip ever, was the last coherent thought I had. And then I didn't think for a while as we kissed long, deep kisses, wrapped around one another, her cat purring beside us.

Eventually Sofie pushed up from the quicksand couch and held out a hand to me.

"Come," she said, and I knew that she was taking me to bed.

I let her pull me up. "Where's your bathroom?"

"Through here."

She led me into a room dominated by a high, four-poster bed and pointed the way, then turned to light a candle on the wooden dresser.

I ducked into the tiny bathroom and pulled the door shut. The entire room was white—tiny white floor tiles, white wainscoting, white walls, white claw foot tub. Only the shower curtain, decorated with lime and lavender swirls, offered any color. I stared at myself in the mirror above the sink. In the bright light, my cheeks were flushed, eyes bloodshot, lips slightly swollen. What was I doing? Hadn't Toby cautioned me not to take Sofie's flirting too seriously? Back home I'd made light of the warning, but here I was, my third night in Amsterdam, about to hop in bed with her. Though flirting was perhaps a bit of an understatement. Seduction was more like it.

Not that I was complaining—and that, of course, was the problem. If I slept with Sofie, then our relationship, if it could even be called that, would jump from casual to intimate whether we intended it to or not. That much I had learned from my forays into forgetfulness with Caitlyn and Steph. No matter what you thought you wanted, your body sometimes had different ideas. Funny things, hormones.

As I stood gazing into Sofie's mirror on the second story of her Amsterdam apartment building, an image floated into my mind of my dad seated at the desk in his hotel room on the other side of the city, worrying about the store and waiting for me. I checked my watch. One in the morning. If I left now, I could still get enough sleep to prevent a semi-comatose state the following day as we toured Keukenhof. I thought of how my father had reached out to me during our walking tour of the Jordaan, how he'd apologized over tapas and sangria, how he'd shyly proposed we spend our last day in the Netherlands at Keukenhof, knowing the garden topped my list of sightseeing possibilities. His father had taken him there on his first trip to Holland, he'd told me, and now he wanted a chance to share that experience with me.

He was genuinely trying to make things better between us. And what was I doing? Digging myself in deeper with an intoxicating woman I would probably never, ever see again.

I reached for the door.

Sofie was understanding, generous even, which made telling her I couldn't stay even more difficult.

"You cannot disappoint your father," she agreed once I'd finished my explanation. "Let us get you back to the hotel."

While she called a cab, I sipped my apple juice and tried to convince myself I wouldn't regret my decision later.

"Tomorrow is important for you and your father, is it not?" Sofie asked as we walked downstairs to wait.

"I think so," I said. "We've been strangers for so long, but now it feels like I'm getting to know him again, and he's not at all who I thought he was."

"People do not stop growing just because they have children."

"Maybe not, but I think it can be hard to see your family clearly, especially if you don't ever get any distance from them."

"This is true. I enjoy seeing my family, but they live three hours away by train, so I do not have to see them if I do not want to."

"That sounds lovely."

"You are lovely," she said, repeating my earlier compliment, and waylaid me with a hand, pushing me against the wall and kissing me soundly.

We stayed there, bodies pressed together in all the right spots, until a door slammed nearby. Sofie pulled away, planting little kisses on each of my eyelids and my nose before relinquishing me.

"You had better go now," she said. "Or else I do not think I will let you."

If we had been anywhere near her four-poster bed, I probably would have chucked the idea of returning to my hotel room. As it was, I drew in a breath and followed her down her building's narrow stairwell, my eyes on the delicate bones of her hand on the rail, the graceful curve of her neck, the enticing sway of her hips that only moments before had been grinding into mine.

Doing what you know you should, turns out, is immensely sucky. No wonder I didn't make a habit of it.

The cab was waiting at the curb. Before I guessed her intent, Sofie leaned in and gave the driver money to cover the fare.

"You didn't have to do that," I said.

"I know." She kissed me square on the lips, American-style. "Enjoy Lisse. You will return to town tomorrow?"

"In the afternoon. Should I call you?"

"You should."

She kissed me one last time, laughed a little, and then she turned away, waving over her shoulder. As the cab pulled away, I leaned my head back against the seat. I had done the right thing, I knew I had, so why didn't I feel better? I sighed and waited for my heart rate to slow, watching out the window for wild beasts silhouetted against the dark sky.

CHAPTER TWELVE

"We're here."

I stuffed my book in my pack and followed my father off the tram, glancing around curiously. The Jordaan—no wonder the ride had taken only a few minutes. What was he up to? Over breakfast my dad had informed me that he'd decided to modify our travel plans slightly, but had refused to share any details. I'd been planning to re-read the Keukenhof guidebook Fitzy had given me, but now it looked like I might not have the chance. Fortunately, I already knew what to expect. One of the most photographed sites in the world, Keukenhof is home to more than seven million flowers, and draws nearly a million visitors from March to May each year. With more than a thousand tulip varieties alone, Keukenhof was worth the trip across the Atlantic all by itself, according to Fitzy. Today I was hoping to be converted to the masses of devoted fans.

First we had to get there.

The tram had let us off at a park beside a canal. As we headed toward a nearby bridge, a clean floral scent wafted about us. In unison my dad and I said, "Hyacinths!" The colorful blooms thronged the front lawn of my parents' house. Each spring, their unmistakable fragrance carried through open windows, filling the house.

"Did grandma plant them?"

He followed my non sequitur easily. "She sure did. They were her favorite. After tulips, of course."

My father's mother, born Edith Grace Vandenberg, had grown up in a conservative Dutch Reformed family in Grand Rapids. Sometimes I was relieved I'd never had to find out what she or my dad's father would have thought about me being gay. My mother's mother, on the other hand, probably wouldn't have cared as much. Not that I would ever know. She'd died before I was born.

My dad consulted a hand-written note and squinted at the intersection on the far side of the bridge.

"That way," he grunted, and away we went.

We rounded a corner onto a narrow lane that soon turned ninety degrees again, leaving me hopelessly lost and increasingly curious. Finally, my dad stuffed the sheet of directions in his pocket and honed in on a shop midway down the block—a scooter rental shop, to be exact, with shiny two-wheeled machines gleaming in the morning sunlight.

I stared at him. "You're kidding, right?"

He lifted his eyebrows. "No."

Until this moment, I'd still assumed we'd be getting to Keukenhof the way most tourists did: train to Leiden, then the Keukenhof Express bus to the park, according to Frommer's. But this? This was—crazy. Awesome. So not my dad. And yet, totally my dad in Amsterdam.

"With scooters," he explained, pushing his glasses up his nose, "we can explore the bulb fields near Lisse. You know I have that last meeting this afternoon; this way we have more flexibility." As I continued to stare from him to the shop and back again, he shrugged.

"Also, I thought it might be fun."

"Are you kidding? This is fantastic!" I reached over and kissed his freshly shaven cheek.

"Oh. Well, good," he said, his smile making him look less like a hassled businessman and more like the dad I remembered playing ball in the summer with Jody and me until dark.

Secretly, of course, I was nonplussed by the idea of my father, Eugene Starreveld, tooling around on a scooter. But the real question was whether or not my sisters would believe me when I told them what Dad and I had gotten up to. Good thing I'd charged my camera before we left the hotel this morning. I had a feeling I would need plenty of battery power to document what might be a slightly surreal experience.

At the rental shop, a teenaged boy with a buzz cut eyed us across a dull metal counter.

"May I help you?"

"I called ahead for two of those," my father said, pointing at the row of scooters that lined the curb in front of the shop.

"Certainly, sir. Cash or card?"

As my dad reached for his wallet, I stepped away, pulled out my pocket-sized camera, and surreptitiously snapped a photo of him with the store sign and the line of scooters visible in the background. Just another shocker to add to the growing list.

Once we'd paid, the attendant assigned us our scooters and helmets and provided a short driving tutorial. He explained the controls, and then made each of us drive in a circle around the alley, accelerating and slowing on his command. Even at five miles per hour, my heart beat accelerated each time I revved the engine. Toby, a Harley chick, would have scoffed, but I didn't care. This motorbike thing rocked!

We passed the exam, and after graciously snapping a photo of the two of us posing beside our bikes, the attendant waved us out onto the streets of Amsterdam. My father led, which was fine with me given the morning rush hour traffic. Almost immediately we came to a roundabout populated by tiny cars and windowless Eurovans, all traveling at what seemed to be way too fast. For a moment, I almost forgot my brief driving lesson. But my dad's characteristic poise flowed back toward me along the city lane, and I followed him around the turn gaining confidence as we went. *Everything's going to be okay*, I could almost hear him saying. And despite a somewhat shaky start, it was.

The route my dad had apparently scoped out ahead of time (or traveled before?) kept us mostly on side streets, for which I was grateful. Soon we were leaving the city sprawl behind and speeding along a country road that wound beside a canal through a picturesque village. Though perhaps "speeding" was an overstatement—the scooters wouldn't go over fifty mph. Even at thirty-five mph, the chill morning air blew through my jeans, puffer vest, and thick, black hoodie. But the padded helmet kept my head warm, and on the bike I felt free, unrestrained, traveling a foreign road without glass or steel to divide me from the passing landscape.

Out beyond the village, the land we traversed gradually became flatter even than Ohio, the least interesting state I'd ever visited. It seemed like I could almost see the curvature of the earth here, until a uniform line of trees on either side of the canal signaled our approach to another town—Hoofdweg, according to various signs. Unlike the previous village, Hoofdweg was more like Amsterdam, with old brick buildings and windmills lining the canal alongside modern cement and steel edifices.

I repeated the town name in my mind, ascribing to it almost unconsciously the Swedish Chef's undulating (some might say convulsive) accent, as we crisscrossed canals and came out into farmland again. Though we couldn't see to the coast from here, I knew from map-gazing that the North Sea wasn't far off. As a Michigander I was accustomed to large bodies of water, but not to salt water. The handful of times I'd swum in the ocean, I couldn't stand the taste of salt in my nose, on my lips, in my mouth. Apparently I'd been spoiled by the Great Lakes.

We were almost to Lisse, only twenty miles from the scooter rental shop, before I caught my first glimpse of color in a field awash with orange, yellow, and red hyacinths in full bloom. My father pulled over to the side of the road and I followed. There, we consulted a map of the bulb fields he'd smuggled along and came up with a plan of attack. Given we had to be back in Amsterdam by three, and the guidebooks had recommended allotting four or five hours to wander Keukenhof's display gardens, we decided to take the shorter of two recommended loops through the flower fields near Lisse.

Route selected, I set the timer on my camera and took a picture of the two of us leaning against his parked scooter in front of the hyacinths, and then we revved our motors and resumed our journey. I had seen bulb fields plenty of times in Michigan, but I decided this was different as we swung past field after field in violent bloom. For one thing, I wasn't in a car, which meant that I could smell the tart scent of manure and growing things. For another, I was in a place much older than Michigan, a land that would have been swallowed by the sea if not for the ingenuity—and stubbornness—of its inhabitants. Ditches edged most of the fields we passed, channeling excess water toward the sea.

Mentally I compared the landscape around me to what I was used to back home. Differences between the two nations were less apparent in the countryside, where farm fields and paved roads looked much the same on both sides of the Atlantic. Except for the occasional windmill and wooden shoe display in the small towns through which we'd passed, any distinction was mostly in my head and had to do, once again, with my knowledge of each continent's history. Before white people had settled America, Michigan, like much of the New World, had been heavily forested. A common saying in Colonial America was that a squirrel could travel from the Atlantic Ocean to the Mississippi River without ever touching the ground. But here in Europe, white people had occupied the area for millennia, and the land had long since been cleared of native forests. That meant the land around us had likely been farmed for centuries. I wondered if bulb farms were family-run for the most part, or if corporate-owned farms now dominated the Dutch landscape to the same degree they did in Michigan. Land and crop management was a hotly debated topic back home, where small landowners were increasingly unable to compete with mega-corporations.

We stopped occasionally to ogle fields and record images of each other against blood-red or deep purple backdrops, but mostly we headed determinedly toward Keukenhof. I was cold by the time we arrived and gladly exchanged my helmet for my U of M baseball cap at the park, where we left our scooters in the bike lot near the main entrance. As we approached the gate on foot, I thought of Fitzy. She would have loved this moment. I could picture her on a scooter tooling along ahead of me, her boots perched on the footrests, her graying head held high as we circled the flower fields that probably hadn't changed much since she'd visited on her honeymoon.

My dad had even, somehow, procured entrance tickets ahead of time. The woman who took them narrowed her eyes at me. Women in the Netherlands, I'd noticed, didn't wear baseball caps. My father intercepted the ticket-taker's impolite stare and ushered me away without responding to the woman's belated suggestion that we enjoy ourselves.

Near the main gate, a hostess in traditional Dutch costume handed us a printed guide far less comprehensive than Fitzy's commemorative book. But our attention didn't linger on the printed pages for long as we joined the other tourists wandering goggle-eyed into the gardens. Keukenhof's planners had started with a bang: Just inside the entrance lay formal beds of red tulips, three feet in height, set off by plum-colored snowdrops. They were the largest, reddest tulips I had ever seen, and with morning dew decorating their petals, seemed almost unreal.

"What do you think?" my father asked, holding up the guide. "Do you want to plan a route, or shall I?"

"Can't we just wander?"

"There are displays you shouldn't miss, Elizabeth."

"I'm sure this place is well laid out. Don't you think it would be more fun to discover what the designers intended organically, without a plan?"

But I already knew the answer to this question: My father was a fan of order, a dedicated soldier against chaos in any form it might try to take. When I was a kid, we used to go to plays at the University, and my dad would read through the entire program from start to finish, including act-by-act plot summaries, while we waited for the show to begin. Meanwhile I wouldn't even glance at the program.

He looked down at the guide. "I guess. If that's really what you want."

"It is," I said, and slipped my arm through his. "Thank you, Dad."

"You're welcome." He squeezed my hand.

I had read up on Keukenhof's layout, of course, and knew generally what to expect. In Dutch Keukenhof means "kitchen garden." Located on the former site of a countess's vegetable patch, the park that forms the basis of the current gardens was designed in the mid-nineteenth century by the Zochters, father and son horticultural architects. This same father-son duo also designed Vondelpark, where Sofie had taken me. I seemed to be developing a thing for the architects Zochter. Keukenhof, however, hadn't taken its current form until just after World War II, when the powers that be decided Northern Europe badly needed an infusion of natural beauty to cheer its destruction-weary inhabitants.

I soon realized that the miles of orderly paths at Keukenhof offered abundant beauty, with small ponds, fountains, streams, and canals strategically placed to enhance the garden displays. At just under eighty acres, Keukenhof was only a tenth of the size of U of M's Botanical Gardens. However, its relatively small size did not signify a lack of quality. Around every curve in the path lay a new vibrant color—beds of fire red tulips set off by deep yellow varieties; plots of dark purple (so-called "black" tulips) and red and yellow striped blooms; and not only tulips, but narcissi, hyacinths, daffodils, orchids, chrysanthemums, roses, Azaleas, lilies, begonias, Gerbera daisies, and Freesia, in reds, blues, yellows, pinks, and purples more vibrant (it seemed) than any other garden I had ever visited. The fritillaries were pretty cool, too. Some looked like delicate bells, while others bore distinctive patterns. My favorite, *frittilaria imperialis*, reminded me of Muppets—of Beeker, to be exact—with their long, bare stalks, oblong hanging blooms, and shock of palm-like leaves on top. What was it about my ancestral homeland's connection to Jim Henson Productions?

Fortunately, the abundant visual and olfactory stimulus soon crowded the Muppets from my mind. Seven million flowers, I reminded myself, of more than 1600 varieties, making Keukenhof the largest bulb park in the world. With the mixture of scents assailing my nose at every turn, I had no problem believing the official numbers.

We hadn't gone far when we rounded a curve in the paved path and discovered a group of visitors on a makeshift landing, murmuring and snapping photos.

"This is a new display," my father said, and read aloud from the guide: "'Each year Keukenhof chooses a foreign country around which to build a theme, and this year the honor goes to Germany. This tulip and hyacinth mosaic, which contains more than 100,000 bulbs, depicts the Brandenburg Gate in Berlin.'"

We waited in line briefly, clambering at our turn onto the platform to get the full effect of the mosaic. Beside me, my dad peered over the top of his glasses the way I'd seen him do countless times at the shop, examining the display critically. I looked, too—there, I could easily make out the gate itself, lines of white tulips outlined in blue hyacinth. The other parts of the mosaic were outlined in the same blue hyacinth, too, which was a bit overwhelming color-wise. But overall, not bad, considering what they had to work with.

"Huh," my dad said. "Not bad, considering what they have to work with."

Fantastic. While Jane was becoming our mother, I was morphing into our father.

"What do you think?" he added. "What's your professional opinion?"

"Impressive. I can imagine the work that went into getting it just right, not to mention the transplanting they probably had to do when some of the bulbs failed to flower."

"I hadn't thought of that." He paused. "You know the remarkable thing about mosaics?"

"What?"

"They're proof that things that are separate or broken can still make a whole, given enough distance."

He placed his hand on the back of my neck and squeezed gently, and then we moved on.

As we wandered the varied pavilions and display beds, I took the requisite mountain of photos along with some short video, too, and scribbled in my journal, jotting down ideas both for the corner Fitzy had granted me at the Botanical Gardens and for the ultimate dream garden I would one day fashion in a yard of my own. I knew it would be a while yet before I owned a home, but I still had a folder of notes tucked away in a filing cabinet.

We visited a variety of display gardens, including Scent, Renaissance, Nature, Japanese, and Historical, many of which boasted related art exhibits. One of my favorite installations was *The Grove* by Nika Neelova, a flower-encircled lawn where upended oak trees (felled naturally, not for the purposes of art, a sign assured us) revealed the convoluted beauty of their life-giving roots. Our mutual least favorite sculpture, my father and I agreed, was of a horned Viking decorated with purple and gold flowers—the colors of the Minnesota Vikings, regional rivals of our own beleaguered Lions. We walked alongside rivers of blue Freesia winding beneath the bud-bedecked branches of 150-year-old trees, past flowering shrubs at the edge of ornamental lakes and fountains. Swans graced the inevitable canals, stark white and black against muted greens and browns, mixed in with other breeding birds.

"'The swans are leased annually and returned to their owners at the end of the season,'" my father read from the guide as we paused to look out across a small lake in the center of which was an island planted with bulb beds and flowering bushes. Deciduous trees, buds still only a hint of green, contrasted with the lush blossoms.

"Man-made lakes and rented swans," I said, "and yet I still think it might be the most beautiful place I've ever seen. Thanks for bringing me, Dad."

"You're welcome. You know, I regret that I never got your grandmother here. She would have loved it."

"Why didn't she ever come over with you and Grandpa?"

"She was terrified of flying."

"Did she know about Mom's mom?"

My maternal grandmother had died in a small plane crash when my mother was only seventeen. I hadn't learned until college that my grandmother, trained as a Women's Airforce Service Pilot (WASP) during World War II, had been at the controls of the plane when it crashed.

"It wasn't that. My mother just didn't think it was natural to be so far above the earth."

"It isn't," I agreed. "But look what it makes possible." I gestured, encompassing the gardens, the Dutch countryside, the blue sky peeking out between white clouds.

"Precisely," my father said. "You know, you inherited the best of both of your grandmothers—my mother's love of nature and your other grandmother's sense of adventure. That's one thing I've always admired about you, Elizabeth. You don't seem afraid of anything."

"Really?" I looked over at my father, but his gaze didn't stray from the colorful scenery before us.

"You do what you think is right, and you don't seem fazed by what other people think. That is a rare quality. I admire you for it."

I swallowed. "Well, thanks."

For a while now, I'd imagined that every time my dad looked at me he saw a big and, to his mind, freakish lesbian. But somewhere along the way he must have looked beyond my outward identity and seen me again.

After a couple of hours wandering the gorgeously sculpted grounds, we stopped for coffee at the Queen Beatrix Pavilion, opting for outdoor seating overlooking a canal lined with bright, square flower patches. From our seats on the deck I counted eleven different colors of flowers. The Botanical Gardens back home were designed to blend with the natural environment, a goal that the Keukenhof gardeners clearly did not share. Honestly, I was beginning to see their point.

"You never got to meet Mom's mom, did you?" I asked after a while, sipping coffee and snacking on *krakelingen*, Dutch pastry cookies I knew and loved from the Michigan Tulip Time Festival.

"No, I didn't."

"What was her background, again?"

"She was raised in Delaware. Your mother's family, as you know, is a mix of European heritages. Unfortunately, she doesn't know much about who came from where."

This was a polite way of saying that my mother's ancestors were Euro-mutts. I'd heard him on more than one occasion teasing her about diluting his pure Dutch blood with her mixed lineage. She never seemed to find the joke quite as funny as he did.

"How do you know she was fearless if you never met her?" I asked.

"I've been married to her daughter for thirty-six years. It would be strange if I hadn't formed an impression of her by now."

"But Mom and Aunt Barb and Uncle Gary have such different takes on her. Barb and Gary make her sound like this totally cool woman who took them to live in the West and taught them how to stick up for themselves. Then you talk to Mom, and she says their mother was a flake who couldn't keep a job or a husband. So which version is right?"

"Probably both, and neither," my father said. "You have to keep in mind that Barb and your mom and Gary experienced their early lives differently. Siblings always do. As the oldest, your mom had a lot more responsibility than your aunt and uncle. She had to pick up a lot of the slack for your grandmother, which isn't always good for someone so young. Barb romanticized their mother because she could afford to."

"We never talk about the women in our family," I said. "I know what your father and his father and his father before him did, because it's all there in the store's history. But not the women."

"What do you want to know? Maybe I can fill in some of the gaps."

We spent the next little while talking about the Starreveld women who had come before my sisters and me, beginning with the fiery Ann Arbor innkeeper's daughter who had convinced my great-great grandfather that Ann Arbor would be a better place to settle than Holland, continuing with my father's grandmother and mother, and finishing up with my own mom.

"Can you keep a secret?" my father asked as I licked pastry from my fingers.

I looked up at him. "I'm gay, Dad. It's kind of our specialty."

He released a short laugh. "In that case, I'm going to tell you something none of your sisters know."

"Not even Jane?"

"Not even Jane. Do you promise not to tell them?"

"Well, how long are you talking? Like, forever and ever? Because I'm not sure I can promise that."

"What about for the foreseeable future?"

I shrugged. "Okay. The world is supposed to end next year anyway, so the foreseeable future will probably be fairly limited."

He ignored this and said, "When your grandmother's plane crashed, your mother had to drop out of high school and take a job as a legal secretary to support Barb and Gary. She didn't earn her GED until Jane was already a year old."

"Are you serious?"

"Perfectly. Don't tell her I told you, either," he added. "Your mom didn't want you kids to think that she didn't value education. Keeping her family together was just a higher priority."

"I won't mention it," I promised.

Knowing this about my mom cast new light on my parents' reaction when I'd proposed taking a year off before college. No wonder she'd been so upset—she'd probably worried I would end up with only a high school diploma, locked into low-paying jobs like waiting tables or manual labor.

Wait a minute...

Across the table, my dad balled up his napkin and threw it into a trash receptacle ten feet away.

"Nice shot," I said, and all at once a multitude of images pressed in on me—of my father and me playing catch on our wide, sloping lawn on spring afternoons; raking leaves to jump into on short autumn days; reading quietly in the den on winter evenings; discussing school or the store while manning the barbecue any time of year. I'd missed my father these last years; I just hadn't let myself notice.

"Thanks, kid," he said, and grinned, looking briefly younger. Running the store had aged him. I wondered if he felt it, too.

"What's going to happen to the store?" I asked, then immediately wished I hadn't.

His smile dimmed. "I don't know. I guess we'll find out. Now, let's get going. There is one view you absolutely have to see."

From the pavilion, he led me up a small rise to a century-old windmill at the park's northern-most edge. We climbed the stairs inside to an observation deck that wound around the exterior, from which visitors could gaze out across wave after wave of multi-colored flower fields that inscribed brilliant, parallel lines across the Dutch landscape. This had to be the view that Fitzy and her daughter had beheld a quarter of a century earlier when they posed for the camera, smiling, in nearly this exact spot.

"Good God," I said, leaning on the railing and trying to take in all of the different bands of color, some nearly fluorescent in hue. I had seen these same fields in Fitzy's photograph and the guide books, had even driven my scooter among them, but the live view from above could not be equaled.

"Precisely." My father, who wasn't nearly as agnostic as I was, leaned beside me. "Pretty amazing, isn't it?"

"Um, yeah."

I pulled out my camera for the thousandth time that day and shot a one hundred eighty degree video of the view spread out before us. Northern Holland grows more than ninety-five percent of the world's flower bulb supply, and Dutch farmers export more than two million tulip bulbs every year. But I had never stopped to picture what so many acres of bulb fields would look like, especially not in full bloom.

"See why I couldn't let you miss this?" my father asked.

"Definitely."

The day was warmer now, which meant our time at Keukenhof was growing limited. I thought about opening the guide and picking out likely displays we had yet to see, but the sun on my face felt good, and it was peaceful to stand on the observation deck gazing out across the colorful flower fields and dark canals populating a landscape I couldn't be sure I'd ever see again, particularly not if the apocalypse indeed struck on the following year's winter solstice. Personally, my money was on aliens. I only hoped they wouldn't be too pissed with what we humans had done to the earth since the last time they'd visited.

My dad seemed disinclined to move on, too. Maybe, like me, he was thinking of our return trip home the next day—the hassle of schlepping luggage, catching trains, making connections that would swallow up an entire day. Or maybe he was thinking of his final meeting this afternoon, after which he, my mother, and his older sister would have to decide the fate of the family business. We stood together in companionable silence as people from a variety of nationalities moved around and below us, ogling the natural beauty of Keukenhof.

Then my dad shifted beside me and said, "Can I ask you about something you said yesterday?"

I suppressed an impatient sigh. What kind of Midwesterner of Northern European descent was he, wanting to Talk About Things when we could just as easily stand in the sunshine pretending everything was fine?

"Of course," I said, bracing myself.

"You mentioned you don't like it when people say being gay is a choice. You don't think it is, then?"

"The only choice gay people face, Dad, is whether to accept themselves for who they are or to cave to societal pressure and live a life of lies. Either way, there's no guarantee of happily ever after."

"There's no guarantee for anyone," my dad pointed out. "But I've always been told homosexuality is very much a choice."

"By actual homosexuals? Or by straight people like Pastor Laughlin?"

The pastor at the church I'd grown up in had only ever had negative things to say about gays and lesbians, all couched in transparently hateful "Love the sinner" terminology. That man did not believe gays and lesbians were worthy of God's love, no matter how often he claimed he did.

My dad squinted out at the flower fields. "Point taken."

"Now let me ask you something. Did you choose to love Mom?"

"No. In fact, to be honest, she wasn't your grandmother's first choice."

"What—a non-Dutch, working class, high school dropout? I can't imagine why your parents would object."

He laughed and shook his head. "I see you still have the same way with words, Lizzie. You and Jane both. I have no idea where you get it."

Aunt Barb, I thought, but refrained from pointing out what seemed glaringly obvious to Jane and me.

"Anyway," he said, "I think one of the reasons I reacted the way I did when you told us you were gay was that I saw you making this choice that I didn't believe would ever make you happy. My whole life, I've seen how people in our community treat anyone who is different, and I couldn't bear to think of that happening to you."

"Because of how it would affect me, or because of what it would mean to you?"

"A little of both," he admitted. "You're not a parent, so you won't understand that when your child hurts, you hurt. And when someone acts hatefully toward your child, you feel that, too."

I turned away from the flowers and faced him, my stomach

suddenly tight. "But *you* were the one acting hatefully. Not other people, but you, my father, the person who was supposed to love me no matter what."

"I did love you!" He lowered his voice as heads all around us swiveled in our direction. "I do love you, Elizabeth. I just, I don't know, I come from a different world. I was raised to do what my parents expected, to accept their judgment. My generation didn't think of refusing what our parents asked."

"That's not true at all. You just said yourself Mom wasn't your mother's first choice, but you married her and built a life with her anyway. And P.S., your generation marched against Vietnam and fought for civil rights. People your age started the gay rights movement."

He shook his head. "Only some of us, and even then, we were usually following older, more experienced leaders. You wouldn't know this, but it was only ever a small number of disproportionately vocal individuals out there making waves. Most of the people I knew were brought up to respect the status quo and fulfill their obligations. You said yourself, the media distorts reality. In point of fact, only a narrow echelon back then had the luxury to rebel, knowing they could always fall back on family money. The rest of us did what was expected, even if it wasn't necessarily what we wanted."

It sounded as if he didn't realize that he was one of the fortunate few, that our family was privileged in a way that much of the rest of the country wasn't. We may not have had a second home or a garage with an elevator for our cars or a wing of the U of M library named after us, but we had always had more than enough of everything. The store had seen to that.

Something else in what he'd said caught my attention, and I honed in on it: "Does that mean you would have done something other than work at the store if you'd thought you had a choice?"

"I don't know," he said, rubbing his chin. "Anyway, it's too late now to consider. I made my decision long ago, and I don't regret it."

He sounded determined, as if this would be true if only he could say it resolutely enough. I pictured him as a young man, the way he appeared in the photos on our family walls—in his high school baseball uniform, swishing home a basket during some big game, smiling into the camera with a football under one arm and his U of M helmet under the other. He'd been a talented athlete with accolades and job offers, but he had given it all up to work in the store, like his father and grandfather and great-grandfather before him. Thus was the fate awaiting the Starreveld men—until my generation, with its dearth of males, came along.

Perhaps my sisters and I were lucky to have the justification of gender freeing us from generations of expectations. If I had been born a boy instead of a boi, would I have let myself be browbeaten into taking up my father's mantle? It seemed inconceivable, but maybe that was because I didn't have large amounts of testosterone coursing through my blood, impacting my every emotion and action.

Even as a girl, though, I might have ended up following in my father's footsteps. A few years before this trip, if he had suddenly embraced me the way he had both of my brothers-in-law, shown me even half the respect and affection he routinely offered them, I would probably have done whatever he asked just for a shot at being accepted, respected, loved. But not now. I had been out in the world on my own for too long, disconnected from him and from the family legacy. I no longer felt the sense of ownership or obligation I would have needed to sacrifice my as-yet unfocused dreams to Starreveld & Sons, as my father had done before me apparently to his regret, no matter what he was telling himself—and me—now.

"Be honest, Dad. If you hadn't had the store waiting for you, what do you think you might have done with your life?"

"I'm happy with the life I've led," he said, turning his authoritative parent look on me.

It had been a long time since that look had worked; I wasn't sure why he still had it in his arsenal. He certainly didn't use it on the grandkids, no matter how lippy they (okay, Joey) could be. My parents were outrageous pushovers when it came to the babies of their babies.

"I didn't say you weren't happy," I countered. "But you started this. I've answered your questions truthfully, and was hoping you would be willing to do the same. But not if you're not comfortable, I guess."

Appealing simultaneously to his sense of honor and a guilt I hadn't known existed until now was a stroke of genius, if I do say so myself.

"No, I'm comfortable," he insisted, and then turned from the railing. "Can we continue this as we walk? I'm sure other people would like to enjoy the view."

I followed him down the steps of the windmill and back across the park, letting him pick the route. He walked quietly at first, his hands in his pants pockets, not seeming to see the flowers or the sculptures or our fellow tourists crowding the walkways. I waited, figuring he would either talk to me or he wouldn't. Whichever path he chose, I was fine with the outcome. We'd already accomplished more than I would have thought possible, him and me, during our time together in Amsterdam.

"I think I might have wanted to be an engineer," he said at last.

"Yeah?"

"Maybe. When I was a kid, you probably don't know this, but I used to take apart all the electronics in our house to see if I could figure out how they worked. I put them back together, too, and sometimes they even worked afterward."

I didn't think he'd ever mentioned anything about this, but then I hadn't always been the best listener. Joey, Mary's ADHD kid, had nothing on me.

"Did you tell your parents?" I asked.

"There would have been no point. I was the only son. I always knew I would work in the store after college, and someday take over when my father retired. I'm not like you, Elizabeth."

I frowned and dodged a woman with a double stroller. "What does that mean?"

"If you'd been in my position, I don't doubt that you would have gone off and done whatever it was that made you happy, even if it didn't match what anyone else wanted for you."

Kinda sounded like he was saying I was a selfish brat. Or maybe I just remembered him calling me that the night I told him I was gay, hurling the insult at me after I refused to recant.

He might have been remembering that moment, too, because he caught my arm and pulled me closer as a smallish boy, clearly hyped up on too much Dutch pastry, nearly bowled me over.

"I don't mean—" my father started. He stopped, tried again. "Do you know what I think when I look at you?"

"Haven't the foggiest," I said, not sure I really wanted to know.

"How tough you are. You came into the world already fully formed, this little self-contained being who didn't seem very happy to be an infant. When you cried, you weren't like your sisters who mainly wanted comfort or security. Your mother and I both thought you seemed angry that you might need other people. As you got older, I never really felt like I knew you, only glimpsed the parts of you that you allowed me to see, fragments that became smaller and smaller over time. Sometimes, when you were in high school, I'd look out the window and there you'd be in the garden with Felix, and you would be smiling and chattering away. And I wondered why you weren't like that with me anymore. I didn't know when I'd lost you."

I digested this, trying to reckon his perspective with my own wildly different view of our shared past. In a way, it made sense. But he was the parent, wasn't he? I'd always thought that made him more responsible for the level of closeness that existed between us. Or didn't.

"With a sister like Cat, I had to be tough," I told him. "Not to mention Jane and Mary. They were so much older and always busy with their own friends, their own lives. They liked having me around as a pet. Sometimes I think I was like the dog they never had."

He smiled. "That sounds about right."

We paused in front of a giant rust-colored metal turtle that appeared to have been forged from recycled materials, perched with its mouth open on a matching metal stand in a patch of green grass made nearly transparent by the mid-day sunlight.

"You know what Cat said to me at Christmas last year when Mom gave me those tickets to *The Laramie Project* in Chicago? She said I always get everything she wants. She told me that right after you brought me home from the hospital, she fell and skinned her knee, only no one came to check on her because you were all too busy oohing and ahhing over me."

He sighed and shook his head. "That is not even a little bit true. Your mother and I worked so hard to include her. We knew she was going to have a harder time than Jane or Mary did at not being the baby anymore, so we read and talked to the pediatrician and did everything we were told to do. But it didn't matter. Cat is Cat, and nothing we did could change how she was going to react to having a new baby in the house. Kids just kind of come into the world the way they are, and become more themselves over time. You'll see..."

Trailing off, he looked away across the colorful blooms and budding trees, and I could see the wheels spinning in his head: Would I ever see what it was like to be a parent? I hoped so, but I couldn't be sure either.

"Who knows?" I said, slipping my arm through his and tugging him along the path. "Maybe someday I will. I'm gay, you know, not reproductively challenged."

"For my generation, I believe it was the same thing."

"You guys had sham marriages to fall back on—yet another reason gay marriage should be legal. But it's different now. Haven't you heard of the Gayby Boom?"

He shook his head again as we strolled past a green space filled with people lounging on bean bags, soaking up the sun, shade, and scents.

"You kids... I feel old when I talk to you, Elizabeth."

"That's because you are old."

"You're probably right. And I know better than you just how much things have changed. You know, I voted Republican my whole life for the economic policies. But this isn't the Republican Party I grew up with. Their focus on social issues seems like subterfuge to me, a carefully designed tactic to prevent the rest of us from looking too closely at policies that are no longer about farmers and small business owners, the people who built this nation, but instead designed to line the pockets of the very wealthy."

I stared at him. "Have you and Mom been watching Jon Stewart?"

"It's possible. I'll tell you something else—your mother has always voted Democrat to cancel out my vote. But in the last election, she didn't need to."

"Geez," I said. "I think that means even more to me than your apology yesterday."

He stared at me, and I wished I could take the crass statement back. Why did my need to seem clever constantly interfere with my ability to say what I actually felt? Because his apology, of course, had been the best moment so far in a year filled with many more crappy moments; better even than when I saw Sofie for the first time, coming across the sidewalk toward me, smiling her adorable smile.

"I'm sorry," I said quickly. "I didn't mean that. Your apology was amazing, Dad. It meant so much to me. Means so much."

"It's okay," he said, and patted my hand where it lay on his arm. "I know you were kidding. But here I am talking about me again when what I wanted was to talk about you. That friend you wanted to bring to dinner at the house—what was her name?"

I bit my lip. "Maddie."

"That's right. Are you still together?"

"No. We broke up a few months ago."

"Your Mom and I wondered. You seemed down for a little while, but lately you seem better. Are you—" he cleared his throat—"seeing anyone these days?"

This new openness we were attempting clearly had its drawbacks. What was I supposed to tell my dad, that I'd tried monogamy and it hadn't worked out, so now I was giving the whole lesbian slut thing a whirl?

"No," I said, "although there is someone I'm interested in here in Amsterdam."

"The friend of a friend?"

I nodded. "Just my luck to meet someone amazing in a city halfway across the world."

"Well, there's the Internet, though, isn't there? You could Skype, or whatever it is people your age do."

I sent him such a scathing look that he held up a hand in defense.

"Sorry," he said, laughing a little. "I'm sure you'll meet someone else, honey. You're young, and any woman would be lucky to have you."

I thought he was blushing as he said this, so I decided to take pity on him. "Thanks, Dad. Hey, before I forget, I've been meaning to ask if you've ordered your season tickets yet."

He perked up at the change of subject. "Why, are you interested in a seat?"

"Maybe," I said, "assuming they're going to be any good this year."

A challenge like that could not be left undefended by Eugene Starreveld, starting running back for the Wolverines from 1970 to 1973. As I'd known it would, my statement sent my father into an enthusiastic description of all the returning football players, both on offense and defense, who would help deliver yet another winning season at Michigan Stadium, starting with local god Denard Robinson. I strolled along beside him, asking questions here and there, enjoying the lighter conversation as we moved through Keukenhof arm-in-arm, a father and daughter with little in common, perhaps, but somehow maybe able again, after years of silence, to talk to each other about almost anything.

Too soon we were back at the park entrance, joining the crowd of visitors coming and going. We climbed on our scooters and headed the long way back to Amsterdam, following a different return path through the tulip fields. Perched ramrod-straight on his bike, my father led the way northeast toward the village of Noordwijk and the sea beyond. I followed, alternately speeding up and slowing my scooter along the flat roads. Neat rows of tulips and daffodils stretched to the horizon, orderly stripes of color broken by thatched-roof cottages and glass-walled greenhouses, by small settlements and tame forests edging the roadway. Occasionally I glimpsed a farmer pacing a field, wide-brimmed hat blocking the sunlight, wooden clogs maneuvering muddy trenches and rows of delicate green shoots equally well.

What would it be like to work bulb fields, to grow up in a family of flower farmers instead of jewelers? The pressure might be intense, with the competition to genetically mutate known varieties into that one new flower that might earn awards, fame, money. Still, given the choice, I was pretty sure I would pick pacing muddy rows of incandescent flowers beneath the spring sky of Northern Europe over helping rich Detroit suburbanites purchase the perfect engagement ring or anniversary gift in the hush of my great-great-grandfather's store.

Later, back in my hotel room, I transcribed my Keukenhof notes into my plant journal, picturing Fitzy's excitement when I shared my observations—and photos—with her. In one day alone, I had added more than thirty new flower varieties to my life list.

The door between my room and my father's was open, so I called over to report the final tally, as he'd requested.

He leaned in the doorway, knotting his tie. "I take it you liked the Spring Gardens of Europe, then?"

"Loved them. Keukenhof is my new favorite spot in the world."

"High praise, indeed."

His tie was crooked, so I rose and fixed it for him. Then I punched him in the shoulder.

"What was that for?"

"Thanks for bringing me. This has been such an awesome

experience."

"It has been awesome, hasn't it?" He smiled down at me. "I'm only sorry we don't have more time."

"Me, too."

He watched me for a moment longer, nodded, and went back to getting ready for his final meeting of the trip. I turned back to my journal, but my mind wandered as I listened to him moving around on the other side of the wall. I couldn't remember the last time my father and I had made it this many hours without bickering. The act of traveling—being away from home and the rest of the family and everything that had, until now, defined our relationship—had allowed us to change the way we communicated. Here, he was less my father and more the experienced businessman and traveler, while I was— what? More myself, or less? Different, or more of who I used to be before I came out and had to leave my family behind?

Whichever, I liked the new way of relating that had grown up between us in the last few days. I just hoped it wouldn't end when the trip did.

CHAPTER THIRTEEN

My dad wasn't planning to be back in time for dinner, so at half past six, I left the hotel and caught a tram to Westerkerk. Sofie was waiting when I arrived, still dressed in the gray pin-striped pants and white silk shirt she'd worn to work. She kissed me and asked about my day, and I waxed enthusiastically about the magnificence of Keukenhof as we headed toward an Indian restaurant not far from the Zeemeermin. The maze of streets that got us there tangled hopelessly in my mind, but I remembered from the guidebook that the best thing to do if you got lost in Amsterdam was to follow a canal. Like getting lost in the wilderness—if you followed moving water, you were bound to find someplace populated eventually.

At the restaurant, we ate quickly, each of us talking over the other as if we had only just comprehended the brevity of our remaining time together and were determined to share the most pertinent facts about ourselves while we still could. At Sofie's prodding, I described my recent history with my father and highlighted the developments in our relationship since we'd landed on European soil, including that day's revelations. Sofie, whose own parents had accepted her sexuality without much fuss, nonetheless seemed readily able to empathize with my cautious excitement about the distance my dad and I had traversed in the past week.

"See?" she said, reaching across the narrow table for two to brush a smudge of curry from my chin. "The Netherlands is good for you, I think. Perhaps your ancestors should not have left."

"Perhaps," I agreed, staring at her mouth and imagining the spicy taste of her lips.

She smiled and leaned across the table for me. "No one here will mind."

And true enough, they didn't.

We lingered over a second basket of naan and a pot of herbal tea, holding hands and talking about work, family, friends. Everything she told me seemed fascinating and she acted similarly delighted with me. I knew our infatuation was heightened by my impending departure, but I couldn't shake the feeling that what was between us, undefined and unconsummated as it might be, didn't come along very often.

By eight o'clock, we had clearly worn out our waiter's welcome, so I paid the bill with the last of my Dutch money and followed Sofie out into the cool, damp night. Arms around each other, we strolled the few short blocks to the Zeemeermin, where Sofie had promised her friends she would bring me to say goodbye.

"But we do not have to stay long," she said as we neared the tavern, her hand on my ass squeezing meaningfully. "I have other plans for you tonight. If you are agreeable, that is."

I pictured her draped across her four-poster bed, my lips on her silky breasts, her hips arching into me.

"I could probably be persuaded," I said, even though nearly all the reasons I'd thought I shouldn't sleep with her the night before were still in effect. My body had apparently missed the memo, though, and I was beginning to think that the only conceivable way for this night to end would be with me naked in Sofie's bed. Truth was, I could think of worse ways to say goodbye.

Inside, the Zeemeermin was warm and rowdy on a Sunday night. Butch women brandishing pool sticks again occupied the lower floor, while upstairs a group of twenty-something lesbians had gathered for what appeared to be a private party.

Juliana was working again, and greeted Sofie with kisses and a few words I didn't catch. Sofie glanced toward the upstairs party and shrugged.

"Two beers, please," she said to Juliana, loud enough that I could hear.

"Okay." Juliana muttered something in Dutch as she turned away.

"Howdy, mates," Jackie said as she swooped onto the bar stool beside me. "And how does this lovely Holland evening find my favorite couple?"

I blinked. Maybe in Aussie English *couple* meant the same thing as *pair*.

Beside me, Sofie frowned. "Fine."

"And what have you gotten up to, Junior?"

"My dad and I went to the Anne Frank House yesterday and Keukenhof Gardens today. Oh, and Sofie and I went out for coffee last night."

"Regular coffee or wacky coffee?" Jackie asked with a wink.

"Wacky."

Sofie leaned across me and said to Jackie, "There is to be nothing wacky for Junior tonight. Do you understand?"

"Got it. No need to be so dire, Sofie dear." She grabbed me by the hand and pulled me from my stool. "Come on. You Americans play pool, don't you? I need a doubles partner."

I waved at Sofie and followed Jackie down the short staircase to the bottom floor of the bar, occupied by a pinball machine, photoplay, pool table, and the afore-mentioned seriously butch lesbians.

"We're going to play them?" I murmured.

"Yep. Get ready to rumble." She winked again and handed me a pool stick.

I glanced up at the main floor of the bar where I could see Sofie speaking to Juliana and gesturing toward the upstairs sitting area. Then Jackie broke, and I turned to find out which we were, stripes or solids. By the time I looked again, Sofie was on her way down to our level, where she set our drinks on a nearby table and leaned against a stool to watch us play.

Our opponents Femke and Iris, the two toughest looking women in the bar, ran a daycare business in the Old Center. They were friendly and smiled a lot, but were terrible pool players. Jackie was good and I was decent, so I didn't think the match would take long, which was just as well—Sofie was clearly upset. She smiled whenever I caught her eye, but she didn't really seem to see me. Once, when the upstairs party roared raucously, she flinched a little, and I almost felt like slapping my forehead. Of course, she was too attractive not to have dyke drama lurking in the wings. At some level, I'd always known this.

When the game ended, Jackie tried to convince me to keep playing.

"No, thanks."

"Come on. You know you want to," she said, elbowing me.

"Sorry, mate, but you're not the one I'm interested in going home with," I said over my shoulder.

When I reached Sofie, I brushed my hand against her cheek. "What's wrong?"

"Nothing," she said, and handed me my beer.

"Is it safe for me to drink alcohol tonight, then?" I teased, trying to coax her into a better mood.

"Yes," she said tersely, wincing as laughter once again erupted from the upstairs party.

I sipped my beer and watched her, certain now that her past and/or present had finally caught up to us. "What's up, seriously? You might as well tell me."

I didn't hear Jackie until she was beside me, her lanky arm around my neck.

"Did you see our little American pool shark at work? Too bad she's heading back to the States tomorrow. We could have had quite a good hustle going."

"She is good, isn't she?"

Sofie eyed Jackie defiantly, then moved closer and kissed me, a slow, lingering kiss that convinced me she might be able to forget about her drama after all, at least for a few hours. If she could, then so could I. By this time tomorrow I would be somewhere over the Atlantic, and what would it matter then whether or not Sofie had girl trouble?

"Let us find a table and finish our drinks," Sofie said, excluding Jackie. "Then I will take you somewhere more private."

Jackie whistled. "I can take a hint. Junior, if I don't see you later, friend, it's been fun." She gave me a high-five, nodded to Sofie, and sauntered off.

"Ready?" Sofie asked.

"Sure."

I followed her up to the main floor of the bar. How bad could her drama be?

I heard Kim before I saw her. The creak, creak of the narrow wooden staircase that led to the upstairs sounded again, and this time, Sofie's glance stayed put long enough that I turned to see who she was watching.

A short-haired woman with blonde streaks and a nose ring stepped heavily down the stairs, eyeing me with obvious displeasure. I checked her out as she reached the main floor and headed for the bar. Lean and tall like me, she wasn't bad-looking, I decided. Actually, she looked a lot like me.

"Who's that?" I asked.

Sofie ran her index finger around the rim of her pint glass. "No one."

"Come on. I might not speak Dutch, but I'm not blind."

"I do not know of what you speak."

"Bull honkey," I said, borrowing from Fitzy.

Sofie's brow furrowed. "This is American for what?"

"It's American for tell me already."

After some additional cajoling, Sofie finally gave in. Turned out she wasn't quite so single after all. The glowering woman from upstairs was Kim, her girlfriend of a year. From the beginning, they'd agreed that theirs would be an open relationship, meaning they were both free to see other people should the opportunity arise. But neither of them had strayed until a few weeks before, when Kim had casually mentioned she was going out on a date with another woman. Sofie had tried to accept the situation, but it had become too painful.

"I told her I could not see her as long as she wanted to see other women, and we have not been together since," Sofie said, rubbing furiously at a glass ring on the table.

"Is she still seeing the other woman?"

"I do not know. I do not care. It is over with us."

"Right," I said.

She looked at me. "What is this tone?"

"It's not over, and you know it."

"I do not know it."

I shrugged insolently. "Whatever you say."

She expelled a breath. "Why is it you Americans always think you know more than everyone else?"

"I don't know. Why do you Europeans always think it's okay to make sweeping generalizations about Americans?"

We eyed each other over our pint glasses. Could the honeymoon really be over this quickly? But then I saw her gaze wander to the bar, where Kim was deep in conversation with Juliana. The flash of pain in Sofie's eyes, quickly hidden, reminded me of my own heartache, only recently reduced to manageable, non-ulcer-producing levels. Betrayal sucked, whether you had agreed to it in theory ahead of time or not.

For a moment, I thought of Caitlyn camped out on my doorstep the week before, waiting in vain for me to open up. Not that this was the same situation. Not at all.

"The thing is," I said, touching Sofie's hand, "I know what I see. And from where I'm sitting, it doesn't look like you two are over."

"No?" Sofie asked, the tinge of longing in her voice telling me all I needed to know.

My hopes for the evening tanked further as Kim stalked past on her way back to the party, scowling openly at me with a look that clearly stated how much she would like to kick my ass. *Sjit*. A starring role in a local dyke drama wasn't really what I'd had in mind for my final night in Amsterdam.

"Do you want to get out of here?" I asked.

Sofie hesitated only a moment. "Yes. Sure."

I said goodbye to Jackie, Anne, and Juliana, and then glanced upstairs as Sofie and I left the bar. Sure enough, Kim was watching us. I saw her start forward, but then the door swung shut, blocking my view. And all at once, I couldn't do it. Now that I knew Kim existed, I couldn't go home with Sofie and pretend I didn't, no matter how hot the sex might be.

I stayed where I was outside the Zeemeermin, breathing on my hands as Sofie started down the sidewalk.

She stopped and turned back. "What are you doing?"

"To be honest, I'm thinking of going back to the hotel."

"No, you cannot," she said, pouting attractively as she returned to my side.

She was adorable, but she was already attached, and I knew how it felt to watch the woman I loved leave with someone else. Although, admittedly, Maddie had never actually mentioned her apparent desire to boff my best friend.

"I have to be up early in the morning, and anyway..." I trailed off as the door to the Zeemeermin opened. Wait for it, wait for it... And there was Kim, right on cue.

"Sofie," she said, approaching us with her hands out.

"What are you doing?" Sofie demanded in English, her eyes narrowed, and suddenly I was glad I wasn't in Kim's shoes.

My Dutch doppelganger stopped before us and spoke rapidly in Dutch. Sofie responded in the same language, forcing me to block out images of quarreling Muppets. I moved a little ways away, looking up and down the narrow street. With the mist, I wasn't sure which direction to take for the Westerkerk tram stop. Then again, even had the night been perfectly clear, I probably wouldn't have found my way out of the jumble of angled streets. Where were those danged church bells when you needed them?

They went on for a few minutes, these Dutch lesbians suffering from a universal anguish. I could imagine what they were saying: *How could you? But it didn't mean anything. I love you!* It was the same no matter what language you spoke. The same whether you were straight or gay, too, as far as I could tell from observing my sisters, though they didn't seem to relish their relationship strife nearly as much as some of the lesbians I knew.

After a brief negotiation, Kim embraced Sofie, who stood stonily in her arms for a moment before relenting and hugging her back. Then she pushed Kim away and waved her back into the Zeemeermin. With a clipped nod at me, Kim returned to the bar.

"I am sorry about that," Sofie said, coming over and touching my shoulder.

"Hey, no worries. I have to fly home tomorrow, remember?"

"I remember." Her hand moved up to my cheek before she let it fall. "You are a good person, Junior."

"Thank you. Now how do I get out of here? I have no idea where we are."

Sofie walked me out to the main street. She even offered to ride back to the hotel with me, but I insisted she go back to the Zeemeermin. After a brief but sincere-seeming protest, she agreed, and then waited with me until the tram came. The conversation that had been so dynamic over dinner was stilted now, awkward even. I kept peering down the fog-socked street, looking for the train that wouldn't come.

Finally it rattled into sight. As it neared the stop, Sofie put her arms around me, resting her head on my shoulder. Her warmth seeped into me, and as I inhaled her scent, earthy and somehow feminine, I remembered for a moment why I'd wanted to go home with her in the first place. She was amazing. Kim, on the other hand, was a schmuck.

Sofie breathed into my ear, "You should follow your dreams, Junior, even if it they are not what your family wishes for you."

"And you should be with someone who treats you the way you deserve to be treated," I returned.

She pulled away and looked at me, shrugging a little, her smile wry. Each of us was right about the other's life, but knowing didn't always equate with doing. We kissed softly, and then the tram shuddered to a stop beside us.

What do you say to someone who it was just possible could have become the most important person in your life, but hadn't? I couldn't think of anything other than a lame, "Take care, Sofie."

"You as well. You have made a hard time for me better, Junior. I will not forget that."

I wouldn't forget her, either, but I didn't tell her that. I just stepped onto the tram and found a window seat near the back. She stood at the curb watching until we turned a corner and bounced out of sight. I leaned my forehead against the cool glass of the window, until a particularly significant bump jostled me painfully. I rubbed my head. Kim was either an idiot or mentally unbalanced. If I'd had a girlfriend like Sofie, I wouldn't have screwed it up the way she had. Of course, I'd managed to botch every relationship I *had* been in, so maybe it was just the lack of opportunity talking.

Back at the hotel, I paused outside my father's room. His light was out, and I was pretty sure I could hear his telltale snores echoing inside. Sighing, I unlocked the door to my room, kicked off my Doc Martens, and lay down on the bed fully clothed. The mingled scent of cigarette smoke and Belgian beer heavy on my skin, I stared at the shadows on the ceiling, thinking about the events of the last few days. So much had changed, and not just with my father. Being with Sofie had shown me that my relationship with Maddie had never been quite right. I had felt an ease these with Sofie that I was fairly certain I had never felt with the woman I'd expected to spend the rest of my life with, though maybe it was just the novelty of a near-affair in Amsterdam I found so appealing. Still, things with Maddie had been deteriorating for a while. Without Dez, I might not have escaped her clutches so soon. Really, I should thank her.

Well, maybe not.

And all at once, alone in a strange room in a foreign country, I felt the gloom of homesickness settling over me again. I wanted to be at home in my own bed, the familiar hum and glow of the growth lights on their night setting keeping me company in my studio apartment, the willow tree outside watching over me as it always did. I told myself that the sooner I fell asleep the sooner I would be home, but I didn't feel at all sleepy. I had half expected to go home with Sofie tonight, Sofie of the soft lips and subtle curves, appealing smiles and the bossy exterior that I suspected would give way to a delicious pliancy beneath my touch. Not that I would ever find out now.

Snippets of conversation and freeze-framed images swirled through my head, my mind spinning on overdrive. I had done more, experienced more in the past five days than I had in months, and my Amsterdam adventures were all pointing me to the same realization: My life in Ann Arbor had stalled somehow, a fact that everyone else seemed able to see clearly even if I couldn't. My father and Sofie were right. I was old enough to choose the life I wanted. Probably it wouldn't be what—or where—my family would pick for me, but after watching my father finally open up to the one part of my life he had always been unable to accept, I had a feeling that, given time, my family would probably come around. If only I would let them.

And if they didn't, I still had Fitzy and Toby and Alex and others to fall back on.

Fitzy. Would she still be there when I got home? Of course she would. I'd logged on to the hotel computer before dinner to check my U of M email, and there'd been a brand new note from her about the upcoming spring concert in the Gardens, only two weekends away now. She was still working, and still obviously planning to be around for at least the next couple of weeks. I couldn't wait to show her my photos from Keukenhof. Maybe I would even print them out as a surprise for her.

I lay in the dark waiting for sleep, the memory of bulb fields and city lights flashing against my eyelids as my father's snoring sounded slow and steady on the other side of the wall.

CHAPTER FOURTEEN

My body did not appreciate being schlepped from time zone to time zone, abused with a multitude of controlled substances, and denied sleep. When my father dropped me off at my apartment the following night, it was early evening in Ann Arbor, but my watch, still tuned to Amsterdam time, registered three in the morning. I left my bags on the floor, watered any plants that might need sustenance, and flopped on my bed. How I loved my bed. How I had missed my bed.

Disappointingly, I had been too tired to sleep even on the plane. The first hour my father had stayed awake with me, and we'd played virtual pinball and pool on his laptop. He beat me soundly at both, explaining smugly that his skill derived from frequent business travel. Then he dozed off, which was a relief given that we were captive seatmates and I'd worried he would want to have more Important Discussions. While I was a lesbian and therefore expected to enjoy long, drawn-out conversations about relationships and the symbolism of language and the state of my chi, when it came down to it I wasn't a big fan of talking. Yet another quality Maddie and Dez had in common—they were better lesbians in that sense than I would ever be.

While my father slept, I tried to read the novel Toby had loaned me, but I couldn't seem to concentrate. Giving up, I leaned my forehead against the window and watched as the distant earth gave way beneath us to the blackness of the Atlantic Ocean. I remembered what my father had said about my grandmother's fear of flying, how it just wasn't natural to be this high. She was entirely right, but how cool was it that we land-locked creatures could fly? For some reason, I didn't worry about a repeat of September 11th on the way home. Had our safe, terror-free flight to Europe allayed my fears, at least temporarily? Or was I simply too sleep-deprived to care if armed anti-American terrorists stormed up the aisle and forcibly took control?

Back in my own bed half a day later, I didn't have any trouble falling asleep. When I opened my eyes again, the spring sky above my willow tree was a pale gray. I checked the clock radio on my bedside table—a Christmas gift the year my parents mixed up my presents with Cat's; while I loved the radio, she was less than thrilled to receive my Star Wars action figures—and discovered that it was six in the morning. I had slept ten solid, beautiful hours. I stretched, a luxurious laziness curling through me. This moment was perfect—I was home in my own apartment after a hectic trip to Europe, warm and sleepy under my comforter, the near future safe and known. The far future was a different story, but it could wait.

I snoozed a little while longer, then rose and ate a huge breakfast before getting ready for work at the Botanical Gardens. I was early and the day looked to be nice, so I decided to skip the bus and ride my bike to work. Wasn't quite the same as riding a scooter through the Dutch countryside flanked by luminous tulip fields, but familiar and comfortable in a way I hadn't felt the past week. I liked Ann Arbor, always had. Despite the perspective I'd gained in Europe, now that I was home, I wondered if I really needed to blow up my life, as had seemed to be the case when I was an ocean away. Things weren't that bad, were they? It was only that regular life couldn't be as exciting as a trip abroad. It was never supposed to be.

At the Gardens, I chained my bike to the rack outside the Conservatory, noting the relative dearth of bikes there compared to the abundance of autos in the staff parking lot. The ratio in Amsterdam had been the exact opposite, with bikes appearing to outnumber their motored counterparts throughout the city. Sofie had told me that even more bikes lurked beneath the surface of the canals—apparently another tradition Amsterdammers and their visitors observe involves getting drunk and dumping unsuspecting bicycles in the city waterways. As a result, the canals have to be dredged regularly.

I walked slowly through the Conservatory, headed for the offices in back. Normally Fitzy would already be at her desk this time of the morning, but would she today? Or would I find some staff member from the Provost's or Dean's office going through her email inbox, filing the financial records on her desk, boxing up her personal belongings?

As I rounded the corner at the back of the Conservatory, I took a calming breath. Everything would be fine, I told myself. Most days this was perfectly true.

Like today—through the open doorway I caught sight of Fitzy at her desk, frowning at yet another pile of receipts, her fingers working the keys of her calculator. She was here, and looking no worse than the day I'd left. Which might not be saying much, but at least she'd kept her word. She was still here.

"Hi," I said, trying not to smile too broadly, and set a lumpy envelope on her desk.

"Starreveld. Welcome back." She finished her calculations and recorded a figure in the Excel document on her screen, and only then picked up the envelope. "More bills?"

"Open it."

She slit the envelope with the African elephant letter opener I'd given her for her birthday and emptied the contents onto her desk.

"What's this?" she asked, holding up the tiny brown bottle with the hand-lettered label.

"Lavender emulsion," I said, and only then remembered that her sense of smell had faded.

She opened the vial and took a whiff, and then smiled brilliantly up at me. "I can actually smell it."

"I was hoping it would be strong enough," I said, thanking my unnamed deity of choice for the small favor.

Still smiling, she touched the other object on her desk. "You brought me a magnet?"

"It's from Keukenhof," I said unnecessarily.

The magnet was in the shape of a delft blue shoe filled with a rainbow assortment of tulips, the park's name scrawled underneath. I'd originally planned to order tulip bulbs, but they wouldn't have bloomed until the following spring. Fortunately I'd realized the inherent cruelty of *that* gesture in time.

"Thank you," she said, and set the magnet on the base of her computer monitor. "It's perfect. Now, how was your trip? How were the tulips?"

"Incredible. Even, dare I say, life changing."

At her urging, I described the new additions to my life list, my wanderings in Belgium and Holland, and the glories of Keukenhof and Vondelpark. (The horticultural architects Zochter were old favorites of hers, too.) My account of the tulip farms near Lisse inspired her to reminisce about a barge trip she and her husband had taken in the area many years earlier. She had already told me about the trip at least once, but I smiled and nodded as if it were the first time.

Then she asked, "Did you and your father manage to tolerate one another's company?"

"We did. Turns out you were right. He wasn't really trying to convince me to take over the store, after all. He mainly wanted us to spend time together."

"I'm glad to hear it. Occasionally we old folks manage to get something right."

"You're not old."

She just shook her head and turned back to her computer. "Go on, now. I have to finish this paperwork if I'm going to get outdoors anytime soon. You gracing us with your presence all week?"

"Yes, ma'am."

"Good. Now go find something to keep you busy. Shouldn't have to look too far."

I lingered in the doorway, watching her squint at the computer screen over her glasses, her breathing slow and ragged. How much longer would she be able to work? At least this way she would never have to retire to Florida, I'd once heard her joke. Socializing with suburban retirees sounded like her version of hell.

She didn't take her eyes from the screen. "I'm not going anywhere yet, remember?"

At this, I turned tail and practically ran out of the building. Maybe not yet, but sooner than I cared to acknowledge, Fitzy really would be gone. For eight years, her doors—home and work alike—had always been open to me, offering a sanctuary I had come to depend on. When she did go.... Well, it didn't bear dwelling on, as she would have said.

I headed outside to see what work needed to be done, the weak spring sunlight dappling my back, the scent of mud in the air. Gone was the blankness of winter, cold air devoid of any intelligible scent. Back was my favorite season in the city I'd lived in my whole life. Ann Arbor wasn't bad, I told myself. Multiple generations of Starrevelds couldn't be all wrong. Anyway, I couldn't just pick up and go whenever I felt like it. Leaving Ann Arbor would take some planning, in addition to an intended destination.

Besides, a permanent removal wasn't an option until Fitzy—I cut off the thought and walked on beneath the still-bare branches of trees that I couldn't help noticing would have dwarfed the piddly urban offerings of Amsterdam.

"Yo, jet-setter," Toby greeted me when I stopped by Boadicea that afternoon to drop off her backpack and books.

"How was Amsterdam?" chimed in Cassie, a college student from Midland who worked more shifts than anyone else on staff to help pay for school.

"Fantastic."

"And Sofie?" Toby asked.

"Let's just say she's now my favorite Dutch person ever."

"That's our Junior," Toby said, and clobbered me on the shoulder.

Over coffee, I filled Toby in on the trip—on Sofie and the Aussie girls and the Magic Pill, the Van Gogh museum and the Anne Frank House, my father's surprising conversation starters. "He even asked me about the history of the gay rights movement and why we use the pink triangle as a symbol. Can you believe it?"

"Actually, I do," Toby said, handing a customer more hot water for her Echinacea tea. To celebrate the advent of spring, a nasty cold was working its way through the Ann Arbor women's community.

"He was really interested," I added. "It was amazing."

"Sounds like it."

She counted a bundle of tens and slid them under the drawer in the cash register. Boadicea seemed to be doing well despite the economic downturn pummeling Michigan. It had been the central meeting place of the Ann Arbor lesbian/ hippie/ leftist student scene for nearly a decade now, and Toby was even thinking about expanding to include a used book section. She'd always dreamed of running a bookshop, but with the mega-bookstores and the growing e-book market, she knew she couldn't compete. Adding a used book corner to the café, though, might fulfill the urge without putting her out of business.

"So when did he hit you with coming to work at the shop?" she asked. "On the way over, or did he wait until you were on European soil?"

"Neither, really."

Toby paused in counting one-dollar bills. "What do you mean?"

"He asked me what I wanted to do with my life, and there was definitely some tension there," I admitted. "But he didn't ask me along to convince me to take over the store. He said he thought it would be a chance for us to spend some quality time together." I smiled, thinking of the quality of our time together in Amsterdam. "You know what else?"

"What?"

"He apologized for everything, said he should have reacted better when I came out, should have accepted me for who I was. He even said that God made me who I am."

"Your father said that?"

"I know, right? And you're going to love this—he asked about

Maddie, and when I told him we'd broken up, he said any woman would be lucky to have me."

"No shit," Toby said. "That's really something. I'm happy for you, kid. I told you to give your parents time, remember? Sometimes that's all it takes."

"Yeah sure, you betcha. I bow to your superior intelligence."

"As well you should. When's the next family dinner?"

"This weekend."

She slipped her arm around my shoulders.

"It's gonna be great," she said. "Because you know what? It sounds like your father is finally realizing any parent would be lucky to have a kid like you."

I hoped she was right, and that the shifts in my relationship with my dad would have long-lasting effects. Positive long-lasting effects, preferably.

Late Sunday afternoon, I rode my bike slowly up my parents' long driveway, taking in the changes four weeks in the spring had wrought. Like Fitzy's home garden, which I had weeded and dead-headed that morning while Fitzy offered helpful pointers from the patio, my parents' front yard was ablaze with flowering bulbs interspersed among budding deciduous trees and shrubs. As I looked out across the lavish plantings, I finally understood my mother's decision to hire grounds-care professionals. I couldn't blame her for not wanting to assume direct responsibility for a landscape design formulated by her highly critical mother-in-law. She'd probably been under the scrutiny of her in-laws for most of her adult life. Had they known she dropped out of high school? For her sake, I hoped not.

I left my bike in the driveway with my siblings' cars and entered the kitchen through the side door, feeling unusually magnanimous as I greeted assorted family members. As usual, I was the last Starreveld to arrive. I helped myself to a beer from the refrigerator and started outside to say hi to my father and brothers-in-law, but my mother waylaid me before I could reach the back door.

"Honey, can I speak to you?" she asked, and for a moment images of our last meeting flooded my mind—dirty laundry, empty beer bottles, forgotten bras. That danged bra. I still needed to return it to Caitlyn, a necessary confrontation I was unofficially putting off for as long as possible.

Without waiting for a response, my mother guided me into the pantry, a windowless walk-in closet that smelled comfortingly of cinnamon. It was crammed to overflowing with baking supplies, dried herbs from the vegetable garden, cereal boxes, baby food, and staples of all sizes and types. Ever since my mother had discovered Sam's Club, available closet space in my parents' house had dwindled considerably.

"What is it, Mom?" I asked, feeling, for the most part, generous in my newfound understanding of her psyche.

"I wanted to thank you."

"Thank me? For what?"

"For being kind to your father."

She meant well, I knew she did. But did she have to sound so incredulous that I had managed to spend a cordial, even friendly week with my dad?

"What did he tell you?"

"Not much," she admitted, tightening the twist-tie on a nearby package of dried basil leaves. "He just said that the two of you had a good time together, which is saying quite a bit considering his reasons for being in Amsterdam."

"We did have a good time," I said. "In fact, I'm going to go say hi to him, okay?"

"Okay." She surprised me with a sudden hug. "I'm proud of you, Elizabeth."

I hugged her back, amazed that both of my parents had embraced me of their own volition within the past week. The times, they were definitely a-changing.

Back in the kitchen, I caught my sister Jane watching me with raised eyebrows. I gave her a thumbs-up, and she turned back to stir a bubbling pot on our parents' stove.

Jane, my self-appointed protector, had bought me lunch at Boa before my shift on Friday so that I could fill her in on the trip. Like Toby, my big sister had been excited about our father's fence-mending. But her response had been less generous than Toby's: "About effing time. Mike and I were thinking we might have to intervene."

"That's sweet, but what could you have done?"

"We talked about making grandparent time contingent on his talking to a counselor who specializes in this sort of thing, and *not* someone from the church."

"You wouldn't do that, would you?" I'd asked, half-scandalized, the other half touched.

"Well, maybe not. But only because we enjoy grandparent time as much as Mom and Dad do, if you know what I mean."

"Ew," I'd said, throwing a potato chip across the table at her. "I don't mind straight people, as long as you don't flaunt your sexuality in public."

"Don't worry," she said. "Whatever we do happens in the privacy of our own home. Much to Owen's dismay—did I tell you he walked in on us last month?"

And we were off and running on another parental teaching moment in the Starreveld-Thompson household.

I squeezed her arm as I passed the stove, thinking how lucky I was to have her on my side.

She smiled at me over her shoulder. "Welcome home, Junior."

Conversation at dinner that night revolved around the trip. My father fielded his share of questions at one end of the table while I handled my own debriefing at the other. My sisters—well, Cat was envious, so I tried to downplay my descriptions of Brussels, Antwerp, and Amsterdam, spending more time than was truly necessary on the minutiae of the IAJ convention. I also skipped over my extracurricular activities, such as tripping on a mystery drug and failing to hook up with the woman who may or may not turn out to be the love of my life. The only part I didn't hold back on was describing the splendors of Keukenhof and Lisse.

As anticipated, shouts of disbelief sounded around the table at the news that Dad and I had scooted our way across the Dutch landscape on our last day in Holland. The denials were so spirited that Owen put his hands over his ears and hummed to drown out the cacophony of adult voices.

At a lull, my sister Cat asked, "So, Lizzie, what was your favorite part of the trip?"

I hate it when Cat calls me that—it's too close to the ever-so-original invective she's been known to toss at me in private, "Lezzie." I paused, picturing Sofie's lips, the spinning lights at the Getto, the feel of every inch of my skin aglow with music, dancing, possibility. Then I thought about the morning my father and I had spent at the gardens in Lisse with the familiar scent of earth, the shine of sunlight off water, the miles of tulip and hyacinth fields stretching red, pink, orange, purple toward the flat horizon.

"Keukenhof Gardens," I said. "Hands down."

There was silence, and it occurred to me that no one in my family really knew me, except maybe Jane who was nodding at me from the other end of the table. Cat had probably put me on the spot hoping I would say something to demonstrate why my father shouldn't have taken me, as she had argued within my earshot the night my father made the offer—and at every other dinner before and after the trip, including this one.

"What about you, Dad?" Jane asked. "What was your favorite part?"

And my father, known better for his glass thumb than his sense of humor, answered, "The Mannekin Pis. Without a doubt."

I laughed and held up my beer in a toast to him while all around the table, my sisters asked each other what he had said.

CHAPTER FIFTEEN

In the weeks following my return to Michigan, while rains came and went, leaves budded and burst, and the sun's rays grew inexorably warmer, for me the comfort of being home after a long trip morphed into a familiar inertia only exacerbated by Fitzy's steady, visible decline.

My days adopted their pre-Europe rhythm, slipping past as I worked on spring installments at the busy Botanical Gardens, took care of the household chores Fitzy was increasingly unable to manage, and made coffee and flirted at Boadicea. I didn't hear from Steph again, and even Caitlyn seemed to be avoiding me, which was, frankly, a relief. My rebound debacle had demonstrated how badly I needed to be alone and get my head together before attempting to join the civilized dating world again. If I didn't, if I just leapt headlong into the next new thing that came along, then the dyke drama that I claimed to despise risked becoming a permanent fixture in my life, as it had in the lives of other lesbians I knew. I still wanted a wife and, down the road, a couple of kids to read to and cuddle and play soccer with. I just didn't want to repeat the dysfunction of my relationship with Maddie, nor the casual disconnect of whatever I'd been doing since. Being with Sofie had assured me that the possibility still existed of a worthy relationship with a mature, caring partner. Even more, that such a prospect was worth waiting for.

On the home front, I attended family dinners every other week, content again to let the spotlight rest on my sisters' careers, relationships, and children. My father didn't mention the business with the shop again, and I kept his secret as he went through the final stage of negotiations with Van de Jijk, the Dutch corporation. The plans for the store gave us a common bond, something we needed, I thought, after so many years of distance.

As the days and weeks passed, the polish wore off my trip memories, eclipsed by a reality I had no choice but to acknowledge. With Fitzy's breathing more labored and her activities restricted, I threw myself into helping her any way I could. If I could just work hard enough, maybe the emphysema would slow down, possibly even stop progressing. This was a form of magical thinking, I knew, but I wasn't in the most rational of places. Meanwhile, she accepted my assistance without comment, gracious for once in the face of need. I wasn't the only one helping out, either. The same friends and neighbors were still checking up on her regularly, and as her condition worsened, a group of faculty and staff from the Botany Department set up a meal schedule so that Fitzy wouldn't have to cook. A nurse from the Visiting Nurses Association came by every morning and evening to check her oxygen levels and other vitals, and I was dropping by almost daily now, too. Fitzy was less alone than she had ever been, which, predictably, did not make her happy.

Before I knew it, a month had passed, and I was still stuck in limbo wishing I had the power to control time. Toby, who knew I wasn't sleeping well, insisted I take Memorial Day weekend off. At Fitzy's urging, I reluctantly accepted an invitation from Alex and Sarah, another college friend, to spend the holiday weekend in Saugatuck. I only agreed because Fitzy's sister and niece were coming down again from Traverse City, and the last thing she claimed to need was more bodies invading her space. So I made plans to leave town, wondering all the while if I was doing the right thing.

The Saturday before Memorial Day, Alex stopped her Jeep in front of my building and honked. With a last check of the timer on my growth lights, I shouldered a backpack, slapped sunglasses and a baseball cap on my head, and emerged into the humid morning. An early heat wave had slammed the Midwest, tipping thermometers toward ninety. The heat felt good, and as I jogged toward Alex's Jeep, I had to admit that getting out of Ann Arbor also felt pretty good. Four of us would be staying at Sarah's aunt's vacation condo, playing Frisbee on the beach, wandering Saugatuck's artsy shops, and going for drinks at the local bars. For three days, we would be in homo heaven in the gayest small town in the Midwest.

"You ready to go?" Alex asked.

"Totally. Thanks for inviting me, dude."

"No worries. You look like you could use a little fun."

She put the Jeep in gear, turned up Melissa Ferrick, and we cruised a few blocks away to pick up Sarah and her girlfriend Evyn—pronounced "Eve with an n," she informed everyone she met—a wealthy Detroit suburbanite Alex and I weren't yet sure we liked. Sarah, who had never set foot on a rugby pitch, was more the brainy social activist type. Dez and I had gotten to know her sophomore year in our Women's Studies Methods class. Unlike Alex, Sarah was still friends with Dez and Maddie, a fact she and I did not discuss. I didn't care if my friends picked sides or not. I just didn't want to hang with my exes, nor did I want to hear about them. Occasionally Sarah forgot and mentioned them, but for the most part she respected my unevolved need to pretend Dez and Maddie didn't exist.

Passengers and bags stowed in the back, Alex guided the Jeep onto the freeway and headed west out of Ann Arbor. The top was down and the wind was too loud to talk, which was fine, I decided as Melissa Ferrick provided a soundtrack to our journey across the state. In a few hours, we would be lounging in the hot tub on Sarah's aunt's deck, planning the weekend's festivities. It would be fun, I told myself, trying not to picture Fitzy the previous morning forcing herself to eat breakfast at her kitchen bar, hooked up to the now omnipresent canister of oxygen. She'd only shown up at the Arboretum once in the past week and a half, and I had taken to swinging by her house "on my way to work" in the mornings. It was a sign—and not a good one—of what was to come that Fitzy hadn't scolded me yet for going late to work.

I pushed the memory away. For the next couple of days, I wasn't going to think about oxygen tanks or scarred lungs. I wasn't going to remember the previous Memorial Day weekend, either, when Maddie, Dez, and I had gone camping with Alex and Sarah and a few other friends at Hoffmaster, a state park just up the coast from Saugatuck, back when things were still good and Maddie and Dez hadn't yet crossed the line I had assumed existed between them. Of course, focusing on the present and ignoring the shipwreck of my personal life would likely be tough. It had taken Sofie's presence and an important breakthrough with my dad to make the trip to Amsterdam a success.

As we roared down the freeway, the sun and wind in our eyes, I had to wonder if Saugatuck, a town I had been visiting since I was in diapers, had the capacity to make me forget about the looming iceberg of Fitzy's illness.

The gorgeous summery weather hung around throughout the weekend, making me feel downright churlish for not being able to completely hide my angst. I did my best to be friendly to the cute women in town, like us, for the weekend—friends of friends from Chicago and Kalamazoo we met dining out at various restaurants, drinking beer at queer afternoon happy hours, playing pool and dancing late into the night. But I couldn't seem to manufacture interest in even the most attractive of lesbians. I didn't want to get drunk at three in the afternoon and kiss someone who would likely turn out to have a girlfriend or, worse, a recent ex she was still "hanging out" with. I would have preferred to lay out on the beach by myself and read a good book, or go for a dune buggy ride with my friends, or poke around the antique shops in town. But even though I longed for a quiet couple of days, I let Alex drag me along on the traditional outings, all the while wishing I had just said no.

Sunday night found me sitting in a corner of a Saugatuck club alone, nursing a beer and watching my friends dance. I would have preferred to be home in my apartment with my plants and the dog I'd always wanted and still didn't have, smoking a little weed and watching cable. In fact, I was mentally cataloging the cable movies I would rather be watching—*Grosse Pointe Blank,* John Cusack's hit man satire, was always a popular choice among Michiganders, though Evyn insisted it wasn't an accurate portrayal of suburban Detroit—when a woman with red hair walked by, laughing over her shoulder. Sofie? But of course it couldn't be. Now that Sofie and I were Facebook friends, I would know if she were anywhere near the state of Michigan. I'd been stalking her from afar ever since I got home, hoping fervently that there wasn't some Facebook setting or app that I didn't know about informing her I visited her page at least once a day to see if her relationship status was still "It's complicated."

I watched her Michigan lookalike walk away, butt swaying in faded jeans. What was Sofie doing at that moment? Alex would have pointed out I could have known where she was if only I had a smartphone, but Facebook was stalkerish enough for me. Still, it might have been nice to visit her page from my corner of the bar and click through some of the photos she had uploaded—strolling along a canal with friends, having brunch at an outdoor café in the Jordaan, picnicking among the flowers of Vondelpark. How could I miss her? I barely knew her. But for the few days I'd hung out with her, trying new things in a strange city, I'd felt less like the person I had become and more like who I wanted to be.

If I'd had a smartphone to play with, maybe I wouldn't have been looking out at the dance floor just then; maybe I would never have seen Dez and Maddie winding hand in hand through the crowd. They looked fit and tanned, with that glow people who are having lots of sex always have, the glow Maddie and I had once shared. I watched them walk, holding onto each other easily, comfortably. They looked happy. And why shouldn't they be? They got to fall asleep at night curled together (at least, on Fridays and Saturdays), share coffee and newspapers in bed, go out on date night with one hand on their drinks and the other on each other.

I sipped my beer and pictured myself blocking their path. What would it feel like to slap the self-satisfied smile off Maddie's face? I imagined the sting of my palm connecting with the face I used to watch in sleep, her eyelashes dark smudges against her pale cheekbones. In the beginning, I would think how lucky I was to have her in my life, but in retrospect, the luck that had brought us together hadn't turned out to be good for me. Good for Dez, maybe, but not so much for me. I tore the label from my empty beer bottle. Would it feel good to slap her? Would Dez try to defend her from me? I kind of hoped so. She was the one who most deserved the smackdown, after all.

Leaving my bottle on the nearest table, I rose and headed toward the blissful couple. I caught Dez's eye as I approached, and was surprised to see what looked like a flicker of fear in her gaze. Good, I thought, let her be afraid. It was just possible she had reason to be, though in my current state of inebriation, I couldn't be sure. I stared her down as I prowled closer, willing her to feel the anguish she'd caused me, that she was inflicting even now by daring to appear in my presence holding onto Maddie like some shiny prize.

As I neared them, Dez reached out a hand as if to stop me.

"Liz, wait," she said. "Please?"

In her strained voice I could hear all of the days and weeks and months we'd shared since freshman year when we'd bonded over our shared crush on Claudia, the smoking hot TA in our Women's Studies class. Claudia had unwittingly set the baseline against which Dez and I had measured all future women. When I met Maddie, I giddily declared that I'd finally found someone hotter. Apparently, Dez had agreed

This was it. This was my chance to take revenge on my ex-best friend, to make her pay for her betrayal. But she was looking at me with this pained expression on her face, and even Maddie looked pale and scared in the dim light from the bar. I felt sick all at once, beer and pretzels rising at the back of my throat. What was I thinking? I didn't want vengeance. I didn't want anything to do with either of them. They were part of my past, a past as irreversible as death.

Fitzy's image flashed in my mind then, followed closely by a painting I'd seen at the Van Gogh museum, a darkly satirical portrait he'd made of a skull with a smoking cigarette clenched between its skeletal teeth, and I understood at last. Fitzy was the one I was furious with. She was the one I wanted to slap.

My throat tightening, I shoved my hands deep into my jeans pockets, brushed past Dez's outstretched hand, and walked out into the cool night. Fog had rolled in, and for a moment I could have been in Amsterdam, walking back to the Westerkerk to catch a tram. But then the illusion passed and I was back on Water Street in Saugatuck, a stone's throw from Holland, Michigan, but thousands of miles from the real thing.

My phone beeped, and I pulled it from my back pocket, heartbeat skittering as I read Dez's text message: "I'm sorry. I miss you so much. Will you ever forgive me?"

Effing dyke drama. But I knew exactly what she meant, even if I didn't know the answer to her question.

Blinking hard against the sting of tears, I turned up my shirt collar and walked on toward the main road. The urgency was back, the need to make a real change, to construct a life worth living somewhere other than the city where I had spent nearly all my days and nights. When had my life split into a before and after? Had it happened when Dez showed up on my doorstep in the middle of a snowstorm to tell me she couldn't stand lying to me anymore? Or was it when Fitzy told me she wouldn't make it through the summer? Either way, my old life in Ann Arbor had become the before. What exactly should come after, I didn't yet know, which must make the space I currently inhabited my own personal purgatory.

I thought of what Sofie had said before I got on the tram my last night in Amsterdam: *Follow your dreams.* Now if I could only figure out what those looked like.

Rain moved in overnight—I heard it rattling against the living room windows at the vacation house, where I failed to sleep on the thinnest futon ever created by man—and continued into Memorial Day. We'd planned to stay through Monday for the traditional barbecue and town parade, but as it was, Alex, Sarah, Evyn, and I ate breakfast and skedaddled. By mid-day, I was home alone in my studio, lying on the floor listening to Ani DiFranco and watching wind whip the branches of my willow tree. I hoped the storm wouldn't get much worse. The predictability of tornadoes in Michigan did not make them any less terrifying.

"Untouchable Face," one of my all-time favorite Ani songs, came on, and I pictured Dez and Maddie as I'd seen them the night before. When I wasn't channeling Glenn Close, I knew it wasn't really their fault they'd fallen in love. I had been so naïve, never thinking to question the nights when the two of them had hung out together when I was working late, never picking up on the looks that must have passed between them when we were all together. It had simply never occurred to me that the two people I cared about most would come to prefer each other over me.

The one thing they could have helped was how they'd chosen to handle the situation. Lying and sneaking around behind my back… At least Dez was torn up over her behavior. The pleading look in her eyes the night before, along with her text, proved that. Still, I didn't know if I would ever feel comfortable around her again, not as long as she and Maddie were a couple.

Four months after she'd upended my life, I missed Dez more than I did Maddie. While Maddie may have been the lone woman I'd ever pondered settling down, buying a house, and having kids with, Dez was my boy, my bro. It was almost as hard to imagine my life without her as it was to face having to say goodbye to Fitzy. Dez and I used to do everything together, from studying and drinking to chalking main campus for various political causes. We'd gone to Gay Pride in Lansing together every summer for seven years running, and I wasn't looking forward to guzzling cheap beer from oversized cans and cheering on the drag queens without her. But how could I ever accept her back as a friend?

Ani's ultimate pissed-off relationship song ended, and I changed over to the Indigo Girls, opting for their usually life-affirming optimism over Ani's often bitter cynicism. One of my favorites of the Girls, "Love's Recovery," came on, and I sang along with it, wanting their simple faith in love to seep into me and remind me that goodness and truth were indeed still out there, if you only knew where to look. I wished I were a trinity, too, so I'd still have two of me left to live, left to give, after this shit storm of a year. Because it wasn't over yet, not even by half.

Late that afternoon, I was still listening to the Indigo Girls and watching the storm pick up force beyond my window when my phone rang. The caller ID blinked, and I shivered in the damp coolness of my basement apartment.

"Yes?" I said, and bit my lip, waiting for the news I'd been dreading.

A woman's voice sounded at the other end: "I'm sorry to call like this, but I'm Grace Collins, Margaret Fitzgerald's niece."

"I know. Is she okay?" Visions of exploding oxygen tanks danced in my head.

"I'm afraid she isn't," Grace said, her voice gentle. "Her condition worsened over the weekend. I'm here at the hospital with her. She asked me to call you."

"I'll be right there," I said. "Where are you?"

She gave me directions, and then I was hanging up and scrambling around the apartment, assembling my wallet and keys. I started for the hallway where I kept my bike, and then stopped. The rain was still coming down, and it would be dark soon. I couldn't show up at the hospital soaked to the skin. I hesitated only a moment before punching in a number I'd never forgotten.

Marjorie, a sales associate who had been with the store more than a decade, answered the private line. I could hear sounds in the background—Starreveld & Sons held a huge Memorial Day sale each year just in time for the summer engagement season. The store would be open for a few more hours yet.

"Hi Marjorie, it's Elizabeth. Can you get my dad?"

"He's with a customer. Can I take a message?"

"I really need to talk to him. Could you bring the phone to him?"

She hesitated.

"Please? It's important."

"Just a minute."

He came on the line, his voice deep and warm. "Elizabeth? Are you all right?"

"I'm fine," I said, pacing the length of my apartment. "I'm sorry to bother you, but I need a favor."

"What is it?"

"Fitzy's in the hospital, and with the storm…"

"I'll be right over. Stay put, okay?"

"I will. Thanks, Dad," I added. But he'd already hung up.

I sat on my couch, trying to gauge how bad it had to be for Fitzy to ask her niece to call me. I'd met Grace and her husband a few times over the years when they'd dropped by to tour the Gardens, and again more recently at Fitzy's house. They lived just south of the UP with their nearly grown children and Grace's mother, Fitzy's older sister Helen. Fitzy spent Thanksgiving and Christmas with them each year, and went up north every summer to vacation on Mackinac Island with the entire clan. Grace and I had exchanged cell phone numbers back in April. Just in case.

Starreveld & Sons was less than a mile from my apartment. I didn't have to wait long before my father sounded the Volvo horn out front. I was down the walk before the sound faded, rain pelting my waterproof jacket.

"Who did you say is in the hospital?" my father asked as I slid into the passenger seat.

"Dr. Fitzgerald," I told him, and for some reason, saying her name out loud brought tears to my eyes. I swallowed past the constriction in my throat. "Thanks for coming, Dad."

"Of course. I'm glad you called," he said, and guided the Volvo away from the curb.

The University of Michigan Medical Center took up several blocks just northeast of main campus. To the south of the complex lay the sprawling Forest Hill Cemetery, with its pristine lawns and tall old trees. Now, driving past the rain-slicked headstones, the proximity of Forest Hill to University Hospital struck me as unforgivably morbid.

As we parked in the Medical Center garage and walked quickly toward the nearest entrance, I filled my father in on Fitzy's illness.

"She doesn't have much time," I told him. "But I thought, I don't know, I just didn't realize—" I stopped, unable to force more words past the lump lodged now in my throat.

"I know," my dad said, slipping an arm around my shoulders. "It'll be okay, honey."

I leaned into him and swiped at the tears threatening to overflow. I couldn't show up in Fitzy's room crying. She would not appreciate such a maudlin display.

Inside the hospital my father took charge, guiding me to the information center on the first floor and then leading me to the correct elevator bank. As we rode the wide, fluorescent-lit elevator to the cardiac intensive care unit, I was glad I'd called him.

We reached Fitzy's private room before I was mentally prepared. In the doorway I stopped, my mind struggling to take it all in. Lying in the hospital bed with an oxygen mask covering her mouth and nose and an IV protruding from her arm, she looked smaller than I'd expected. More wires wound from her chest to another machine behind the oxygen tank. In her faded blue hospital gown, surrounded by medical equipment, she looked fragile, her skin pulled taut across the bone and sinew beneath.

She caught sight of us and pulled the mask down far enough to say, "Don't just stand there. Come in."

I hesitated before entering the room, my dad close behind me. Grace, a plump middle-aged woman who resembled Fitzy only peripherally, rose from her seat by the bed to give me a hug and shake my father's hand. He shook Fitzy's hand, too, grasping it where it lay against the sheets, and she moved the mask aside again.

"I'm pleased to finally meet you."

"Same here," he replied. "I've heard a lot about you."

Fitzy replaced the mask and seemed to breathe hard for a few minutes. Tactfully, Grace and my father made small talk. I stood awkwardly in the middle of the room looking everywhere but at the bed while they chatted about Ann Arbor and Traverse City, where my father had vacationed as a boy. They discussed the spring storm holding over the city, agreeing that in Michigan, if you didn't like the current weather, all you had to do was wait.

At last Fitzy recovered and waved me closer. As I took the seat by the bed, I heard my father ask Grace, "Could you show me where they keep the coffee? I could use a warm-up."

"Of course," she answered, and they moved out into the hallway.

Fitzy moved the mask aside and smiled at me, her eyes glinting. It took her a while, but she managed to grate, "I'm glad to meet your father, but kiddo, I called you so you could break me out of this joint."

Still the same Fitzy, I thought, relaxing a little. I took her hand in mine and held it lightly, tracing the breakable bones and the blue veins just beneath the surface of her skin as she caught her breath again. This level of intimacy was new for us, but it felt right. I sat at her side while she lay in bed fighting her recalcitrant lungs for another breath, another minute, another hour.

She appeared to doze briefly before jerking awake and staring at me wide-eyed. When she slid the mask aside, I leaned closer to hear her whisper, "I'm so glad you're here, Amanda. I've missed you, my sweet girl."

And she smiled up at me with so much joy that all I could do was squeeze her hand and say, "Me, too."

Her eyes closed again and she seemed almost to deflate, shrinking back against the pillow. Her eyes were sunken, her skin thin and gray, almost translucent. She couldn't have long, even I could see that. And to think I'd wasted all that time in Saugatuck when I could have been here, with her, doing... what, exactly?

As she lay there, lost to the world around her, I sat quietly beside the bed, still holding her hand. In a little while, Grace and my father returned. He touched my shoulder and pulled a chair close to mine.

Once Fitzy's niece had settled into her seat again, I glanced over at her. "Can I ask you something?"

She lowered her knitting. "Certainly, dear."

"Fitzy said her daughter was born in Seattle. Is that true?"

"Yes. Has she been talking about Amanda again?"

"Just a little." I looked down at Fitzy's small form, her bruised-looking eyes still shut. "What happened to her? Amanda, I mean."

"It was meningitis. She passed right here in this very hospital. Didn't you know?"

I shook my head.

"Well, most of what I know comes second-hand, but I'm sure she wouldn't mind me sharing it with you."

As the sky darkened and the rain and wind beat steadily against the window, Grace told us the story of Fitzy's life. Some of it I knew—her love of green things, which had taken her first to graduate school and then all over the world lecturing, collecting specimens, studying rare species. But much of it I didn't: her marriage in her late twenties to Tom Fitzgerald, a mild-mannered entomologist with an abiding interest in butterflies; her first and only child, Amanda, a precocious girl who inherited both parents' fascination with the natural world; her teaching positions at the University of Washington and the University of Chicago; and the tragedy that had swallowed up her little family.

"Amanda was so like her mother," Grace said, her knitting needles clicking together rapidly. "Fiery and headstrong, and passionate about her studies. She moved to Ann Arbor to earn a doctorate in primate studies, I think it was. But in her third year, she fell ill. By the time her roommate brought her to the hospital, she was in a coma. Margaret and Tom were still on the road from Chicago when she died. She was already gone when they got here."

Tears stung my eyes again, and beside me, my father shifted in his chair.

"How awful," I murmured, watching the subject of our discussion struggle to breathe.

"Tom was never the same," Grace continued. "You see, he and Amanda had parted ways a few years earlier over her—well, political beliefs."

Political beliefs? Grace had also referenced a "roommate," a word that always made my homo-sensitive ears tingle.

I looked from Fitzy to her niece. "What beliefs?"

Next to me, my father cleared his throat. Admittedly, the question was personal. But so was everything else about this moment.

Grace peered down at the scarf she was knitting for her first grandchild, due the following month, she'd told us. "Oh, you know, feminism, those sorts of things."

"Was Amanda gay?"

Her gaze shot upward, and she considered me for a moment. "Yes, she was. What makes you ask?"

"Fitzy has always been so great to me, I guess I always wondered if there was a reason." I returned to the story. "You said Tom and Amanda weren't on good terms when she died?"

"They were barely speaking," Grace said, and her knitting needles resumed their clack-clacking. "Tom's heart broke the day Amanda died. Literally—his heart gave out less than a year later. He was a good deal older than Margaret, but even so, my mother always believed that Amanda's death killed him. The year after he died, a job opened up here at the University, and Margaret has been in Ann Arbor ever since. Mother says she thinks Margaret feels closer to Amanda here."

She fell silent and we sat together, the sound of her needles and Fitzy's assisted breathing the only accompaniment to our vigil. Outside, evening fell as the storm wore on, spot-lit tree trunks in the hospital courtyard swaying in gusts of wind. Fitzy slept, the oxygen mask fogging with her irregular breaths. She seemed to be growing smaller against the pillows, her hold on life more and more tenuous as she prepared to take leave of the world in the same hospital where her daughter had died. As I sat beside her, waiting for something to happen, the thought comforted me somehow.

We stayed a couple of hours, talking quietly on and off with Grace. She told stories of the old Fitzy, before Amanda died—the energetic woman who traveled the world, collected motorcycles, and worked on an organic farm long before the term had been invented—until visiting hours for non-family members ended. When a nurse indicated it was time for my father and me to leave, I squeezed Fitzy's hand, but she still didn't wake up. Grace had told us she'd only stayed awake earlier because she was waiting to see me.

"Goodbye," I murmured to my old friend, and with a last look at her resting motionless in the hospital bed, I followed my father from the room.

Grace walked with us down the dimly lit hallway, rain blurring the windows and our view of the hospital courtyard.

"Thank you so much for coming," she said. "I know that your presence means a lot to Margaret. She talks about you often, Elizabeth. She thinks of you as family."

Nice to know the feeling was mutual.

"I don't have to work tomorrow afternoon," I said as we reached the elevator. "I could come by again."

"That would be so kind of you," Grace said, and gave me a hug.

My father and I made our way to the parking garage in silence. In the car, he set his hand on my knee for a moment before turning the key in the ignition.

"She seems like a phenomenal person."

"She is."

I watched out the window as we left the parking ramp and entered the wind-blown streets. Hard to believe that I'd awakened in Saugatuck that morning, never imagining where I would spend my evening. My anxiety over seeing Dez and Maddie seemed so trivial now.

"Thanks again for bringing me, Dad."

"Of course. What do you say you come home with me for a late dinner? I talked to your mom earlier, and she has a roast warming in the oven."

He never remembered that I was a vegetarian. "That's okay," I said. "I'm not that hungry."

"I forgot, you don't eat red meat, do you?"

"No, but thanks anyway."

When the Volvo slowed before my building, I hesitated before leaning over to kiss him on the cheek.

"Love you, Dad," I said, and slid out of the car.

"Love you, too," I heard him reply as I slammed the door and sprinted off through the rain.

Inside my chilly apartment I didn't turn on the lights, only kicked off my shoes and dropped onto my couch in the dark, wishing I had that dog to greet me with wagging tail and snuffling nose. I pictured Fitzy as I'd seen her at home on Friday morning, shuffling around her kitchen, oxygen tubes snaking into her nose. Of course I'd known she was going downhill, but her transition from functional to bedridden still seemed sudden somehow. Maybe that change always seems sudden, even when you have time to prepare.

I folded my hands behind my head and stared up at the shadows on the wall cast by the bars on the window, trying to decide which was worse: watching someone you loved waste away until the person she had been was barely recognizable, or losing her in the space of a single day. Amanda Fitzgerald had died so suddenly that Fitzy and her husband—and Amanda's "roommate"—wouldn't have had a chance to adjust to the idea of losing her. She was just abruptly, terribly gone, like my Aunt Karen who struck a tree on a downhill course in the UP and died instantly. My uncle remarried, but I knew my cousins Susan and David still missed their mom every day.

Why hadn't Fitzy ever told me her daughter was gay? She'd always known more about me than I knew about her, and had seemed content to keep mostly to the periphery of my life, only popping up when she thought I might need her. Now at the end she was reaching out more—or maybe I was the one reaching in further, insinuating myself in her life just as she was about to lose it. We were like strangers on an airplane—quiet for most of the flight as we passed refreshments and used napkins back and forth, and then suddenly garrulous for the last thirty minutes, sharing family photos and intimate stories as the flight attendants prepared the cabin for landing. Once the passengers de-planed, they usually never saw each other again.

I rose from the couch and turned on the overhead light. It was going to be a long night, no doubt about it.

CHAPTER SIXTEEN

By the next day, the storm had blown itself out, leaving the streets damp and the air crisp. After a long morning at the Arboretum where I had the unfortunate honor of sharing the news with co-workers, I grabbed a bagel and cream cheese from Boadicea and rode my bike to the hospital, weaving in and out of rush-hour traffic. I had always loved riding my bike, and this morning as I darted between cars, the sun shining down on streets cleansed by the storm, I felt stronger and more alive than I had in a long time.

At the hospital, I made my way to Fitzy's room and paused in the doorway. She was still there, her breath rattling irregularly, Grace knitting in the seat at her side. Other visitors dotted the room today, too—a burly man I recognized as Grace's husband, Bob, and an older woman who sat in a chair by the window.

"Hello, Elizabeth," Grace said in a quiet voice, rising when she saw me. "Come in, dear. Margaret's asleep, but I know she'll be happy to see you when she wakes up."

Grace reminded her husband who I was and introduced me to her mother, Fitzy's sister. Helen looked me over and nodded once before turning back to her novel. Apparently Grace had inherited her gregariousness from the other side of the family.

"What's in the bag?" Bob, another friendly sort, asked, gesturing at my backpack.

"Let me show you," I said.

First came my laptop in its protective sleeve. I set it on a small, wheeled table near the bed and booted it up, then reached into the pack again and pulled out an envelope of photos.

"I was in the Netherlands last month," I told Grace and Bob, "and got a chance to spend some time at Keukenhof Gardens, one of Fitz—Margaret's favorite places. She's seen the photos already, but I thought they might brighten up the room."

"I'm sure they will," Grace declared, and set about extending the arm of the table across the bed.

I organized the photos in piles—one stack for the scooter trip through the fields of Lisse; one for the best of Keukenhof, where I had taken more than a hundred shots; and the last for my other photos of Holland and Belgium. Not included, of course, were assorted shots I hadn't remembered taking of Sofie, her friends, and me in varied inebriated states. Those were stashed safely at home or, in a couple of cases, set to private on Facebook.

Fitzy woke up before I finished. She squeezed my hand, her fingers warm and dry on mine.

Hoping she recognized me this time, I squeezed back and said, "Feel like watching a movie? Thought I might as well take advantage of a captive audience."

She braced herself, slid the oxygen mask to one side, and said, "I could leave if I wanted. I'm only staying for the food."

Near the window, Helen sniffed audibly. I had the impression that, compared to her sister, curmudgeonly Fitzy was the one with the still functioning sense of humor.

Grace and Bob and even Helen crowded around the bed so that they could see my laptop screen. I navigated to a folder on my hard drive and started the video. The music sounded first, the opening bars of Mozart's *Eine Kleine Nachtmusik*, one of Fitzy's favorites, and then the images began, twisting and turning across the screen. As the resident techie at the Botanical Gardens, I subscribed to the web-based video production application Animoto, which we used mainly to create marketing clips and event promos. The night before I'd spent a couple of hours on Animoto arranging photos and video into a five-minute movie of the day my dad and I had spent at Keukenhof.

"Isn't that where you and Tom went for your honeymoon?" Grace asked when the photo of the main entrance danced across the screen.

Fitzy nodded, and I could see her smile through the mask. I couldn't imagine her on her honeymoon, but I could picture her easily at Keukenhof. She would stride purposefully along the walkways, pen in hand, stopping to feel the texture of the leaves and record details in her field notebook. I'd learned my own technique from her.

The video clip of nearby flower fields from the deck of the Keukenhof windmill came exactly halfway through the movie. As the viewpoint panned across the rows of colorful flowers, Fitzy took my hand. Even Helen offered an appreciative grunt.

When the movie ended, Fitzy slid her mask to the side. "It's beautiful. Has your father seen it yet?"

"Nope—this is the official premiere. But don't worry, I'll share it with him, too, seeing as he is one of the stars."

I closed the laptop so that the five of us could look through the photos I'd printed out at Walgreen's the week after the trip. Grace asked me about traveling with my father, and I waxed enthusiastically about the time we'd spent together. I told them that I came from a large family, and that my father and I had grown apart in recent years.

"I wouldn't have believed it possible," I added, my eyes on Fitzy's, "but the trip managed to bring us closer."

"He seems like a lovely man," Grace said.

"He is."

Fitzy touched my hand, and I wondered if she was thinking about Amanda and Tom and how they hadn't ever had the chance to heal the rift between them. Had they reunited somehow in death? Would Fitzy join them in some other, peaceful place? I wasn't sure what I believed, but I knew I hoped they would see each other again.

"These copies are yours," I told Fitzy as she leafed through the photos. "Maybe, if you want, you could pick out your favorites and we can hang them on the wall near your bed," I added, pulling a glue stick from my backpack. I'd borrowed the idea from one of my favorite movies, *Fried Green Tomatoes*.

Grace looked around nervously. "I don't know that they'll let us put anything on the walls."

Bob patted her shoulder. "I'll talk to the day nurse," he said. "Becky, I think it is. I'm sure the hospital won't mind."

Obtaining permission was more of a production than I'd anticipated—wall tacks were most certainly not allowed—but once Becky had been by to examine the glue stick and set limits on the wall space we were allowed to tamper with, we went to work. Fitzy picked the photos, and Bob and I took turns covering up the dull gray paint with the bright flowers of Keukenhof.

When the designated wall space had been filled, we stood back to examine our work. The room felt more alive now. You could almost smell the rich earth and the fragrant blooms waving in the breeze.

Almost.

Fitzy had kept out the photo the boy at the scooter shop had snapped of my father and me. We were standing in the Dutch sunshine, his arm across my shoulders, both smiling widely in anticipation of the adventure awaiting us. She made me tape this photo to the rails on her bed, the flower photos a blur in the background.

"This," she said, tapping the photo with a shaky forefinger, "is my favorite."

"Mine, too," I said, and smiled at her.

My days that week took on a routine: Up early, shower and breakfast, and leave for the Arboretum. Putter around the Gardens for a few hours, answering questions about Fitzy's condition and collecting good wishes to pass along, and then leave for the hospital. Arrive during visiting hours and spend the afternoons reading aloud from one of Fitzy's favorite publications (*Edinburgh Journal of Botany*, *Fine Gardening*, and *Atlantic Monthly*) or, if she was dozing, playing cards with Bob or another visitor. Once the word got around on campus and in Fitzy's neighborhood, someone new stopped by almost hourly.

By Wednesday, she was sleeping most of the time I spent there, and on Thursday, she only woke up once all day. On Friday, from a quiet conversation with Grace before my afternoon shift at Boa, I learned that the doctors were saying it wouldn't be long. I almost called Toby to tell her I was staying at the hospital, but Grace assured me I had been there when it mattered most. There was nothing I or anyone else could do now.

The following morning, shortly after I'd stepped out of the shower, my phone rang. I froze by my dresser. This was it, I thought, knowing even before I saw the name on the screen. As I stood there in my apartment with only a towel around my waist, Grace told me gently that Fitzy had passed away in the night. Linda, the night nurse, had contacted Grace.

"I wanted to catch you before you went to the hospital," she added. "I didn't want you walking into an empty room."

"I appreciate that."

Phone tight against my ear, I waited to see if I would cry. But my eyes remained dry. I'd grieved some the night before, alone in bed in the dark after an inauspicious shift at Boadicea. The rain had returned, bringing with it a wave of irritability in the crowds who frequented the café. Still, my tears had owed more to the loss of Fitzy's steady presence in my life than to the patronizing straight girl who'd lectured me about putting too much milk in her latte.

"I have your photos," Grace said, "along with a few other items Margaret wanted you to have. Do you think you could come by the house this morning?"

"Of course," I said, wondering what the "other items" could be.

"Good. We'll see you soon."

I hung up the phone and moved aimlessly about my apartment, picking up a book here, a shoe there, and putting them down again all without focusing on what I was doing. Fitzy was gone, I told myself as I paused in front of the closet near my bed, waiting for the reality of her death to sink in. But she'd slept through the last couple of days; the news that she'd slipped away in the night was almost anti-climactic.

Meanwhile, Grace and Bob were waiting. I donned jeans and a sweatshirt, munched a quick breakfast of bagel and cream cheese, and rode my bike out of town toward Fitzy's house. As I pedaled through the quiet streets east of campus, lined with tall old trees, wide yards, and classic older homes, I realized that this was probably the last time I would ride my bike to Fitzy's house. No more Arboretum events, no more dinner parties, no more mucking about the garden she'd taken such pains to build over the past fifteen years. What would happen to her house? I wished I'd thought to ask her while she was still alive. I hated to think of someone else living there, someone who would let weeds take over the plant beds and forget to dead-head the perennials.

I leaned my bike against the corner of the house and walked around to the back door. A second after I knocked, Grace appeared and waved me in. I took the kitchen steps more slowly than usual, knowing that from now on forever after, I wouldn't find Fitzy standing at the stove stirring a giant pot of cold cucumber soup, or mixing a salad on the counter with the wooden tongs she'd bought in a West African village market. In her place, I found Bob at the table beneath the picture window, drinking instant coffee and reading the *Detroit Free Press*. He nodded at me over his newspaper and I nodded back.

"Come in, Elizabeth," Grace said, smiling at me as she went to tend a side of bacon sizzling on the stove. "How are you this morning, dear?"

"Okay," I said, trying not to picture the happy fat pig the bacon had once been. I didn't begrudge other people their right to eat meat. I just didn't want to have to watch. "How are you guys doing?"

"As well as can be expected," Grace said. "It wasn't a surprise, was it. But then I think it's always a shock when someone passes, even when they've been sick for as long as Margaret has."

I'd thought nearly the same thing, but somehow, hearing someone else express the sentiment aloud made it seem trite. I just nodded.

"Anyhoo, can I get you some breakfast?"

"No, thanks," I said quickly. "I ate before I came."

"Oh." She seemed disappointed. Then she rallied. "You know, hon, you should take a turn through the house and see if there's anything you'd like. We're going to box up anything with sentimental value to take back with us, but I think we'll end up leaving most of the rest."

"What's going to happen to the house?"

"That's up to the University. Margaret left her estate to the Botany Department."

I should have guessed as much.

"If there are any books or artwork," Grace continued, "or anything else you would like to keep to remember Margaret by, you let us know. We'd be happy to set it aside."

"Thanks," I said, and ducked out of the kitchen before Bob could bite into the bacon Grace was setting before him.

In the dining room I paused before the floor-to-ceiling bookshelves, trailing a hand over the smooth spines of the books Fitzy had seen fit to collect over the years. I didn't really want to window shop among her things. It felt disrespectful, as if the only reason I had come here was to help myself to her possessions.

"It's not," I murmured, stopping before the framed photo of Fitzy in her fedora, laughing. Well, maybe I'd ask Grace if I could keep this one. The one of her and Amanda at Keukenhof, too.

Still: "I'm not here for your stuff," I repeated to the photo, and waited for a moment. No response was forthcoming.

Each room of her house, so uncharacteristically silent, contained its own set of memories. I let the images wash over me, picturing Fitzy on my very first visit when she'd paced the dining room choosing book after book she thought I absolutely had to read. She'd been fit and strong still, the emphysema that would pillage her lungs as yet undiscovered. I remembered her a few years later standing near the French windows at the front of the house, motionless for once as a music professor friend played Mozart on the baby grand piano that took up half the living room. She'd seemed far away that night as the music drifted through the open doors and out across the lawn. I had wondered at the time if she was thinking about her husband and daughter, and now I knew that any thoughts she must have had about her family would have been more complex than I could have guessed then. Another time, late one spring evening after a volunteer dinner when her exchange student Tomiko and I were the only ones left, I'd wondered why she'd seemed so sad as the three of us sat quietly on the back patio watching the moon rise over the fruit trees.

Half a decade later, I finally knew the reason for her sorrow—now that it was too late to offer her comfort. But maybe the presence of friends and the energy she must have sensed flitting between Tomiko and me as we sat on a wicker love seat, careful not to touch, maybe those things had been comfort of a sort, even as we reminded her of what her daughter would never have again. All these years, I'd never realized I was a reminder of what she'd lost. Was I just a stand-in? Or had she really cared about me?

Even as these questions elbowed their way into my mind, I could imagine Fitzy slapping me on the back and saying something like, "If you're not bright enough to figure out who loves you, my girl, then I worry for your future."

And I knew, she loved me and I loved her, too, even if neither of us had ever said so.

As I wandered down the hall from the living room, I caught a glimpse of Helen in Fitzy's bedroom. She was seated on the side of the made-up bed, hands folded neatly in her lap, feet flat on the floor. She was just sitting there staring straight ahead, silent tears on her cheeks. I took a step back, then another, and returned the way I had come.

Back in the kitchen, I sat with Grace and Bob as they breakfasted, chatting pleasantly and avoiding looking too closely at their plates. When the table had been cleared and Bob had lifted his newspaper again, Grace paused beside my chair.

"Elizabeth, honey, could you come outside with me?"

"Sure."

Hands in my jeans pockets, I followed Fitzy's niece out into the driveway. We passed the backyard and I wondered again who would take over tending the yard and garden. Maybe I should organize a committee at work, at least until the University decided what to do with the property.

"I think I mentioned," Grace said as we neared the detached garage beside the greenhouse, "that my aunt thought of you as family."

"Oh. Well, yeah. That's how I thought of her, too."

"Last weekend, before the hospital, Margaret made me promise something." She paused before the closed garage door and reached into her pocket. "She wanted you to have these." And she held out a keychain.

I recognized that keychain, with its glass-encased lavender bloom, car fob, and single black key.

"Wait—what?"

"She wanted you to have her car," Grace clarified, pressing the keychain into my palm. As I stared at her, speechless, she pulled a garage door opener from a pocket and pressed the button. Gears groaning, the garage door rose slowly to reveal Fitzy's silver Subaru Forester. Resting on the hood of the car was the framed photo of her and Amanda at Keukenhof and a pot that contained a plant I recognized immediately—the Christmas cactus from her office at the Gardens.

"I can't accept it," I said, almost automatically.

This car was Fitzy's baby. She'd kept it shiny and clean even on the inside, no small feat for a gardener. Two winters earlier when the car was brand new, she'd taken me for a ride, excited to show off the heated seats and climate control dash. Michiganders spend an inordinate amount of time thinking about temperature control.

"Too late," Grace said, smiling. "She already signed the title over to you. There's something else, too. Take a look in the glove compartment."

I hesitated, thinking of what my parents would say. I couldn't accept such a gift, could I? I slid into the passenger seat and checked the glove compartment, where I found a large brown envelope folded in half. I opened it and withdrew a bundle of papers. Clipped to the front was a check written out to me. I counted the zeros, and then stared at Grace.

"What is this?"

"She said to tell you it's for Seattle—now you don't have any excuses."

I leaned back in the passenger seat. Now I knew why she'd asked me where I would go if I ever left Ann Arbor. Here, in my hand, was the means to go wherever I wanted. The packet of papers contained the title to the nearly new Subaru, signed over to me just as Grace had said. There were two smaller envelopes as well, both addressed to me. One read, "Open now." The other instructed, "Open one year from today. I mean it, Junior."

Grace patted my shoulder and said, "Come inside when you're ready, hon."

I watched her walk back to the house, one of Fitzy's old cardigans pulled close about her plump frame. What could she think of her aunt's generosity to someone who wasn't a blood relative? I held the letters for a moment, feeling their weight in my palm. Fitzy was gone, and yet here she was in the garage with me. I took a breath and tore the flap on the first envelope. Inside was a single sheet of paper. I unfolded it and beheld the inscription, "Carpe Diem, my girl—All my love, MAF," scrawled across the page in Fitzy's scientist's chicken-scratch hand.

Shaking my head, I folded the paper back into its envelope and hefted the second letter. It was thicker, and I wondered what she might have written that couldn't be read for an entire year. Secret botanical designs? Dirt on the U of M Botany Department? Looked like I would have to wait to find out, assuming I could successfully master the urge to open it for the next twelve months.

Twelve months. Where would I be in a year? I shivered a little, considering the changes that Fitzy's gifts made suddenly, unbelievably possible. Not possible, even, but compulsory—with these gifts came an obligation, just as she must have intended. No longer could I just hang around Ann Arbor, waiting for something to happen. She was charging me with action that I could only refuse at the peril of my conscience. I'd known she was devious, but this was downright Machiavellian. If Machiavelli had been in the habit of helping others achieve their stated goals and dreams, that is.

Papers tucked under my arm, I slipped out of the car and stood back to look her over. I'd always assumed my first car would be a beat-up Ford purchased from my cousin's dealership with tip money scraped together over a period of months or years. Fitzy's Forester was a far cry from even my loftiest expectations. Seriously, what would my parents say? But I wouldn't have to face them, not yet. Anyway, they were probably going to freak out more about my potential desertion than the vehicle in which I planned to abscond.

Pocketing the car keys, I left the driveway to wind through the backyard, past the greenhouse where Fitzy had spent many of her waking hours experimenting with hybrid flowers and flowering bushes. On the patio, I dropped onto the love seat where Tomiko, the exchange student, and I had once sat without touching as the moon rose over the greenhouse. I could picture that night so clearly, and so many days and nights before and since. But I couldn't imagine what leaving Ann Arbor might feel like. I couldn't imagine going more than a week without seeing Fitzy traipsing about her wood-floored house or seated behind her overflowing desk at the Arboretum. She was someone it was impossible to ignore, and she had taken up space in my Ann Arbor life for so long that without her, nothing in that life could seem quite right.

Gazing out across the summer-lit yard, I caught sight of the tiny mound of earth where we'd buried Curly the previous fall, now grown over with the Brandywine crabapple tree Fitzy had planted. In a way, I was glad the little dog had left before Fitzy could. The sweet-hearted mutt had followed Fitzy wherever she went, content to lie near her, sometimes touching, sometimes not, but always nearby while Fitzy pulled weeds or read the *New York Times* or chopped vegetables from the garden for a salad. I didn't think I could have stood seeing Curly wander the house anxiously, whining and scratching at each door in succession as she looked for her owner. Would they be together again now, too? Had they already found each other, and were even now frolicking together with Tom and Amanda through some perfect field, neither too hot nor too cold, no mosquitoes or black flies or ticks to find them, just an unending early summer morning like today, the scent of recent rain in the air, the threat of autumn not even on the horizon?

The tears I'd expected earlier that morning came finally, and I sat quietly in Fitzy's backyard, crying and listening to the chatter of robins flitting among the forsythia, the buzzing of insects and hummingbirds about the columbine. After the lonely silence of winter, the birds were back now, evident in recent weeks in morning calls and evening trills. Including the sparrows my mother battled every year—she hated the non-native pests who insisted on noisily raising their young in the same spot just outside our attic each summer. She'd knocked the nests down one fall when I was in high school, but the sparrows had rebuilt the following spring. Unfortunately, the head builder was inexperienced, or had lost out when it came to the nest-building gene pool, and since then, a baby bird or two had dropped each summer from their poorly constructed home to their deaths on the brick patio below. I pictured their vulnerable bodies now, naked wings twisted beneath them. If I was lucky, I would be gone before the first casualty.

The thought occurred almost of its own volition. This was it, I realized. I was really going. I was leaving Ann Arbor—Fitzy had seen to that.

I wiped my eyes and rose from the love seat, papers secure beneath my arm.

"Thank you," I said to the backyard, my voice rough from crying. "I'll miss you both."

But the only answer I received from the garden was the steady hum of bees moving from one nectar-laden bloom to another.

CHAPTER SEVENTEEN

The memorial service took place the following Saturday at the Unitarian church near campus where Fitzy had been a longtime member—for the fellowship, she'd once told me, not for the ritual practiced by even the most progressive of churches. In her usual efficient fashion, she'd made service arrangements well in advance. At my invitation, my father came with me. Grace and Bob and their daughters, including the exceedingly pregnant one, invited us to sit in the family row. The church was packed—Fitzy's illness hadn't been a secret, and as soon as her death had been reported, the emails and Twitters and Facebook posts had taken wing. Former students and colleagues, neighbors, local gardeners, botanists, zoologists, and biologists from across the country came to listen to the eulogy by the minister who had known her for more than a decade, to hear from friends and relatives who shared the stories of their connection with Fitzy, and what her life and passing meant to them.

In keeping with Fitzy's personality, humor outweighed sorrow throughout the service, and I found myself laughing more than I cried. The slide show that played on-screen behind the podium was something that I had put together, at Grace's request, and contained photos that Helen had provided along with others, both official and unofficial, from Fitzy's time in Ann Arbor. Mozart, naturally, played accompaniment.

After the service, my father and I milled around the religious education room together, mingling and munching from a buffet of Fitzy's favorite foods—cucumber soup, her signature dish, among other regional and foreign exotics. Fitzy's offhand manner was legendary, but everyone we spoke with had a story to tell about how she'd helped them or someone they knew in some selfless, direct fashion. Including, of course, me.

There was to be no funeral, no burial in the cemetery beside the hospital. Fitzy had been cremated, like her husband and daughter before her, and had left instructions that anyone who wanted to could take some of her ashes with them and scatter them wherever they saw fit. Plastic bags were piled near her urn at the front of the sanctuary, along with a steel garden trowel with a hardwood handle. Before we left, my father and I returned to the sanctuary so that I could take a piece of Fitzy with me.

Trying not to think too deeply about what I was doing, I dug into the ashy mixture that had been my friend and carefully placed a scoop into the bag my father held open for me. As he sealed the bag, he asked, "Okay, Elizabeth?"

"Fine," I said, and set the trowel back on the table.

And then it was over, and my dad and I were leaving the church and walking back to the Volvo. I hadn't told him about Fitzy's generosity yet. I wasn't sure how I was going to tell him or my mother or sisters about Fitzy's gifts or the obligation inherent in my acceptance of them. I would have to tell my family, and soon. But not this week. Our next family dinner wasn't until the following weekend. That left me plenty of time to plan my announcement—and to worry over every possible reaction such a declaration might provoke from the Starreveld clan.

Alex called shortly after my dad dropped me off.

"Change out of your funeral clothes," she ordered. "I'm taking you for veggie burgers at Mama Cassidy's."

A vegetarian restaurant half a block from Boadicea, Mama Cassidy's was owned by two gay men who had worked as chefs for years in San Francisco before moving back to their Midwestern roots. The restaurant was usually crowded, especially on weekends.

Alex and I ordered at the front counter, then stood for a second, craning our heads for a table.

"There's one," she said, pointing toward the back corner. "Why don't you grab it and I'll wait for the food."

For the past two weeks, my world had consisted of hospitals, grieving, and work. At the Arboretum, we'd packed up Fitzy's office and handed it over to the interim director, a Botany professor who had already been doing Fitzy's job for the past month. But I still expected to see Fitzy in the director's office, out on the grounds, in the Conservatory. I doubted that would change anytime soon.

Today, though, it felt good to be out among strangers who hadn't known Fitzy. I wove between narrowly-spaced tables, eavesdropping on hipsters and neo-hippies as I crossed the restaurant.

"And then he whipped it out, and I was all, 'Girlfriend, you better know what you're doing with that,'" from a thin African American man in an orange wife-beater tank top and camo pants.

"I was thinking of cutting off my dreads before my mom comes," from a white college student in tie-dye.

And, "I think she just didn't know what she wanted."

This last statement, delivered in a familiar voice, originated from a table not far from the one Alex had scoped out. My stomach clenched as I zeroed in on the conversationalists in question. Not five feet away sat Steph and Caitlyn, talking amiably over smoothies.

Steph spotted me first. "Speak of the devil," she said, her shapely eyebrows raised. I hadn't seen her much lately, and I'd almost forgotten how cute she could look with her nose ring and dyed blonde pixie cut.

Caitlyn, sporty in a navy Adidas zip-up she'd "borrowed" from my closet, turned a level gaze my way. "Hi, Junior."

"Hi," I said, trying to gauge the distance to the door. Could I turn and flee the restaurant without being totally obvious? Probably not, seeing as we'd already placed our orders.

"Don't worry," Steph said. "We won't throw our smoothies on you, will we, Caitie?"

"We'll see." But she smiled at me with eyes surprisingly free of anger.

"Um, sorry I haven't been in touch," I tried, looking from one to the other.

"It's fine. Caitie and I are actually really glad you introduced us," Steph said, and reached across the table to take Caitlyn's hand. They smiled into each other's eyes, and I took a step back. That one, I had most definitely not seen coming.

"Wow. Um, cool. I'm happy for you guys." I moved away some more. "I'm just going to grab this table before someone else does."

"Are you here by yourself?" Caitlyn asked. "Because if you are, you could join us."

"Totally," Steph said, nodding.

"No! I mean, that's okay. Alex brought me," I clarified, gesturing back toward the order counter where my buddy waited, her eyes fixed on us. After a second, she gave a half-hearted wave. "Anyway, it was good seeing you both." I backed away, offering a toothy smile with a panicked edge that likely outshone its rakishness.

"Bye, Junior," they said in unison.

A moment later, I sat down at the empty table in the corner, my back to the two women I'd slept with most recently, who were now, apparently, sleeping with each other. As I pondered the patchy sunshine beyond the nearest window, I reflected that all signs in the universe seemed to be pointing to the fact that Ann Arbor and I were no longer meant to be together. I couldn't get out of Dodge soon enough, apparently.

"Damn, Junior," Alex said when she reached me, setting the tray on our table, "is this what they call the luck of the Dutch?"

"That's the Irish. About the Dutch they say, 'You ain't much if you ain't Dutch.'"

"I thought they just called you cheap, conservative bastards and let it go at that."

I threw an organic potato chip at her. "Zip it."

She grinned and bit into her soy burger.

A little while later I said, "You don't think they could be comparing notes on me, you know, like in bed, do you?"

Alex wouldn't meet my eyes, and paused just a little too long. "Nah, I'm sure they're not. But don't worry. We'll go over to Boa after this and Cassie will make us chocolate strawberry milkshakes and you'll forget all about them."

"Right. Okay. Thanks, Alex."

"No worries. What are friends for?"

Stealing your girlfriend, I considered replying but decided it might sound bitter. I glanced around, making sure Dez and Maddie hadn't shown up to raise the awkward encounter stakes. Nope, I was safe. Wait, were Steph and Caitlyn really making out? *Ew...* Actually, it was kind of hot.

Funeral, I reminded myself, fixing my eyes back on my plate. *You were just at a funeral.* I had read that sex and death were inextricably linked in the human psyche. Apparently those researchers knew what they were talking about.

"I'm thinking of moving," I announced suddenly.

"I thought you liked your studio. Or are you doing the roommate thing again?"

Note to self, specify the move will be out of state.

"Um, well, probably the roommate thing—Lesley and Steven have always said I can stay with them for a while."

"But they live..." She put her burger down and stared at me. "Are you saying what I think you are?"

I nodded.

"No way!" Alex reached over and punched me in the shoulder. "Junior finally grew a pair. What do you know!"

I rubbed my arm. For a skinny girl, Alex could pack a wallop. Probably why they'd named her player-coach of the rugby team back in the day.

"Have you told your parents yet?"

"Nope. I haven't even told Lesley and Steven yet."

Her eyes narrowed. "Are you really moving to Seattle? Or is this another one of those things you mean to get to and never do, like our road-trip to Florida?"

Senior year, I'd promised to drive to Florida with Alex and Dez, but when spring break had rolled around, I'd hopped a plane to Vegas with my then-girlfriend instead. For years afterward we said we would do a make-up, but we never had.

"This is something I'm really doing," I said. I quickly told her about Fitzy's legacy, and the guilt I would feel if I didn't at least give Seattle a try. "And by the way," I added, "if I can do this, you should be able to ask Ariel out. Calling someone up takes considerably less planning than moving cross-country."

"I did ask her out," Alex said, ducking her head.

"Dude, that's amazing!" It was my turn to pummel her. "What did she say?"

"She said yes, and now I'm freaking out. That's why I asked you to dinner—I was hoping I could pick your brain. That, and I thought you might want company after your boss's funeral. I know what she meant to you."

"That's sweet," I said. "You know what we'll have to call you if you guys get married and have kids and live the dream, don't you?"

She eyed me quizzically.

"A squared."

"Funny. First we have to get through dinner, though."

"True. Pointer number one: Lose the visor. I'm completely serious, man."

"I knew you were going to say that."

She didn't argue this time, though—apparently change was in the air. We spent the rest of the meal planning her date with Ariel. Alex was so excited, and it was such a relief to focus on something as inherently hopeful as a first date, I even managed to forget about Fitzy for a little while.

When I got home that night, though, the packet of papers Fitzy had left in her glove compartment were waiting for me on my desk. I stared at the check. Now that I was free to go, I wasn't sure I was strong enough to cut my Starreveld ties and set out on my own. Not that I would be on my own in Seattle. Lesley and Steven were there, along with a posse of gay boys they regularly hung out with.

The night my dad and I had visited Fitzy in her hospital room, they'd left a cheerful message on my voice mail: "Hey, girl, just calling from out here in the Pacific Northwest to see how your Memorial Day is going. Say hello to Junior, boys!" And a male chorus had whooped greetings over the phone line. "Anyway, we're having a little barbecue in the sunshine here, you know, close friends and their friends and some people who wandered in off the street. The mountains are out, the grill is hot, the keg is tapped, and we wish you were here! When are you coming out for another visit? Let's talk soon, sweetie. Kisses."

When I heard their happy tipsy voices and pictured their house on Capitol Hill lit up in mid-day sunshine, I'd wished I were there, too. Now I lay down on my floor and looked up through the willow branches waving gently in the breeze. I could picture the view from the guest room on the third floor of their house, a territorial panorama of Puget Sound and the Olympic Mountains. All but one of my ten days in Seattle the previous summer had been sunny, warm, and clear. When I'd commented on it, Steven had confided that the city's rainy rep is a lie circulated by locals to prevent even more droves of outsiders from invading. Between May and October, Seattle gets less rain even than Michigan.

I could do this. Besides, I'd already told Alex. The more people I told, the more real it would become. For reasons of pride alone I would have to follow through.

I reached for my phone and hit speed dial. What if they didn't pick up? Or worse, what if they hadn't been serious?

"Is this the party to whom I am speaking?" Lesley answered.

"Did you guys mean it about wanting help with the rent?" I asked.

"Hello to you, too, Miss Junior."

"Come on, Lezzie," I said, channeling my sister Cat. "Does the invitation still stand, or not?"

"Of course! Does this mean you're actually considering leaving the Dutch Mafia? Will they even let you?"

"I'm not just considering it, I'm doing it," I said. "I'm moving to Seattle."

I'd thought that the words, spoken aloud in the privacy of my apartment, would have some sort of dramatic effect. That maybe my voice would stop working or an earthquake would strike or Fitzy's ghost would appear beside me. Instead, my breath eased out slowly and I felt my shoulders relax. My body even knew it was time.

Lesley shouted for Steven to pick up the other extension, and the three of us laughed and spoke over each other in a cacophony of planning. They wanted me to be there by the end of the month for Seattle Pride, a spectacle they claimed was not to be missed. But given it was already mid-June, there was no way I could make it all happen in time for Pride. We haggled back and forth before finally deciding I should move to Seattle in mid-July. That would give me a month to tell my family and give notice at my apartment—and at work.

"Toby is going to hate us," Steven said.

"You're right. So is my family."

"Don't tell them where you're going, okay?" Lesley said. "I don't want the wrath of the Starrevelds shadowing me the remainder of my days."

"Seriously," Steven seconded.

"Come on, guys, it won't be that bad."

"You keep telling yourself that, sister. Now, you're sure you're sober? You'll remember all of this tomorrow when I call to remind you?"

"I'm sober, and I'll remember."

"Can we post it on Facebook?"

"Not unless you want my sister Jane to come after you. Don't tell anyone until I say you can, got it?"

"Uh, yeah. Your sister Jane is scary."

"Totally," Lesley agreed. "You have to be a little bit S&M to want to be an orthodontist, don't you?"

If the association of bondage with my straitlaced older sister hadn't been so ridiculous, I might have lambasted my future roomie. As it was, I just giggled.

After we hung up, I was too antsy to stay in my apartment, so I took my bike out for a ride through the streets of Ann Arbor in the warm summer-like rain that had moved in while I'd been on the phone. Better get used to this weather, I told myself.

I paused on the sidewalk by my favorite willow tree and lifted my face to the warm rain falling from its branches. *About time, Starreveld*, I imagined I heard Fitzy say, her eyes crinkling at the corners in a not-so-tough smile, the brim of her trusty Fedora dipping with each step she took away from me.

CHAPTER EIGHTEEN

For the next few days, I hoarded my plans and tried to figure out how to tell my friends and family. Would they be happy for me? Jane would, I imagined, and my father, maybe. At least, in the context of our new relationship. But I couldn't predict how my mother would react. She was a fan of settling down, probably because of the unsettled state of her own childhood. I didn't think she'd be happy to hear that I'd inherited even a smidgeon of her mother's wander lust.

On Thursday night my doorbell rang, startling me. I considered not answering. The day before, I'd checked out a handful of library books on cross-country moves and the job market in Seattle, and currently wanted nothing more than to hole up and plan. My visitor, however, leaned on the buzzer until I finally answered the intercom.

"Who is it?" I asked, bracing myself for Caitlyn's voice.

"It's me," my father said. "Is this a bad time?"

I looked around, checking for inappropriate items, but luckily I'd picked up that afternoon. So I buzzed my dad in and waited at the open door, not sure he would remember which unit was mine.

He appeared in the hallway dressed in his usual suit, tie, and shiny shoes—straight from the store, from the looks of him. In his arms he carried a paper grocery bag.

"Hi, Elizabeth."

"Hi, Dad. This is a nice surprise," I said, kissing his cheek. He smelled of aftershave and sandalwood incense. "Come on in."

He entered the apartment ahead of me and looked around curiously. His gaze didn't linger long on the Botticelli but skipped along to my plant collection, arranged on a long table under the growing lights.

"Those look healthy," he said. "Your grandmother would be proud."

"Thanks."

"Anyway," he added, reaching into the bag, "I brought you this. It's Belgian. I had one of my suppliers ship it with our last order."

He held out the six-pack of beer still cold from the store's refrigerator. I didn't recognize the label, but given my previous experience with Belgian beer, I didn't doubt I would love it.

"Awesome. Thanks," I said again.

"You're welcome. I thought maybe we could have a chat over a drink. With everything that's been going on, we haven't had a chance to catch up lately."

"Of course. Have a seat," I said, waving at the futon couch as I rummaged in a kitchen drawer for a bottle opener.

He sat down on the couch and picked up a book from the stack on the coffee table. I had arranged them so that the top book, a Ray Bradbury novel, wouldn't alert him to my upcoming plans, but moving *Fahrenheit 451* revealed the next book, *Newcomer's Handbook for Moving to and Living in Seattle*. I couldn't tell if he'd seen it as I handed him the beer and dropped onto the papasan chair facing him.

"How are your allergies?" I asked. "I haven't heard you sneeze yet."

"I got a new prescription after our trip. I've been congestion-free ever since."

"That's great, Dad."

He held out his beer and I knocked mine against it.

"How have you been holding up since the memorial service?" he asked.

"Okay, I guess. It still hasn't sunk in all the way, I don't think." I hesitated. This was the perfect opening to tell him about Fitzy's bequest. "You know, we never talked about Memorial Day. Did you guys have the family over?" Each year, my parents hosted a Memorial Day brunch before my father went into the store for the big sale.

"Yes, but the barbecue was rained out. We ended up frying hamburgers and watching a Disney movie. And here I'd thought I was well past my Disney days." He took a pull on his beer. "This is good, hmm? Really smooth."

My father usually drank wine. "I thought you didn't like beer."

"I just don't like American beer."

"I bet you'd like microbrews."

"Possibly. Seattle has a lot of microbreweries, doesn't it?" he asked, watching me.

"Yeah, I guess." I shrugged, peeling the label from my bottle of beer in small strips.

"Anyway, I've been meaning to tell you we missed you at Tulip Time."

For the first time in years, I'd missed the annual mid-May family pilgrimage to the other side of the state. Fitzy had had a rough week, and I hadn't felt comfortable leaving her alone for so long. I'd tilled her vegetable garden that weekend, even though she had suggested I might consider saving my energies.

"How was it?" I asked.

"Spring came a little early, as you know, but it was still peak bloom time. Nothing like Keukenhof, of course. Which reminds me, I have something else for you."

He reached into the paper bag he'd brought and removed a thin box and a Walgreen's packet that contained a stack of photos.

Setting aside the box, I leafed through the pictures. Half were of buildings and flowers and the two of us in Europe, the other half of the rest of the family at Tulip Time.

"They're duplicates," he said, "so you can keep them."

"I have some for you, too. I'll bring them to dinner this weekend. But what's in the box?"

"Take a look."

I pulled out a wooden photo frame and held it up. Inside was the picture of my father and me beside the Homomonument at Westerkerk, his arm around my shoulders, both of us smiling.

"Cool," I said, glancing up at him.

"That was the best picture of the two of us from the trip, I thought."

I looked again, closer this time. The upraised pink stone was barely visible protruding from the sidewalk, but it was a good shot of the two of us in front of the church whose bell tower we'd seen and heard from trams, over rooftops, beyond canals our few days in Amsterdam. You would have had to look closely to see the slight bewilderment in my eyes, the tilt of my head away from my father. He, meanwhile, looked genuinely pleased, his eyes focused squarely on the camera, his arm tight around my shoulders.

If you had told me only a few months before that my father would present me with a framed photo of the two of us standing beside an international tribute to gays and lesbians, I would have called you a wing nut. But here it was, and here we were, sharing a beer in my apartment, growth lights droning in the background.

"The photos aren't the only reason I wanted to see you," my father said. "I wanted to tell you about the store. We signed the final papers today."

"You did?"

"The lawyers finally got everything ironed out. The deal is done."

"Was Mom there?" I asked, remembering how she and I had sat together just like this the day before the trip.

"She was. Your Aunt Trudy came down from Saginaw, too."

"What about the other girls? Do they know?"

"Not yet. I'm going to make an announcement at dinner this weekend."

"This is huge, Dad. How do you feel?"

He leaned forward, elbows on his knees, and rubbed his forehead. "Tired, mostly. But I'm relieved it's done. The store will remain after I'm gone, and that's what matters. The name will even stay the same."

"That's good to hear."

Starreveld & Sons had been an Ann Arbor fixture for so long, surviving recession, war, the rise of the chains. It was part of the city's landscape.

My father nudged the pile of books in front of him. "It looks as though you might have an announcement of your own to make this weekend. Your friends who live in Seattle, what are their names?"

"Lesley and Steven."

"I seem to recall they invited you to move in with them last time you were out there. I take it you're thinking of accepting the offer?"

"Maybe," I said, the urge to chicken out threatening to overwhelm the urge to get it over with. Then my eyes fell on the keychain hanging over my desk. Fitzy's keychain. If there was one thing she had never been in all the time I'd known her, it was a coward.

I took a deep breath and looked my father in the eye. "I mean, yeah, I'm going to do it. I'm moving to Seattle."

He nodded slowly. "I see. When, exactly?"

"I was thinking July."

"Next month?"

"That's the one."

"How will you get there?"

"The thing is, Fitzy left me her car and a little bit of money. I didn't know until Grace told me, you know, after."

"That's a very generous gift," he said. And yet, he didn't seem surprised. "What will you do for work?"

"I'll temp while I look for something in landscape design. Then in a few years, if I like what I'm doing, I'm thinking about going for a Master's in landscape architecture so that I can run my own business."

My father blinked, and then nodded again. "You've obviously put some thought into this. It sounds like a good plan, Elizabeth. You know, in a way you'll be following in family footsteps."

"I will?"

"We wouldn't be sitting here if your great-great grandfather hadn't left his family and everything he knew. I'm going to share a story with you now, one that has passed from father to son for four generations of Starrevelds. But you have to promise to keep it to yourself. Can you do that? Can you keep the family secret until it's time to pass it on?"

"Of course." I felt the hair rise on the back of my neck.

"I'm serious, Elizabeth."

"I promise, Dad." I leaned forward, almost tipping the papasan chair.

As it turned out, the version of my great-great grandfather's immigration to America I'd always heard had been sanitized for general consumption. The ancestor in question had not set off for America to find his fortune, but had fled the Netherlands because he'd gotten a young peasant woman in trouble. His family had planned to force him to do the honorable thing and marry the girl. But only days before the wedding, Wilhelm had absconded with a handful of diamonds from his father's vault and stowed away aboard the first ship he could find—bound, incidentally, for America.

On the ship, he joined up with a band of families headed for Holland, the Dutch colony in Michigan. He never made it that far west, however, as I knew. What I hadn't known was that an Ann Arbor innkeeper, my other great-great-great grandfather, found him in a compromising position—a naked, compromising position—with his daughter and forced him at gunpoint to marry the girl. With nowhere to run to, Wilhelm had succumbed and made a go at the straight life, opening a jewelry shop with the backing and support of his well-to-do in-laws. His first pieces were diamond rings made from the stash he'd brought to America sewn into the lining of his jacket.

"And that's how the Starrevelds really got started in America," my father finished. He drained his beer. "Now the secret rests with you, Elizabeth, the last of the Starrevelds."

"You don't know that for sure," I said. "I might have kids someday, Dad, remember?"

"I know, you said that. It's just," he shook his head, "it's hard to keep up with you kids."

"Judging from the story you just told me, it always has been."

"True enough," he said, and clinked his bottle against mine.

He asked me more about my Seattle plans, and we chatted about moves, jobs, and the store deal over a second beer. It was nice, sitting in my warm apartment and talking with my dad, the Indigo Girls crooning in the background, the sky darkening beyond the window.

When our bottles were empty, he rose from the couch and announced that he'd better be going. My mother was waiting for him at home.

I walked him outside and hugged him on the front stoop. "Thanks, Dad. For stopping by, for the beer, for the story."

"You're welcome, Elizabeth. I don't think I've said it enough, but I'm proud of you. You've become a fine woman. I look forward to hearing what Seattle holds for you."

"I'm proud of you, too, Dad," I said. "The store will be fine, thanks to you."

He shrugged and looked down the block. "Maybe it will and maybe it won't. But it doesn't matter as much to me as you girls do. By the way, promise me something?"

"Okay."

"Don't raid the vault on your way out of town, eh?"

I punched him on the shoulder, laughing. "I'll try to resist."

He jogged down the steps, light on his feet as ever, and started down the sidewalk. "See you Sunday?" he called back over his shoulder.

"See you Sunday," I answered, and lingered on the stoop a little longer, watching my father's shadow recede.

CHAPTER NINETEEN

At the Arboretum the day after my father's visit, I officially gave notice. Dr. Allen, the interim director, accepted it without question and even offered to be a reference. Then she pulled out a file that Fitzy had left. Inside were glowing letters of recommendation she'd painstakingly typed up for all the long-term Arboretum staff, including me.

Later at Boadicea, my morning success still fresh in my mind, I asked Toby to join me outside for a smoke break. Only I didn't light up. I'd given up cigarettes for good the day after Fitzy died, and so far, I hadn't had much problem breaking my only ever mild addiction. I still enjoyed weed, but had decided to limit myself to once a week. Whenever I thought about crossing the line I'd set for myself, I pictured Fitzy in the hospital, shrunken and gray and gasping for breath. Fairly effective negative reinforcement, as it turned out.

We sat down on the back steps in the alley behind Boadicea and inhaled the scent of summer in the city—the inimitable odors of rotting trash and stale urine.

"I've got something to tell you," I started, and then hesitated.

The words I'd been rehearsing were suddenly difficult to get out.

Toby was one of my oldest friends, and one of the few who had always seemed to care about me for myself. How could I tell her I was abandoning Ann Arbor for the lure of a new start two thousand miles away?

"You're not sick, are you?" she asked. "Is that why you've lost so much weight? Damn it, Junior, I told you to be safe! HIV isn't just a gay man's disease anymore, you know."

I held up a hand. "Wait, I'm not sick, okay? I'm negative, as far as I know. It's just been a rough year."

She expelled a breath. "Glad to hear it. But you should still be careful. So what is it, then?"

"Remember how I said the other day that the last few weeks have sucked?"

"I believe you referred to the previous month as an abomination."

"Right. But the thing is, it hasn't been a complete disaster. Something happened, something I think is really good, and I need to tell you about it."

Only I still couldn't seem to, so I stopped again.

"Oh, God, don't tell me you're going straight. Tell me you're not off girls because of those two lying sacks of shit."

This was starting to get funny. I was tempted to draw out the conversation just to see what other theories Toby might concoct. Maybe I should tell her I had decided to accept Jesus Christ as my lord and savior. That would go over well.

"It's nothing like that." I hesitated again, trying to form the words.

"Out with it already," she said, sliding her arm across my shoulders.

"Okay. It's not that big of a deal. I mean, I guess maybe it is. It's just, I figured out where I should be and what I should be doing. It actually started in Amsterdam when I was hanging out with Sofie."

"I told you not to take her seriously, Junior. If she has you convinced you should move to Amsterdam and start a new life with her just because you're both on the rebound, forget about it."

Sofie was on the rebound? Interesting. Clearly I had not been on Facebook enough recently.

"Not Amsterdam, but Seattle. I'm moving to Seattle to look for a job in landscape design. You know, still working in gardens, but more residential-based than institutional."

"Seriously? Those queens finally got to you, huh."

"They didn't get to me. I've been thinking about leaving Ann Arbor for a while, you know that. I was born here. Isn't it time I got out?"

She sighed. "Yes, it is. Past time, in fact. Seattle could be really good for you. It's just hard to watch you leave. You're my favorite person in Ann Arbor, you know?"

"I know," I said, "and you and Sheila are mine. Are you okay with me going, then? You don't feel like I'm leaving you in the lurch?"

"'Course not. There are plenty of good kids who want to work here. I'm actually glad to see you moving on to bigger and better things. I would have had to kick your butt sooner or later if you didn't come up with a plan. You're too smart to stay a barista forever, kid. Have you told your family?"

"Only my dad. He was really cool about it, but I still have to tell my mom and my sisters."

"Good luck with that," Toby said, her hand heavy on my shoulder. "Let me know if there's anything I can do."

"Thanks," I said. "I will."

That Sunday, as I set the table in my parents' dining room, I decided to save the topic of my move for another week's meal. Or, perhaps, to send them all a group email regarding my plans. Having my parents and my sisters (Cat didn't count) happy with me at the same time was almost too unusual to risk losing. But after the main course, while my mother and I cleared the table and Mary brought out strawberry shortcake with the first strawberries of the season, my father made the decision for me.

"Ahem," he said, tapping his glass with a knife. "I have an announcement to make regarding the store. But first, I think Elizabeth has something she'd like to share with all of us."

Ten pairs of eyes swiveled my way. I stared at my father. "Excuse me?"

He smiled, a little mischievously I thought. "It's okay. I told you I don't mind going second."

Obviously he wasn't going to let me get away without coming clean, and had deduced that the only way I was going to announce my intentions was against my will. I paused. My sisters and I had shared all sorts of things at this table, from graduation and pregnancy announcements to engagements and first home purchases. No one had ever told the family they were planning to leave the state, though. Or even the city limits.

"Go ahead, Elizabeth," my father prodded. "We're listening. Cat, shush."

Cat, who had been whispering to Mary, scowled at me.

"Okay," I said, and took a deep breath. "I'm moving to Seattle. My friends Lesley and Steven have a house there, and they're looking for a roommate."

Everyone looked from me to my father. I looked at my mother, though, waiting.

"What are you talking about?" she asked. "When?"

"Next month. I'm going to try to be settled by the end of July."

"You can't be serious," she said. "What will you do for work?"

"I'm going to temp while I look for something I really want to do, something to do with gardens or landscaping."

"But why now? Why the sudden change?"

"I need to try something different, Mom."

It didn't have anything to do with her, I wanted to add. But I didn't.

"I, for one, think it's a good idea," my father said, his eyes on my mother.

Two of my sisters gasped. One of my brothers-in-law choked on a strawberry.

A look passed between my parents, a wordless message I couldn't read despite the years I'd lived with them. Whatever it contained, my mother nodded slowly. "All right, then. Elizabeth, we'll talk more about this later. Now, Gene, didn't you have something to share with the family?"

And just like that, the spotlight shifted from me to my father. It took him the rest of dessert and coffee to answer everyone's questions about the upcoming merger. Afterward, when Cat and I were doing the dishes—it was our turn on the rotation, according to the schedule posted on the fridge—she pumped me for information.

"You knew he was going to sell the shop, didn't you?"

"He's not selling it," I pointed out, scrubbing a plate my great-grandmother had had shipped across the Atlantic from Rotterdam. "We retain 51% of the business. We're just no longer solely responsible for the cost of operation."

"Semantics," Cat the lawyer dismissed with a wave of her blue-and-white checkered dishtowel. "You knew."

"Maybe."

"And he knew about your little Seattle deal, didn't he? That's why he didn't flip out."

"No," I lied. "The only people who knew were Steven and Lesley. And my boss, Toby." Not to mention, everyone I worked with at Boadicea and the Arboretum, Alex, Sarah, and my other friends in the lesbian scene. They were already planning a series of going-away parties, to which Dez and Maddie would definitely not be invited.

Cat shook her head. "You two are completely alike, you know that? You're just like him, totally secretive and bull-headed."

For once, a comment like that from one of my sisters didn't elicit a stream of insults from me in return. Just then, it didn't seem like such a bad thing to be like our father.

"You're right," I said, and smiled as Cat stared at me, confounded.

Behind us, our dad cleared his throat. I hadn't realized he was there. Obviously, Cat hadn't, either. I nodded at him. He nodded back, then took a couple of beers from the refrigerator and slipped out.

"You always were his favorite," Cat said. "Probably because you're the closest thing to a son he'll ever have."

"I am, aren't I," I agreed, and continued washing the mountain of dishes in my parents' kitchen sink.

A few days later, my mother called to tell me that she and my father had decided I should let her drive out to Seattle with me. She didn't like to think of me driving all that way alone, and anyway, it would be a chance for the two of us to spend some time together. Besides, who knew when she would get to see me, her youngest child, again?

Despite the fact that it meant untold hours alone together in a cramped space, I accepted her offer, and not only because her guilt trip had worked. Frankly, I could use the help. I was planning to build a wooden frame for the back of the Forester to hold my plants. Once we hit the road, I would cover my babies with a layer of damp cheesecloth to keep them cool on the cross-country trip. Our bags would go in the back seat, with an overhead luggage carriage for overflow. As we planned the trip, my mom and I decided to drive out via Glacier National Park in northern Montana—slightly out of the way, but definitely worth a few extra hours on the road, we agreed. When she told me that she and my father had road-tripped there on their honeymoon, I tried to imagine my father honeymooning in a place with bears and moose, and failed. Amsterdam, yes; an allergen-infested national park in Montana, not so much.

The Fourth of July came and went, with the usual lesbian barbecues fit around an evening celebration at my parents' house. As I held a sleeping Brittany, the youngest of my nieces and nephews, I thought about all the milestones I would miss in her life—first steps, first words, first day of pre-school. I had been around for each of those moments in Meredith, Owen, and Joey's lives, and was having a hard time getting accustomed to the idea that from now on, other than the twice-yearly visits home I was planning, I would see my nieces and nephews only on Skype and in photos. The thought was more painful than any other aspect of leaving, and as I sat on the back deck of my parents' house, where I had learned to walk and crawl and run myself all those years ago, I almost quit. I almost told my family that I couldn't leave, couldn't go off by myself to a city none of them had ever visited while they continued to have Sunday dinners and Saturday pee-wee soccer, birthday parties and grandchildren time without me.

But it was too late to change my mind now, and anyway, I did want to go, even as I didn't.

The week after the Fourth, I packed up my apartment, gave the plants that were too delicate or too large to make the trip in the back of the Subaru to Toby or my mother, partied with my dyke scene friends, and said goodbye to everyone except Maddie and Dez. I thought about calling Dez, or at least texting her. The Ann Arbor scene was small, so I knew she'd probably heard about my impending move. But I didn't run into her around town and I couldn't bring myself to reach out, a fact that bothered me and yet, at the same time, seemed perfectly in keeping with the messy way things had ended.

And then somehow it was the Sunday morning I'd chosen for the Big Day. Toby, Sheila, and Alex came over to my parents' house for an early breakfast. The whole family was there, trying to be cheerful but stealing furtive glances at me as if I were about to go off to war. The only one missing was Fitzy, but she was there in spirit, I decided.

After breakfast, we headed outside en masse. In the driveway, I hugged Toby and Sheila and Alex and each member of my family, plastering kisses on all of the kids, who didn't really get what was going on.

Mary cried as she hugged me goodbye, and Jane and I exchanged a look over her head. I could see my own question reflected in her eyes: Was Mary pregnant again?

My father hugged me last, a long, drawn-out embrace that brought tears to my eyes. Finally he pounded me on the back and pressed a padded envelope into my hand.

I looked up at him. "What's this?"

"You'll see. Open it when you get there, but only after your mother flies home. Okay?"

What was it about letters with conditions lately?

"Okay." I hesitated, then hugged him again. "Thanks, Dad. For everything."

"You're welcome," he said, "Junior." Then he winked. "Drive carefully, ladies."

My mother and I both waved to the gathered clan and took our places in the laden Forester, which was already pointed toward the street. I realized I was glad she was with me as I turned the key and headed down the driveway. In the rearview mirror, I could see everyone I loved most standing in front of the house, waving and smiling and calling after us. Except my dad—he just stood with his hands in the pockets of his pressed Dockers watching the car drive away.

"Ready, honey?" my mother asked as I pulled the Subaru up to the stop sign at the end of our street.

"Ready, Mom."

She touched my shoulder. "Let's go."

I put my turn signal on, glanced back at the house on the hill where everyone except my father had already started to file back to their normal lives, and pressed the gas pedal.

We took turns driving and sleeping, air conditioning keeping my cheese-clothed plants cool as we crossed Middle America. My mother slept through most of the seemingly endless plains of South Dakota—"Once you've seen the Dakotas, you really never have to see them again"—and I drove as fast as I dared to push Fitzy's baby, occasionally cracking the windows when the air conditioning got to be too much.

With my mother asleep and a mix CD I had burned especially for the trip playing such gems as "Life is a Highway," "Wide Open Spaces," "Ol' 55," "Take it Easy," and the gay classic "Go West," I could almost pretend I was heading alone into my new life. Behind me was everything safe and known, while up ahead waited a couple of friends and a city I had visited exactly three times. This was going to be quite the year by the time it ended—losing my best friend and girlfriend in one fell swoop, finding my father during a trip to Europe, losing Fitzy to the ravages of disease, and removing myself to Seattle, home to happy queers and a fault line nearly as active as the San Andreas.

"You're not planning to stay there forever, are you?" my mother had asked anxiously a few days earlier when she came over to help me pack. "Because I've read that the entire West Coast, from LA to Canada, is going to end up in the ocean eventually."

I paused in cramming my sweatshirt collection into my already overloaded suitcase. Pretty soon I was going to have to resort to plastic bags. "I don't know, Mom. We'll see. Anyway, 'eventually' means like a million years from now."

She frowned at me. "I know that, Elizabeth, but it doesn't change the fact that the West Coast is earthquake-prone."

"Good thing you made me take all those swimming lessons when I was little, then."

"Elizabeth Anne Starreveld!" My mother smacked my butt lightly as she crossed to my closet to survey the pile of shoes still remaining. "You may think you're all grown up, but I'm still your mother. Don't you take that tone with me."

"Sorry," I offered.

"You are not," she said, and we both laughed.

Now, driving along a mostly empty freeway lined with green and brown farm fields, the smell of earth and manure heavy on the air, I wondered if I would stay in Seattle forever. Right now I couldn't imagine settling there permanently, but maybe I would meet the woman of my dreams and we would get married and buy a house overlooking the Sound and have dogs and kids running around our huge yard by this time next decade.

Anything at all was possible in that moment, as I drove away from my old life toward an entirely new, as yet mysterious existence. Driving through South Dakota, I had that wonderful feeling of being on the edge of beginning, the sense of a home yet undiscovered and friends yet unmet. I couldn't wait to know the people and places that would feel foreign to me at first, and then eventually become commonplace. I couldn't wait for someplace outside of Michigan to feel like home.

But even if Seattle did capture me permanently, it didn't mean I wouldn't have a home to come back to in Michigan. Unlike my ancestors, I lived in a world easily traversed by automobiles and airplanes. I didn't have the option of boarding a ship bound for a distant land, knowing I would likely never see my family again. Which was good, because despite what I had always regarded as the iron grip of the Starreveld clan, I was starting to think that maybe the tightness with which my family held to one another wasn't such a bad thing, after all.

Beside me my mother stirred and sat up. "What did I miss?"

"Not much," I said, and smiled at her.

She smiled back, and we both looked ahead at the small Dakota town creeping into sight over the flat spine of the horizon.

"I like this song," she said, turning up the stereo as Van Morrison came on.

We drove onward in Fitzy's Forester, belting out "Brown-Eyed Girl" as we left the Midwest behind. In a matter of days, I would be in Seattle settling into my new life, and my mother would be back in Ann Arbor, settling into a life without me. But for now, we rode together past sunlit farm fields, laughing and blending our voices to a song we both knew by heart.

EPILOGUE

On the first anniversary of Fitzy's death, after a long day of working on a property on the shore of Lake Washington, I came home to my third floor sanctuary, lit a candle, and curled up on my window seat, Fitzy's unopened second letter on my lap. With my dog Tyson sleeping at my side, I sipped a cold Full Sail amber and looked out at the sun setting over the Sound. In a few weeks, it would be the longest day of the year. Steven and Lesley and I were planning a solstice party. Those boys loved any excuse to party. Not that I minded.

Living with Steven and Lesley was awesome—I had the whole top floor, with its territorial views and widow's walk, to myself. They hadn't charged me rent my first month in Seattle. In exchange, I'd built a deck and patio off the back of the house. Steven's uncle, who owned the house, paid for materials, while I provided the sweat and tools. When I was done, their friend with the landscape design business put me to work on one of his crews. Turned out summer was a good time to arrive in the Northwest. Landscape work had kept me busy into November.

Over the winter, when the outdoor jobs weren't as plentiful, I'd worked part-time at Lowe's and free-lanced in indoor construction. If you knew the right people, there was always building and remodeling work to be had. Fortunately, Lesley and Steven and their friends knew plenty of DINKs—double income no kid couples—looking to improve their properties. With steady work and low expenses, I'd been able to tuck a chunk of change into savings every month, building on the nest egg Fitzy had left me. In another year or two, I might even be able to buy a house with a yard big enough to hold my dream garden. Assuming I stayed in Seattle, I had my eye on the Central District, the neighborhood south of Steven and Lesley's, which was well on its way to transitioning from run-down to gentrified.

Ty whined in her sleep, and I turned back to the letter in my lap. Slowly, I slid a permanently dirt-stained finger under the back flap of the envelope and pulled out a single sheet of paper. There was Fitzy's sloped handwriting, talking to me from beyond the grave:

Elizabeth,

If I know you, and I think I do, you've done as I asked and it has now been a year since, well, you know. There are plenty of things I wish I had told you, things you may or may not know about me. But there's one thing in particular. You may not be surprised to learn that I've never been very maternal, and far from the grandmotherly type. Just the word grandmother conjures for me the story of Little Red Riding Hood and the woman who was sweet and kind and couldn't tell the difference between a sheep and a wolf. I know the difference, and I also know that sometimes they are the same. But what I want you to know is that if I had been blessed with a granddaughter, I always imagined she would be like you, smart and true and loyal.

Perhaps it will also be of no surprise to learn that you remind me of another young woman, one I loved very much—Amanda. She died too young, and since losing her, I suppose I've felt more dead than alive myself at times. The best cure for sorrow that I've found over the years lies in immersing myself in the growing season, watching seeds take shape first as shoots and then as mature plants, growing fuller and more resilient with the combination of sunshine and water. At the end of summer, though, even the hardiest of varieties loses its leaves, only to rebound the following spring—assuming we're talking perennials here, of course.

I won't turn sentimental and compare you to a young flower, so don't worry on that account. But I will say that it has been a pleasure and a joy at times for me to watch you change over these last few years from a teenager with a chip on her shoulder to a young woman certain of who she is. I am happy for you that you've reconnected with your family. There were times when I thought about paying your father a visit to tell him he didn't know what he has in you. But thankfully I kept my mouth shut on that score, and you and he appear to have found your way back to each other on your own.

Wherever you are right now, reading these words from a long-since-gone old lady, I wish you joy and a lifetime of interesting work and generous spirits. May you be as lucky as I have been, but luckier, too. And know that you leant to my time in Ann Arbor the love and joy—yes, my girl, joy—that I didn't know I would ever find again. Take care of yourself, my girl. Live well.

–MAF

Beneath her initials, she'd inscribed the following quote, which had been on the bulletin board above her desk at the Arboretum: "Study nature, love nature, stay close to nature. It will never fail you. - Frank Lloyd Wright"

I folded the letter and returned it to its envelope, then pulled Tyson onto my lap. She stretched her legs out and licked my chin, her tail thumping against my leg. She wasn't a puppy anymore, but I wanted puppy kisses, and she was more than happy to oblige. A little pit bull lab mix, Tyson had found me a few weeks after I moved in with the boys. At six months she was all brindle ribs and skittish chocolate eyes. Probably she wandered away from a group of Bellevue runaways sleeping at the Reservoir just off Broadway. She showed up collarless at the front gate while I was laying out a vegetable garden, and whined plaintively until I came and let her in. After a few minutes of belly rubs, she curled up and fell asleep in the sun, where she stayed while I played in the dirt.

The boys fell in love with her almost as quickly as I did, and no one ever came looking. So I took her to the vet for her shots, registered her with the city, got her chipped, and enrolled her in obedience training. And then I realized she was really mine. I finally had a dog. A year later, she had just started to mellow out of puppydom. It now appeared to be safe to leave my shoes lying around without fearing she would decorate them with her tooth marks.

Steps sounded on the landing, and Tyson leapt off me, her rear end wiggling at the knock on the door.

"Come in," I called.

"Are you decent?" Lesley asked. "Because I'm about to get my gay on, and the last thing I need is for real boobs to put me off."

"I'm decent," I said. As he entered the apartment, I added, "But what are you talking about? Your gay is always on."

"True." He flopped onto a beat-up old couch that was surprisingly comfortable. In Sofie's honor, I called her Mini. "Are you coming out with us tonight?"

"Where are you going?"

"Man-Ray, of course."

I wrinkled my nose. "I'm not in the mood for boy-fest tonight."

"Maybe we'll find a girl there for you."

Tyson had crawled back up onto the window seat beside me, and I covered her ears. "Don't listen to him, baby. I'm not looking to replace you."

Ty was what you might call a needy dog—she needed to be touching someone at all times, if possible. At night she slept in the crook of my legs or with her back pressed to mine. Sometimes I woke up and found her head on the pillow next to me, her eyes gazing adoringly into mine. Which was a little spooky, but awfully sweet, too.

"Bestiality isn't really in right now," Lesley said.

"Ew. Don't taint my bond with my dog with your perverted mind."

"You just referred to bondage in the same sentence as your dog, and I'm the perverted one?"

"That's it, I'm definitely not coming out with you guys now. I am way too tired to come up with a clever retort. I think I'm just going to chill tonight."

"You haven't been out with us in weeks," Lesley said, frowning. "Maybe hanging out with boys all the time has killed your lesbian mojo."

"If anything has killed my mojo, it's hauling a thousand pounds of rock in nine hours, like I did today."

"You are so butch."

"Thanks."

He patted Tyson and headed for the door. "Brunch downstairs at noon, *capiche?*"

"I'll be there."

And with a swish of his hips, he was out the door.

I looked down at Ty. "What do you think, dinner or a bath?"

She scrambled off my lap and went to stand by the door to the pantry, where I kept her bag of dry food. Not a big surprise. I have yet to meet a dog who would pick bathing over food.

The next morning, I got up early and walked Tyson to nearby Volunteer Park, where only a few people were out. On weekends, I usually tried to get out of the city for a hike in the Cascades or the Olympics, the moss-cushioned mountain forests only an hour or two outside the city. If I didn't manage it on the weekends, then I would throw Ty in the Subaru on a weekday when I didn't have to work late and take her to one of the city parks: Golden Gardens out past Ballard, or Seward Park on Lake Washington, or the Arboretum near U-Dub. In the summer it didn't get dark until ten or eleven at night, so I was usually able to spend some time among trees and ferns a couple of times a week. This kept me sane and able to tolerate city life. I'd thought my little ghetto apartment in Ann Arbor was located in an urban area, but Seattle is a real city. Unbelievably livable for a city its size, but a big city nonetheless.

Today I wouldn't be squeezing in a hike. But that was fine—I had something else in mind, anyway.

Back at the house, I took down a vase from the mantel in my room, removed a bouquet of dried lavender, and fished out the plastic bag of Fitzy's ashes. I returned the vase to its place on the mantel beside Fitzy's old Christmas cactus (which still refused to bloom at Christmas), and set out on my mission leaving Tyson, for once, at home. First I sprinkled a handful of Fitzy's ashes over the flower garden near our front gate. Then I drove the Subaru to the Arboretum and walked among the flowering bushes and fragrant trees, sprinkling ashes like fertilizer every so often. After a brief stop at the Rose Garden on top of Fremont Hill, I parked the Forester downtown and boarded the Bainbridge Island ferry as a foot passenger.

It was a beautiful day, with high clouds and a steady salt-tinged breeze. Halfway across the Sound, I headed to the back of the ship and took a little time writing a letter to Fitzy in my head, telling her about everything that had happened since she'd died. Then I thanked her out loud one last time and emptied the rest of the bag into the wind, the Seattle city skyline visible through the cloud of ashes that floated briefly on the air before settling into the salt water, where the ferry's wake churned them under in an instant. That was it. Fitzy was really gone now, and I was really on my own in a city she had once called home. A place that was no longer strange to me at all.

Right after I arrived, I wasn't sure I wanted to stay. My mom stuck around for a few days, which eased the transition. As someone who had lived in twelve different towns before the age of seventeen, she had the moving thing down pat. By the time she left, I was set up with everything I could need. Everything except my parents and sisters and nieces and nephews, from whom I had never lived more than ten miles. I was so homesick at first I even missed Cat, though admittedly not for long.

The day my mom flew home, I fished out the padded envelope my father had given me the morning I left, sat down in the window seat, and tore it open. Inside I found a card and an oblong mass of bubble wrap taped tightly at both ends. I picked at the tape, then gave up and opened the card, which bore a picture of a lighthouse on one of the Great Lakes. Inside, my father's neat cursive offered the following short message:

> Elizabeth,
>
> As you prepare to leave Ann Arbor, I find myself trying to put into words the nearly inexpressible. Namely, that I am a luckier man than I likely have a right to be. The store is stable, our family's ownership guaranteed, and all of my daughters are leading the lives they were meant to lead. I am proud of you, my youngest child and, by far, my bravest. I admire you for the person you have become. Your honesty and insistence on being yourself in a world that hardly welcomes that self with open arms has, on occasion, taken my breath away. You don't come by that courage from my side; clearly it comes from your mother.
>
> If you haven't already done so, please open the small package included with this card. Go ahead, I can wait.

I was never the kind of kid who wanted to know what she was getting for Christmas or her birthday. Every December Cat and Jane would go looking for presents. More often than not they would unearth the hiding spot, and then Mary and I would spend the next few weeks with our fingers in our ears, closing our eyes and humming as Cat and Jane, amused by our protests, sought ever more creative ways to tell us what we were getting. So when I read my father's instructions, I dutifully set the card down and went to search the kitchen for my Leatherman, which I had already misplaced at least a dozen times in the few days since I'd arrived on Capitol Hill.

Leatherman in hand, I returned to the window seat and made short work of the yard or more of bubble wrap in which my father had wrapped the unknown object(s). I already suspected what I would find as I unwound the last sheet of opaque plastic: three diamonds of varying shapes and sizes, but all, I could see immediately, of high quality. Not that I would expect anything else from my father.

Well, that explained why my mother had insisted on keeping the envelope in her purse and her purse on her person at all times during our trip west. I set the stones on the window sill, picked up the card, and resumed reading:

> I knew you wouldn't read ahead. I also knew you wouldn't ask for money when you left, nor would you raid the vault. So I raided it for you, as I've done for each of your sisters at various times—the store paid for Jane's medical school, Cat's law school, Mary's wedding and the down payment on her and Joe's house. In each of those cases, I wrote a check. But with you leaving your hometown, our home, for a new life in a distant land, much as your great-great grandfather did all those years ago, I liked the symbolism.
>
> These stones are your legacy, and you should do with them as you choose, be it a graduate education, a down payment on a house, or even, someday, a ring for a special someone. I trust that you will make the right decision when

the time comes. (That said, please keep the stones in a safety deposit box in a nationally recognized bank; and if you do decide to cash them in, let me know so that I can recommend a jeweler in your area and a ballpark value.)

In any case, good luck in Seattle. I look forward to visiting you and sharing in the life you construct in your new home. If you ever need anything, I hope you'll pick up the phone. Your mother, sisters, and I are only ever a plane ride away. We love and miss you already—

Dad

That same day, I'd entrusted the stones to a safety deposit box in the Washington Mutual building downtown, my favorite skyscraper in the city. It was nice knowing they were there if I needed them, along with the funds Fitzy had seen fit to bestow on me. For now, I was content to build gardens and decks, to learn, to collect tools for my workshop in Lesley and Steven's garage, to volunteer at the Rose Garden at the Seattle Zoo, to hike as much as I could with my dog in the city's forests and beyond. I wasn't even thirty yet. I didn't have to know exactly how I was going to spend the next fifty or sixty years.

My mother didn't necessarily agree, but she was coming around. I'd been home three times already since I moved, once as a surprise for my dad's sixtieth birthday, another time for Christmas with the family, and my latest jaunt to see the tulips in Holland. During my last visit a month earlier, I'd attended the grand opening of the University of Michigan Margaret Fitzgerald Center for the Study of Native Plants. Fitzy's house had been remodeled to fit its new role, but some things were the same as when she'd lived there—the wall of books in the dining room, the baby grand piano in the living room, the greenhouse and the patio and the crabapple tree over Curly's grave, flowering with spring blossoms. Fitzy would have been proud, those of us who knew her agreed over wine and cheese as University officials made speeches and posed for photo ops.

The Seattle-Ann Arbor pipeline hadn't only run in a single direction, either. Jane and Mike had visited me a couple of months after I moved and loved it so much they planned to bring the kids back this summer and every year in perpetuity. Ditto with Toby and Sheila, and even Alex and Ariel had made it out to Seattle.

My mom returned in September and stayed for a week at a bed and breakfast a few blocks away, run by two gay men. She'd seemed to enjoy herself. We stayed busy with shopping downtown, dining out at seafood restaurants, and visiting Mt. Rainier and Olympic National Parks. I hadn't realized before our road trip out, when we visited the Badlands and Glacier, how much my mother loved national parks. She told me it was because she'd lived for a short time as a child in Flagstaff, only a stone's throw from the Grand Canyon.

My father, on the other hand, flew into Seattle in the spring for a gemology conference in Bellevue, and actually stayed at the house with us. He seemed to like putzing about in my workshop and even in the garden, which I'd transformed into one of the nicest vegetable, herb, and flower patches around, according to our neighbors, mostly queer people with high-paying jobs that kept them indoors the majority of the time.

The picture my dad gave me of the two of us at the Homomonument sits next to the photo of Fitzy and her daughter on the mantle above the fireplace in my third floor apartment. He noticed the picture right away when I brought him upstairs for the first time.

"I'm glad we went on that trip," he said, holding up the frame for a closer look.

"So am I, Dad."

He put the picture back and let me lead him downstairs and out into the backyard for a garden tour, Ty trotting at our heels.

I might not ever be the son my father wanted, but that seems to be okay with both of us these days.

Sometimes, when I gaze out from my window seat at the hills of Queen Anne and Magnolia rising in the distance, I think of Ann Arbor and its quiet, shady streets. The landscapes are so different, but for me, they evoke some of the same feelings. When I was home in May, I went with my family to the Tulip Time Festival in Holland—tulip fields, windmills, Dutch dancers in their traditional garb and wooden shoes stamping out the beat a few miles from the shores of Lake Michigan. I hadn't been to the Festival in a couple of years, and I was happy to learn that old ghosts really do fade away, given time and distance.

Soon after the move I sent Sofie a message on Facebook to let her know I'd done it; I'd kept my promise. She replied that she was happy for me, and looked forward to seeing my new life someday with her own eyes. I suppose our lives are bound to intertwine again. After all, we're lesbians with mutual friends.

Maybe someday I'll be walking down Broadway and catch a glimpse of her red hair, her quick step. Or maybe it'll be in Amsterdam, in the glow of neon in the Red Light district. Or even along a tree-lined avenue in Ann Arbor. There she'll be, and there I'll be. And after that, who knows?

But for now, Seattle is home, with its misty islands, trade winds, mossy banks, and white-tipped mountains in every direction. My dog, my friends, my Forester, my third floor. And my family, distant but not forgotten, content to let me explore the world and my place in it, and to keep on loving me while I do.

This past New Year's Eve, I watched the fireworks over Lake Union with Steven and Lesley and half a dozen of their close friends from the deck of a condo in Eastlake. They actually knew the words to "Auld Lang Syne," and as they sang, I hummed along and watched the multi-colored shells explode overhead, knowing that whatever the coming year happened to bring, I would be equal to the challenge.

So far, so good.

ABOUT THE AUTHOR

Kate Christie was born in Kalamazoo, Michigan, and grew up playing in the waters of the Great Lakes. Of mixed Dutch and Scotch-Irish descent, she remembers the Tulip Time Festival in the nearby town of Holland fondly, and the *oliebollen* (Dutch pastries) her neighbors Hank and Gwen used to share at the holidays even more fondly.

A graduate of Smith College, Christie lives near Seattle with her wife and daughter and their two dogs. *Family Jewels* is the second title from her indie imprint, Second Growth Books, and follows *Gay Pride & Prejudice* (March 2012). She has three other novels in print, all published by Bella Books: *Solstice*, *Leaving LA*, and *Beautiful Game*. For book trailers, first chapters, and more, visit www.katejchristie.com.